CROSS MY HEART

JAMES PATTERSON is one of the best-known and biggest-selling writers of all time. He is the author of some of the most popular series of the past decade – the Alex Cross, Women's Murder Club and Detective Michael Bennett novels – and he has written many other number one bestsellers including romance novels and stand-alone thrillers. He lives in Florida with his wife and son.

James is passionate about encouraging children to read. Inspired by his own son who was a reluctant reader, he also writes a range of books specifically for young readers. James is a founding partner of Booktrust's Children's Reading Fund in the UK. In 2010, he was voted Author of the Year at the Children's Choice Book Awards in New York.

Praise for James Patterson's *Cross My Heart*

'Behind all the noise and the numbers, we shouldn't forget that no one gets this big without amazing natural storytelling talent – which is what Jim has, in spades. The Alex Cross series proves it. It just rolls along, irresistibly. Here's to the next twenty years.' **Lee Child**

'It's no mystery why James Patterson is the world's most popular thriller writer: his uncanny skill in creating living, breathing characters we truly feel for and seamless, lightning-fast plots. I do this for a living, and he still manages to keep me guessing from the first to last page. I've been a devoted Alex Cross fan for twenty years, when the first in the series appeared, and *Cross My Heart* proves that both author and his hero are at the top of their game. It's virtually a one-sitting read, and what a read it is: get ready for sweaty palms and lost sleep – and prepare yourself for one of the most gripping endings of any thriller in recent memory. Simply put: nobody does it better.' **Jeffery Deaver**

'James Patterson is The Boss. End of.' **Ian Rankin**

'Twenty years ago, I wrote, "*Along Came a Spider* is the best thriller I've come across in many a year. It deserves to be this season's No. 1 bestseller and should instantly make James Patterson a household name." A household name, indeed. Congratulations, Jim, on twenty years of Alex Cross and on *Cross My Heart*, which I am loving. You the man.' **Nelson DeMille**

'Every once in a while a writer comes along and fundamentally changes the way people read. He or she is so bright, so innovative, so industrious that what they envision and create becomes the measure by which all others are judged. In 1993 one such writer – James Patterson – began to do just that. Now, twenty years later, with his mission still unfolding, James Patterson is the gold standard by which all others are judged. Bravo, Jim.'
Steve Berry

'Alex Cross is one of the best-written heroes in American fiction, and each Cross novel further defines what it means to be a professional, a husband, a father, and above all, a man. Congratulations to James Patterson on twenty years of Alex Cross – both of you only get better and better.'   **Lisa Scottoline**

'Twenty years after the first Alex Cross story, he has become one of the greatest fictional detectives of all time, a character for the ages. *Cross My Heart* has got to be the most terrifying and shocking Cross thriller to date, full of unexpected twists, savage turns, and electrifying suspense. This is the page-turner to end all page-turners.'
Douglas Preston & Lincoln Child

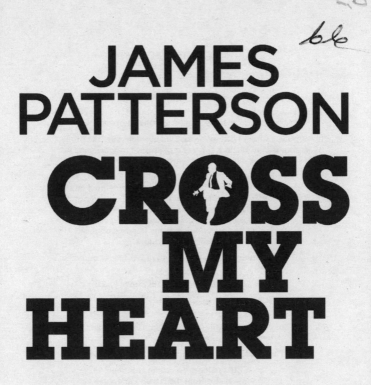

JAMES PATTERSON
CROSS MY HEART

arrow books

Published by Arrow Books in 2014

1 3 5 7 9 10 8 6 4 2

Copyright © James Patterson, 2013

First published in Great Britain in 2013 by Century

Arrow Books
Random House, 20 Vauxhall Bridge Road,
London SW1V 2SA

www.randomhouse.co.uk

Addresses for companies within The Random House Group Limited can be
found at: www.randomhouse.co.uk/offices.htm

The Random House Group Limited Reg. No. 954009

A CIP catalogue record for this book
is available from the British Library

Penguin Random House is committed to a sustainable future for
our business, our readers and our planet. This book is made from
Forest Stewardship Council® certified paper.

Typeset in Berkeley by SX Composing DTP, Rayleigh, Essex SS6 7XF
Printed and bound in Great Britain by Clays Ltd, Elcograf S.p.A.

Prologue

'TWAS THE NIGHT BEFORE EASTER

I TRUDGED AIMLESSLY THROUGH the dark, empty streets of Washington, haunted by the memory of my son Ali telling me that the only way to kill a zombie was to destroy its brain.

It was 3 a.m. Storms punished the city.

I'd been walking like that for hours by then but didn't feel hungry, or thirsty, or tired in any way. When lightning bolts ripped the sky and thunder clapped right over my head, I barely flinched. Not even the pouring rain could slow me or soothe the agony that burned through every inch of my body because of what had been done to my family. With every step I kept seeing Ali, Bree, Damon, Jannie, and Nana Mama in my mind. With every step the horror of what had happened to them ignited inside me all over again, and loneliness and grief and anger.

Is this what Thierry Mulch wanted? I kept asking myself.

Thierry Mulch had destroyed everything I loved, everything I believed in. He'd gutted me and left a dead, soulless man doomed to endless, meaningless movement.

As I walked, I kept hoping Mulch or some anonymous street predator would appear and blow my head off with a shotgun, or crush it with an axe.

There was nothing I wanted more than that.

Part One

SIXTEEN DAYS EARLIER...

Chapter 1

SITTING IN A PARKED work van on Fifth Street on a beautiful April morning, Marcus Sunday used high-definition Leica binoculars to monitor Alex Cross's house and felt a genuine thrill, thinking that the great detective was sure to make an appearance sometime in the next half hour or so.

After all, it was a Thursday and seven thirty in the morning. Cross had to work. So did his wife. And his children had school to attend.

Sunday had no sooner had that thought than Regina Cross Hope, Cross's ninety-one-year-old grandmother, came up the sidewalk from the direction of St. Anthony's Catholic Church. The old bird was tough and moving at a surprising clip despite the cane. She walked right by his van, barely gave it a glance.

Then again, why would she?

Sunday had attached magnetic signs to the van that advertised OVER THE MOON VACUUM CLEANER COMPANY. And behind the tinted glass he was wearing the uniform of said company, a real find at the Salvation Army. Fit perfectly.

The used vacuums in the back of the van had been purchased at a secondhand store out in Potomac for sixty bucks apiece. The phony magnetic signs had been ordered online through FedEx Office. So had the phony badge on his left shirt pocket. It read: THIERRY MULCH.

A lithe, fit man in his late thirties with close-cropped salt-and-pepper hair and slate-gray eyes, Sunday checked his watch as Cross's grandmother disappeared inside the house. Then he took up a black binder stowed between the driver's seat and the center console.

Flipping it open, he noted the tabs on the first five section dividers, each marked with a name: Bree Stone, Ali Cross, Jannie Cross, Damon Cross, and Regina Cross Hope, otherwise known as Nana Mama.

Sunday went straight to the Regina Cross Hope/Nana Mama section and filled in the exact time the old woman had entered the house and from what direction. Then, waiting for more sightings, he flipped to the back of the binder and found a four-page copy of the floor plan of the house, which had conveniently been filed with the city planning board last month as part of Cross's application for permits to redo his kitchen and bathrooms.

Alternately studying the plan and the house itself, Sunday made notes on the diagrams regarding entries and exits, positions of windows, landscaping, and the like. When Cross's wife, Bree Stone, also a detective with the DC Metro Police, came out on the porch to fill a bird feeder at 7:40, he recorded that act as well, and the fact that her backside looked glorious in a tight pair of jeans.

At 7:52, a truck bearing a logo that read DEAR OLD HOUSE pulled up in front of Cross's house, followed by a waste disposal company hauling a construction Dumpster. Out came the great detective onto the porch to greet the contractors and watch the unloading of the Dumpster. So did his grandmother, his wife, and two of his three children: fifteen-year-old Jannie and seven-year-old Ali.

Nice happy family, Sunday thought, studying them through the binoculars in turn. *The future for them seems bright. Looks full of promise. Doesn't it?*

Sunday allowed himself a smile, thinking that a good deal of the fun in any adventure lay in the planning, the preparation, and the anticipation. Maybe more than half, he decided, enjoying the way his ever-fertile brain conjured up various dark ways to destroy the dream scenario unfolding before his eyes.

Then Dr. Alex left with his kids. The three of them walked past Sunday on the other side of Fifth, but the detective barely looked at the work van.

Then again, why would he?

Sunday felt deflated after Cross and his children disappeared. It just wasn't as enjoyable scouting the house with the detective absent, almost like looking at a maze in desperate need of a rodent.

Sunday checked his watch, shut the binder, and put it away, feeling that he was a free, authentic man with a purpose that would not waver no matter the consequences. He started the van, thinking that wavering in any way was almost an insult to one's opponent. You had to want to destroy your enemy as much as he wanted to destroy you.

As Sunday drove off, he believed he was up to his task. He also believed Cross's family deserved the wickedness to come.

Each and every one of them.

Especially Dr. Alex.

Chapter 2

IN A NORMAL YEAR the murder rate in Washington, DC, waits for the stifling days of summer to peak. In July and August, when the air along the Potomac is the consistency and temperature of a rabid dog's mouth, people just seem to snap left and right. In my line of work you come to expect it.

But beginning with the terrorist attack at Union Station on New Year's Day, there had been a steady run of homicides through the winter and on into spring. It was barely April, but this was shaping up already as one of the worst years in three decades for homicide in the District of Columbia.

That had put enormous political pressure on the mayor and the city council, which meant the Metro police chief, too, was under enormous pressure. But the squeeze was especially tight around the homicide and major case squads. Since

I was now a roaming investigator for both teams, the nonstop murders meant the biggest squeeze had been put on me and on my partner and closest friend, John Sampson.

We had not had a day off in nearly two months, and our caseload seemed to grow every day. To make it worse, I was fielding calls from a contractor who was about to remodel the kitchen and put an addition on our house. So the last person I wanted to see around nine thirty that Thursday morning was Captain Roelof Antonius Quintus, who ran Homicide.

Captain Quintus knocked on the door of my office, where I'd been finishing up a breakfast burrito and a second cup of coffee while looking at a cabinet hardware catalog my wife had shoved into my hand as I left home. Sampson, a locomotive of a man, was on the couch, devouring the last of his morning meal.

Sampson saw Quintus and groaned. "Not another one?"

Quintus shook his head. "I just need an update to take to the chief. The mayor's out of her mind and hounding him nonstop."

"We cleared three this week, but you handed us four," I replied. "So the takeaway is that we're making progress but falling behind."

"Sounds about right," Sampson said. "Like that king in mythology who keeps pushing the boulder up the hill, only it keeps falling down."

"Sisyphus," I said.

"Like him," Sampson said, pointing at me.

"C'mon, Cross," Quintus said. "We're counting on you to put some of the higher-profile cases like Rawlins and Kimmel to bed, get the *Post* off our backs. Did you see that goddamned editorial?"

I had. Just that morning they'd run a piece that described the effect the murders were having on tourism, called for the police chief to resign, and floated a proposal to have the FBI take over the department until the murder rate could be lowered.

"Tell you what, Captain," I said. "You tell people to stop killing each other, and we'll have more time to work on cases like Rawlins and Kimmel."

"Funny."

"I wasn't joking."

"No, really, you should try stand-up at open-mike night, Cross," Quintus said, turning to leave. "I think you may have missed your calling."

Chapter 3

DRESSED NOW IN A black leather jacket, black jeans, black polo shirt, and black harness boots, Marcus Sunday hurried toward the New North building at the center of the Georgetown University campus. Weaving through a throng of students, he reached the 120-seat McNeir Auditorium and went in, passing a sign outside that read, THE PERFECT CRIMINAL. LECTURE TODAY. 11 A.M.

The place was abuzz with anticipation. And as Sunday moved down the aisle toward the front rows, he saw that other than an empty director's chair onstage, there wasn't a seat to be had, standing room only.

When he reached the front row, Sunday saw students sitting on the floor in front of the stage. He smiled, moved through them, and bounded up the stairs onto the stage, where he shook hands with the tweedy-looking, gray-bearded fellow waiting.

"Sorry I'm running late, Dr. Wolk," Sunday said.

"I'm just out of class myself," the man said. "Shall I introduce you?"

"Please," Sunday replied, and bobbed his head with deference.

Dr. Wolk turned on the microphone and tapped it twice before saying, "Good morning. I am David Wolk, chairman of Georgetown's philosophy department, and I'd like to welcome you once again to the Spring Series of Lectures by Diverse Scholars."

He smiled and went on: "They say the study of philosophy is not relevant to the real world, but as this crowd shows, that's not true. The creative, resourceful application of philosophical methods to modern problems can be penetrating—ground-breaking, even. Today's guest, who has a PhD in philosophy from Harvard, does just this sort of startling, innovative, and controversial work.

"His first book, published earlier this year, was *The Perfect Criminal*, a fascinating look at two unsolved mass-murder cases told through the eyes of a truly original thinker focused on the depths of the criminal soul.

"Please welcome Marcus Sunday."

Sunday grinned, stood, and took the mike from Dr. Wolk.

Facing the clapping audience, the writer scanned the crowd, his gaze hesitating only briefly on an extremely sexy woman, there in the second row. She had a bemused look about her. Curly, dirty-blond hair hung down over her shoulders and a well-filled white tank top. A colorful sleeve tattoo covered her left arm, depicting a black panther lying on a blooming branch in the jungle. The panther's tail roamed down the woman's forearm and crossed her wrist. The cat had bewitching green eyes, the color of new, wet clover. So did she.

"Five years ago, I set out to find the perfect criminal," Sunday began, forcing himself to look away from her. "To my knowledge he'd never been studied, never been identified. That made sense, because if he was perfect, he would never get caught. Right?"

There was nervous laughter in the room, and nods of agreement.

"So how do you find perfect criminals?" Sunday asked, looking around the room and seeing no confident faces. He focused on that young woman with the ruby lips and the startling clover eyes.

She shrugged, said in a light Cajun accent, "Look at unsolved crimes?"

"Excellent," Sunday said, dropping his head toward his left shoulder. "That is exactly what I did."

The writer went on to describe two unsolved mass murders that had become the heart of his book. Seven years earlier, the five members of the Daley family of suburban Omaha had been found slain at home two nights before Christmas. Except for the wife, they were all found in their beds. Their throats had all been cut with a scalpel or razor. The wife had died similarly, but in the bathroom, and naked. The house doors had either been unlocked, or the killer had had a key. It had snowed during the night and all tracks were buried. Police had found no valuable evidence.

Fourteen months later, the Monahan family of suburban Fort Worth was discovered in a similar state in the aftermath of a violent storm: a father and four children under the age of thirteen were found with their throats slit in their beds. The wife was naked, dead on the bathroom floor. The doors had either been unlocked or the killer had had a key. Again, because of rain and high winds, and the killer's meticulous methods, police had found no usable evidence, DNA or otherwise.

"I became interested because of that lack of evidence, that void," Sunday informed his rapt audience. "After traveling to Nebraska and Texas several times, going to the scenes, reading the files, and interviewing every investigator who worked the cases—FBI, Nebraska State Police, Texas Rangers—I came away understanding that other than the carnage the killer had left, the cases were black holes."

Sunday said that the dearth of evidence had forced him to backtrack and theorize about the philosophical worldview of a perfect killer.

"I came to the conclusion that he had to be an existentialist of some twisted sort," the writer said. "Someone who does not believe in God or any kind of moral or ethical basis for life, someone who thinks there is no meaning to be found in the world beyond what he alone gives to it."

Sunday slowed, seeing he'd lost a few in his audience, and changed tack.

"What I'm saying is that the Russian novelist Fyodor Dostoyevsky almost got it right," he went on. "In his masterwork, *Crime and Punishment*, the central character, Raskolnikov, nearly pulls off the perfect crime. Raskolnikov decides life is meaning-less and he kills a man no one cares about for money.

"At first he's fine with it," Sunday continued, and tapped his head. "But eventually Raskolnikov's mind, specifically his imagination, does him in. Because Raskolnikov can imagine a moral, ethical universe where life has actual meaning, he breaks. Not so, our perfect criminal."

The writer paused, seeing that he held his audience again, before pushing on.

"The perfect killer, I believe, understands clearly that life is meaningless, absurd, without absolute value. As long as the criminal operates from this perspective, he can't be tripped up by his own mind, and he can't be caught."

Sunday went on in this vein for some time, explaining how the evidence surrounding the murder scenes supported his theories and led to others.

He left time at the end for questions. After several nit-pickers fixated on minor notes in the book, the sexy woman in the second row batted her clover eyes and raised her panther tattoo as if she were languidly summoning a waiter.

The writer nodded to her.

"The reviews you got were pretty solid," she said in that rich southern voice. "Except for the one that Detective Alex Cross wrote in the *Post*. I think you'll agree he trashed it, disagreed with almost everything you said. Claimed you changed his words after you interviewed him to fit your thesis."

Sunday gritted his teeth a moment before replying, "Miss, as any journalist will tell you, sources saying they didn't say something are commonplace. What Detective Cross and I have is a strong difference of opinion. Nothing more."

After a long moment of awkwardness, Dr. Wolk cleared his throat, said, "I have a question, Dr. Sunday. As I indicated, I found your book riveting, but I, too, have a quibble about one of your conclusions."

Sunday forced a smile onto his face. "Which one is that, Doctor?"

"At one point in the book you describe the antithesis of the perfect criminal," Dr. Wolk replied. "A detective who believes in and is emblematic of the moral, ethical universe, and so of a meaningful life."

Sunday nodded.

"But I was surprised at your suggestion that

someone like your perfect detective could be made to see that life was meaningless and valueless, and . . ."

"In so doing become a perfect criminal himself?" Sunday asked. "Yes. I wrote that. I believe that it logically follows, Doctor. Don't you?"

Chapter 4

SUNDAY DID NOT GET to his apartment in Washington's Kalorama neighborhood until almost five. There had been a few books to autograph after his lecture, followed by an unavoidable lunch with Dr. Wolk, who drank too much and often reduced philosophical arguments into object lessons worthy of Dear Abby.

To make matters worse, Dr. Wolk had pressed Sunday repeatedly about the sort of research or writing he was doing while on sabbatical. Sunday finally told the chairman of Georgetown's philosophy department the unvarnished but completely vague truth: "I'm conducting an experiment that tests the dimensions of an existential world and the role of human nature in that world."

Dr. Wolk had seemed genuinely intrigued, wanted more, but Sunday had gently and firmly

22

refused, telling his colleague he'd be able to read all about it someday when his research was complete. In fact, he'd promised, Wolk would get the first read.

Hearing zydeco music inside the apartment now and smelling garlic frying somewhere, Sunday used his key to open the door and entered a room with white walls, a white ceiling, and a pale-gray rug. Several pieces of chrome-and-black-leather furniture faced a flat-screen television tuned to a music channel; that was the source of the zydeco.

A woman was in the room, dancing to the music. Her back was to him as her hips swayed and shimmied. Her riot of dirty-blond hair was tied up on her head. She was barefoot, wore loose, flowing olive-green pants and a tight-fitting white tank top that showed off the damp skin and muscles of her shoulders as she reached high overhead, revealing the colorful tattoo of the lounging panther that covered most of her left arm.

Sunday smiled and shut the door loudly. The woman stopped dancing and looked over her shoulder at him with those clover-green eyes. She grinned, clapped, and turned. She ran to him, kissed him hungrily on the mouth, and said in that light Cajun accent, "Thought you'd never get here, Marcus."

"Couldn't be helped," Sunday said. "Had to keep up appearances."

She jumped up into his arms, locked her powerful thighs around his waist, and kissed him again. "But I had something to show you, sugar."

"Been reading *Fifty Shades of Grey* again, Acadia?" he asked, amused, as he stared into her impossible irises.

"Better," Acadia said, unlocked her legs, and slid from his arms. "Follow me, sugar?"

The writer trailed her down the hall, watching her rear sway, imagining some carnal delight. But instead of heading to the master bedroom, she turned right into a room they'd been using for storage.

Four seventy-two-inch flat-screens had been affixed to the far wall, creating one floor-to-ceiling screen that was interrupted only by an Xbox 360 Kinect device aiming outward. The screens glowed dull blue.

A scruffy young guy in a denim jacket sat with his back to them, facing the screens, wearing Bose noise-canceling headphones that were blaring hard rock. A helmet of some sort lay on the table.

Beside the table were a server about the size of a large suitcase and an Xbox 360. Cables linked it all to several laptops.

"Ta-da," Acadia said. "What do you think?"

Furious, Sunday grabbed her by her panther tattoo and dragged her back into the hallway and into a bedroom. He whispered fiercely, "I didn't okay this, and who is that guy?"

Furious right back at him, Acadia hissed, "Preston Elliot. Computer genius. You want state-of-the-art understanding, you need state-of-the-art minds and equipment. You said so yourself!"

Before Sunday could reply, she softened, said, "Besides, sugar, Preston picked up most of it at Costco. No-questions-asked return policy on all electronics."

Sunday stayed skeptical. "What about him? What's his fee?"

Her nostrils flared and she looked at him like he was meat. "The eager young man expects two hours of ultra-kinky sex with me. He'll use a condom. Isn't that what you said you needed right about now?"

Sunday cocked his head, appraising her anew. "Really? I didn't notice, is he—?"

"Approximately your height and weight, yes."

Intrigued now, the writer saw all the possibilities. "That means?"

"Don't you think?" Acadia asked. Her breathing was slow. "It has been a while since we indulged, sugar."

Sunday looked into her dark eyes and felt a thrill of primal anticipation ripple through him. "When?" he asked.

She shrugged. "All he has to do now is debug the software. Says he'll be finished tomorrow around this time."

"Who knows he's here?"

"No one," she replied. "Part of the deal. A secret."

"Think he'll keep it?"

"What do you think?" she asked, pressing against him a moment and igniting crazy desire in him. Sunday looked into Acadia's green eyes and saw himself at eighteen, feeling that predatory rush for the first time as he carried a shovel and slipped up behind a figure crossing a dark yard. For a second it was all so real he swore he heard pigs squealing.

"Well, sugar?" Acadia whispered.

"I'll leave," he said, feeling that thrill all over again. "It's better if he doesn't see me tonight."

She put on a saucy look, pressed against him again, and whispered in his ear, "Acadia Le Duc is limitless. No restrictions. None. You believe that, don't you, sugar?"

"Oh, I do, baby," Sunday said, almost breathless. "It's one of the reasons I'm totally addicted to you."

Chapter 5

MUCH LATER THAT SAME day, Kevin Olmstead, a soft-featured man in his late twenties, spotted the neon sign of the Superior Spa, a massage parlor on Connecticut Avenue reputed to offer "happy endings."

Happy endings, Olmstead thought, running his fingers delicately over his smooth skin. Despite all the craziness in his head, he still knew the enduring value of a happy ending. He had enough money in his pocket, didn't he? He seemed to remember withdrawing cash from an ATM sometime that day.

Was that real? Do I still have the money?

Olmstead stopped, blinking, trying to get his thoughts on track again, a common problem recently. Then he dug in the right front pocket of his jeans, pulled out a wad of cash. He smiled again. He wasn't losing the old noodle when it came to sex *or* money.

Excited now, he hurried toward the massage parlor.

A man in a business suit, no tie, darted out the front door, looked furtively at Olmstead, and then scurried past him. Something about the man's demeanor activated searing memories of another massage parlor and another night.

Olmstead remembered most vividly the smell of citrus cleaner. And he vaguely recalled five bodies: three women in bathrobes, a Cuban in a striped bowling shirt and porkpie hat, and a white guy in a cheap business suit, no tie, all shot at close range, all bleeding from head wounds.

Pain ripped through Olmstead's own skull, almost buckling him on the sidewalk. Was that real? Had that happened? Were there five people dead in a massage parlor in . . . where? Florida?

Or was that all a hallucination? Some blip in his meds?

Olmstead's mind surfed to another memory: a hand putting a Glock 21 pistol into a backpack. Was it the backpack on his shoulder? Was that his hand?

He looked at his hands and was surprised to

see that he wore flesh-colored latex gloves. He was about to check the backpack when the front door of the Superior Spa opened.

A young Asian woman looked out at him, smiled luridly in red hot pants, stiletto heels, and a T-shirt that said GODDESS spelled out in glitter.

"It okay," she said in halting English. "We no bite. You want come inside?"

Happy endings, Olmstead thought, and went toward her feeling an overwhelming sense of gratitude for the invitation.

Everything about the Superior Spa was a marvel to Olmstead, even the thumping rap music. But what entranced him most was the smell of citrus disinfectant. As one might with a freshly baked pie, he sniffed long and deep, flashing on the image of those corpses in Florida. Were they real? Was this?

He looked at the little thing in the red hot pants, said, "Any other girls working tonight?"

She pouted, poked him in the ribs. "What, you no like for me?"

"Oh, I like you fine, Little Thing. Just looking at options."

A big, hard-looking man in a black T-shirt came out from behind the maroon curtain. A second

Asian woman followed him. Scrawnier than Little Thing, she gazed at Olmstead with pink, watery, vacant eyes.

"See anything you like, bro?" the big guy asked.

"I like *them* both," Olmstead said.

"You think this is Bangkok or something? Make a choice."

"Cost?"

"Shower, soapy table, massage, seventy-five to me," the bouncer replied. "Anything extra, you talk to the girl. Anything extra, you pay the girl."

Olmstead nodded, pointed at Little Thing, who looked overjoyed.

The bouncer said, "Seventy-five and you gotta check your pack, bro."

Olmstead went soft-lidded, nodded. "Lemme get my wallet."

He swung the pack off his shoulder, set it on one of the plastic chairs, and unstrapped the top flap. He drew back the toggle that held shut the main compartment and tugged the pouch open. There was his wallet deep inside. And a beautiful Glock 21.

Was that a suppressor on the barrel? Was the weapon real? Was any of this?

Olmstead sure hoped so as he drew out the pistol. When it came to happy endings, a wet dream was rarely as satisfying as the real thing.

Chapter 6

JUST AFTER EIGHT THAT night, I was getting ready to pack it in, head home, have a beer, see my wife and kids, and watch the last half of the game. So was John Sampson. It had been a long, grinding day for both of us and we'd made little progress on the cases we were working. We both groaned when Captain Quintus appeared, blocking the doorway.

"Another one?" I said.

"You've got to be kidding," Sampson said.

"Not in the least," Quintus replied grimly. "We've got at least three dead at a massage parlor over on Connecticut. Patrolmen on the scene said it's a bloodbath just based on what they've seen in the front room. They're waiting for you and Sampson to go through the rest of the place. Forensics is swamped, backed up. They'll be there as soon as they can."

I sighed, tossed the Kimmel file on my desk, and grabbed my blue Homicide Windbreaker. Sampson grabbed his own Windbreaker and drove us in an unmarked sedan over to Connecticut Avenue just south of Dupont Circle. Metro patrol officers had already set up a generous perimeter around the massage parlor. The first television news camera crews were arriving. We hustled behind the yellow tape before they could spot us.

Officer K. D. Carney, a young patrolman and the initial responder, filled us in. At 7:55 p.m. dispatch took a 911 report from an anonymous male caller who said someone had "gone psycho inside the Superior Spa on Connecticut Ave."

"I was on my way home from work, and close by, so I was first on the scene," said Carney, a baby-faced guy with no eyebrows or lashes and no hair on his face or forearms. I pegged him as a sufferer from alopecia areata, a disorder that causes a total loss of body hair.

"Contamination?" I asked.

"None from me, sir," the young officer replied. "Took one look, saw three deceased, backed out, sealed the place. Front and back. There's an alley exit."

"Let's button up that alley, too, for the time being," I said.

"You want me to search it?"

"Wait for the crime scene unit."

You could tell Carney was disappointed in the way only someone who desperately wanted to be a detective could be disappointed. But that was the way it had to be. The fewer people with access to the crime scene, the better.

"You know the history of this place, right?" Carney said as Sampson and I donned blue surgical booties and latex gloves.

"Remind us," Sampson said.

"Used to be called the Cherry Blossom Spa," Carney said. "It was shut down for involvement in sexual slavery a few years back."

I remembered now. I'd heard about it when I was still out working at Quantico for the FBI. The girls were underage, lured by the promise of easy entry into the United States, and enslaved here by Asian crime syndicates.

"How in God's name did this place ever reopen?" I asked.

Carney shrugged. "New ownership, I'd guess."

"Thanks, Officer," I said, heading toward the massage parlor. "Good work."

I opened the door, and we took three steps into a scene straight out of an Alfred Hitchcock movie.

The place reeked of some kind of citrus-based cleanser, and stereo speakers hummed with feedback. Sprawled in every ounce of her blood, an Asian female in red hot pants, heels, and a white T-shirt lay on the floor. One round had hit her through the neck, taking out the carotid.

A second victim, also an Asian female, dressed in a threadbare robe, lay on her side next to a maroon curtain. She was curled almost into a fetal position, but her shoulders were twisted slightly toward the ceiling. Her right eye was open and her fingers splayed. Blood stained her face and matted her hair, draining from what used to be the socket of her left eye.

The third victim, the massage parlor's night manager, was sprawled against a blood-spattered wall behind the counter. There was a look of surprise on his face and a bullet hole dead center in his forehead.

I counted four 9mm shells around the bodies. It appeared that the killer had sprayed disinfectant all over the room. Streams of it stained the bodies, the furniture, and the floor. There was an empty five-gallon container of Citrus II Hospital Germicidal Deodorizing Cleanser concentrate by the manager's corpse. We discovered a second empty container of it beyond the maroon curtain in the L-shaped hallway, as depressing a place as I've ever been, with exposed stud walls and grimy, unpainted plasterboard.

In the back room on the right, we found the fourth victim.

I am a big man, and Sampson stands six foot five, but the bruiser facedown on the mattress was physically in a whole other league. I judged him to be six foot eight and close to three hundred pounds, most of it muscle. He had longish brown hair that hung over his face, which was matted in blood.

I took several pictures with my phone, squatted down, and with my gloved fingers pushed back the hair to get a better look at the wound. When I did, the big man's face was revealed and I stopped short.

"Sonofabitch," said Sampson, who was standing behind me. "Is that—?"

"Pete Francones," I said, nodding in disbelief. "The Mad Man himself."

Chapter 7

PETE "MAD MAN" FRANCONES had anchored the Washington Redskins defensive unit for fourteen years. A defensive end with outstanding speed and quickness, Francones wreaked havoc in the NFL, earning a reputation as a tireless worker and an insanely passionate player on game day.

His histrionics on the sideline during big games in college had earned him the nickname, and he'd parlayed the whole Mad Man thing into a fortune in commercial endorsements. It didn't hurt that Francones was good-looking, smart, well-spoken, and irreverent, traits that had earned him a coveted spot commentating on *Monday Night Football* just the season before.

And now Francones was the fourth victim in a killing spree in one of the sleaziest places in DC? This guy?

"Didn't he date, like, Miss Universe or something?" Sampson asked, sounding baffled as well.

"Runner-up. Miss Venezuela."

"So why would he be in this hellhole?"

I could think of several reasons, but I got his point. Francones was the kind of guy who did not have to pay for sex. If you believed the gossip, he'd had women throwing themselves at him for—

Something puzzled me. "Where's the hooker he was with?"

We looked under the bed. We even lifted Francones's body to see if she'd been pinned beneath him. But she hadn't.

"Suppressor," Sampson said, breaking me out of my thoughts.

"Again?" I said.

"Killer must have used a suppressor on the gun. Or Francones would have heard the shots and been up and facing the door."

I saw what he was saying, replied, "So the three in the outer room die first. Then the killer comes down the hall, finds victim number four, shoots to incapacitate, and then to kill."

"Sounds professional."

I nodded, studying the Mad Man's wounds again, thinking trajectories. "He's kneeling when he takes the first shot, and then falls forward. So again, where's the hooker?"

"And what's with the cleanser?"

"Maybe the killer doesn't like the smell of death?"

"Or maybe the killer gets off on the citrus smell."

"Definitely not a robbery," Sampson said, gesturing toward the Breitling watch on Francones's wrist.

I picked up the Hall of Famer's pants, rifled the pockets, and came up with a gold money clip holding a thousand dollars in fifties, and then something I didn't expect to find. The vial held at least three grams of white powder but was capable of holding twice that. I tasted it. My tongue and lips numbed at the bitter taste of high-grade cocaine.

Showing the vial to Sampson, I said, "I don't remember anything to do with the Mad Man and drugs."

"Maybe he wasn't all *naturally* amped up and crazy."

We bagged the cocaine as evidence.

"You seeing a phone?" Sampson asked.

"No," I said. "And no car keys, either. And no third woman."

We went through the rest of the Superior Spa. The manager's office had been lightly tossed. Oddly, however, the unlocked strongbox was untouched and contained nearly four thousand dollars. Untouched as well were a wallet with six hundred dollars and IDs that pegged the manager as twenty-nine-year-old Donald Blunt of College Park, a grad student at the University of Maryland. The only thing we could determine as missing was the hard drive that recorded the feed from the lobby security cameras.

In the women's locker room we found clothes, cash, three cell phones, and documents that identified the two female victims. The woman in the red hot pants was Kim Ho, a twenty-year-old Korean national who'd come to the United States three months before on a temporary work visa. The woman who'd died in the fetal position was An Lu, also Korean, nineteen, also in the United States on a short-term work visa.

"Third cell phone," Sampson said.

"Third hooker," I said, nodding as my mind flashed back to the wound on the Mad Man's lower back, imagining how he had to have been kneeling when—

"Detective Cross?" Officer Carney said.

Sampson and I spun around. The patrolman was standing in the doorway, wearing surgical booties.

"Officer, I clearly asked you to stay outside and maintain the perimeter."

Carney's head retreated by several inches. "I'm sorry, sir, but I thought you'd want to know that there's a hysterical young woman outside who says she knows at least one of the people working in here tonight."

Chapter 8

"I'M ALEX CROSS," I said to the young woman after Officer Carney had brought her under the tape and led her over to me. "Could I see your identification, miss?"

Young, Asian, and wearing jeans, sneakers, and a George Washington University Windbreaker, she seemed not to hear my request at first. She just stared at the door to the Superior Spa. Everything about her looked tortured.

"Miss?" I said softly.

Her voice trembled as she asked, "They all dead?"

"I'm afraid everyone inside is deceased, yes," I replied. "How did—"

Everything about her seemed to dissolve right then. I couldn't catch her before she collapsed to the sidewalk. She choked, retched, and vomited several times. Then she looked up at me and began to sob. "I knew this place was—I . . . I told her. But she always said it was—"

The young woman started hyperventilating and then dry-heaving. I squatted down next to her, put my hand on her back, trying to comfort her. But it was as if I'd put a hot iron on her skin.

She jerked away from me, cowered against the front of a paint store, flinging up her hands, screaming, "No! No! Don't touch me!"

"Miss," I said. "I'm not here to—"

And then I got it.

I stood, took several steps back, and squatted down again. Like I said, I'm a big man, and I was trying to make myself smaller. I motioned with my chin for Sampson, who'd been listening, to do the same.

"Miss?" I said. "Do you work here?"

Her eyes had gone haunted again, but she shook her head violently.

"Did you used to work here?" Sampson asked.

Her eyes darted toward the front door and the tears began to gush out of her. "My parents," she sobbed. "They're going to know, aren't they?"

We spent the next fifteen minutes getting the gist of her story. Her name was Blossom Mai. She was nineteen and a sophomore at George

Washington University, a premed major from San Diego. Her parents were Vietnamese immigrants who'd worked eighty-hour weeks to send her to school. They covered what she had not received in scholarships for room and board, but nothing more.

The job Blossom had at school was not enough to live on, or at least it did not feel that way when she compared her life to her rich classmates'. Last fall, Blossom had made a new friend. Her name was Cam Nguyen. A year older, a junior economics major at GW, Cam came from Orange County, California, and was also a second-generation Vietnamese-American girl whose parents had scrimped for her education.

But Cam wore the latest clothes. And on Saturday nights she went to expensive bars in Georgetown. Cam seemed to have anything she wanted.

"So you asked her how she was doing it?" Sampson said.

Blossom nodded. "She said it was safer working here than as an escort because there was always an armed manager guarding you."

The deal was simple. Each girl paid the house manager five hundred a shift. Each customer paid the manager seventy-five dollars. The girls took everything beyond that. Many nights Cam netted a thousand, sometimes fifteen hundred. But Blossom only worked at the Superior Spa for one night.

"I felt like I was in a filthy nightmare," she told us, crying again. "I . . . I just couldn't do it again. Couldn't even spend the money. I gave it away to the homeless shelter. But Cam, she could turn things off, you know?"

"Why do you think Cam's in there?"

"I *know* she's in there," Blossom said. "We live next door to each other in a building a few blocks from here. I saw her in the hallway two, no three hours ago. She said she was on her way here and tried to get me to go with her again."

"I'm glad you didn't," I said softly.

After a moment, Blossom asked weakly, "She's dead?

Cam?"

"We don't know," Sampson said. "But she's not in there."

"Really?" Blossom said, her eyes wide with sudden hope. "Maybe she decided not to come."

"Got her cell phone number?"

She nodded, gave it to me. I said to Sampson, "Go inside, listen for it."

Sampson understood and left. I waited a minute

and then punched in the number. It rang. My partner answered. "Right here," he said. "The blue iPhone."

"Okay," I said, hung up, and looked at Blossom. "Her phone's inside, but nothing else."

"No," Blossom said, shaking her head. "She would never, ever leave her phone. She was, like, a textaholic."

"What if she'd just shot four people?" I asked. "Would she leave it behind?"

"Cam?" She paused. "I guess I don't know." Then anguish took her. "How am I going to explain this to my parents?"

I was confused but then understood. "Blossom, as long as you are cooperating with us, as far as we're concerned, your parents don't have to know a thing about this. Ever."

"Really?"

"Really."

Blossom Mai broke down all over again.

Chapter 9

AT SEVEN FORTY-FIVE the next morning, Marcus Sunday strode confidently through the lobby of the Four Seasons in Georgetown, knowing full well that no one would ever recognize him in this outrageous getup.

On another man it might have been thought a clown's outfit: purple high-top sneakers, orange shirt and pants, ice-blue contact lenses, two nose rings, and a flaming-red Abe Lincoln beard with matching eyebrows and a matching wig that stood four inches straight up over his head. But Sunday knew that the disguise exuded a certain, well, charismatic threat, especially in a place like this, as if he were some sort of psycho Carrot Top or worse.

Indeed, the maître d' looked mightily upset when Sunday went to the stack on a table and grabbed a copy of the *Washington Post* that featured a story on the death of Mad Man Francones and three others at a local massage parlor, then approached his station, saying in a nasal, whiny tone: "Table for one."

The maître d' tried to look down his nose at Sunday, said, "And do you have a reservation with us, sir?"

"Guest of the hotel," Sunday said. "Room 1450."

Room 1450 was a thousand-dollar-a-night suite. The maître d's attitude shifted measurably, but he still eyed the writer's attire. "Mr. . . . ?"

"Mulch," Sunday replied. "Thierry Mulch. Like the composted stuff."

"Oh," the maître d' said as if he'd just tasted something unpleasant, and snatched up a menu. "Please follow me, Mr. Mulch."

Inside the dining room, the air seemed at a different barometric pressure, as if some vast low had descended over the place. And it bore a smell beyond rueful bacon, sausage, and coffee that Sunday recognized as the rot of power.

Corpulent stuffed shirts with five-hundred-dollar haircuts were wall-eyeing the writer almost immediately. A brassy blond cougar in a brick-red Chanel suit looked up as he passed. Sunday winked her way, licked his upper lip with feline hunger, and almost laughed when her cheeks ignited.

He kept walking, flashing on the mystery that was Acadia Le Duc, and the indescribable fun and desires they would share in just a few short—

"Mr. Mulch?" the maître d' said, breaking into his thoughts with a stiff gesture to a table tucked in the corner by the kitchen doors.

"Why don't you stick me in the john?" Sunday asked in that nasal, whiny voice, then pointed over near the windows. "I'd like to sit there."

The maître d' went stone-faced but nodded and led the writer to a table where almost everyone in the place could see him.

"Thanks," Sunday said loudly. "More like it."

He looked around at the various dignitaries, politicians, lobbyists, and the like, many of whom were either glancing at him or staring openly. The writer gave several of them the thumbs-up. They looked like they'd just felt a tick crawling up their spine.

Brilliant entertainment, he thought, and then analyzed the forces at play.

These sorts of ridiculous people believed in decorum, tact, and manners. Sunday had found that when you brushed up hard against their rules of accepted behavior, you created agitation. And agitation, as far as he was concerned, was a good thing, a very good thing—what he lived for, as a matter of fact.

But when a waiter came over to pour coffee and take his order, Sunday behaved himself. He was hungry and had a busy day ahead.

"The frittata, the lemon and ricotta pancakes, and a large fresh-squeezed OJ," he said.

"Bacon?" the waiter asked.

Sunday made a face as if he might be ill, said, "No, never again."

When the waiter left, the writer read the story about the Francones murder with great interest, especially the fact that Alex Cross had been assigned to the case. *Well, who else, right?*

Rather than getting truly pissed off, however, Sunday refocused on the task at hand. *Make a scene,* he thought.

Looking around again, the writer noticed that a nerdy man in a Brooks Brothers suit that screamed professional boor had taken a seat at the table to his left. The boor was studying his iPhone intently. Sunday recognized him as a syndicated political pundit and mainstay of the morning talk shows, a pasty-faced guy in a bow tie who never used a single-syllable word when a six-syllable one would do.

Perfect target, the writer realized, and began to enjoy himself. Serendipity, that was what it was. Chance fortune.

"Porn?" Sunday called over to the pundit.

The chattering head looked up, confused.

The writer gestured at the phone and observed in that nasal, whiny voice: "I figured you had to be watching something, like, really nasty to be that locked on."

"Hardly," the man shot back in a harsh whisper. "Have some couth."

"That one of the specials here?" Sunday asked, glancing down at his menu. "I must have missed that. Does couth come poached or fried?"

The pundit was studying his iPhone even more intently now.

"I know you," Sunday said. "You're a guy who's got an opinion on everything. So I want to know: Do you think Pooh was right?"

The pundit sighed, looked at the writer, said, "Pooh? As in the bear?"

"Or *Ursus mellitus,* as *you* might say," Sunday replied good-naturedly. "Now, I consider Pooh

Bear to be one of the great thinkers of all time. Right up with Marcus Aurelius, Nietzsche, and Bob Dylan. Especially when it came to breakfast."

The pundit got exasperated. "What *are* you babbling about?"

Sunday acted offended, touched his fingers to his flaming-red hair.

"Babbling?" he said. "Thierry Mulch? Well, no more than you in your latest column. All *I* was doing was discussing Pooh Bear and his immortal disquisition with Piglet regarding breakfast.

"Don't you remember?" Sunday demanded angrily. "Pooh Bear thought breakfast was the most exciting part of the day. There's his thesis, my good man. Agree or disagree? No reason to say 'affirmative' or 'demonstrably false.' A simple yes or no will do."

Chapter 10

SENSING THE BED SHIFTING as a new weight compressed it, I came slowly to consciousness, feeling as if I'd gone to sleep only a few minutes before. But when I groggily opened my eyes, it was broad daylight and my beautiful wife, Bree, lay on her belly beside me, dressed for the gym. She was up on her elbows, her chin cradled in her hands. Tears clouded her eyes, but she was beaming.

"Sorry to wake you up, Alex. I know you got in late and the Mad Man Francones case and all. But I thought you'd want to know."

I blinked dumbly, yawned, and said, "Know what?"

"Jeannie Shelton just called, from the lab?"

"Okay?" I said, glancing at the clock. Ten past nine. What ungodly time had I gone to bed? It had to have been after—

"Alex, the burned body in that old factory wasn't Ava," Bree said.

That was like guzzling a pot of French roast. I sat up, alert and jittery.

"But the identification, the necklace?"

"They ran Ava's dental records against the burned girl's," my wife said. "Not even close to a match. Ava had congenitally missing teeth. The dead girl had a full set."

Relief washed over me like a wave and I felt tears welling to match Bree's. Ava Williams was still alive.

Nana Mama took Ava in when she was fourteen, an orphan and runaway from a foster home. She'd lived with us almost a year. For a time, life in our house seemed to have been good for Ava. Or at least it seemed that way to us. She'd bonded with Bree and seemed to tolerate the rest of us.

But then Ava had started hanging with the wrong crowd. We suspected drug use, maybe alcohol, and quicker and sadder than you'd think, she was gone, until a burned corpse was discovered in an old, abandoned factory in Southeast that was also a reputed hangout for junkies and the homeless. Ava's silver bracelet, which she'd worn constantly, was on the dead girl's wrist. So was a necklace my grandmother had given her. The news had been devastating.

"Isn't that wonderful?" Bree asked.

"Better than wonderful," I said, and wiped at my eyes. "But where is she? And who's the dead girl?"

"Jeannie said no match on her yet. But Jane Doe is definitely *not* our Ava."

Tired as I was, my mind has been conditioned over decades of police work to think a certain way, whether I want to or not. The relief I'd felt at learning that Ava was alive was replaced by a colder sensation as I considered the idea that the young runaway who'd found shelter under my roof could have killed another young woman, planted phony identification on her, and then set her on fire.

But because my wife and Ava had become so close, I said nothing.

"We have to find her," Bree said. "Bring her home."

I thought about Pete Francones and the other victims at the massage parlor and wondered how I was going to make time to search for Ava.

"Let's start tonight if you get home at a reasonable hour," Bree insisted.

"I don't think there will be any reasonable hours for me for a long time," I said. "The Francones case is going to be a media circus."

"Already is," she said. "And I get what a slam this is going to be for you, Alex. I really do. But don't worry. I'll start looking for Ava myself. When you can, you pitch in. Okay?"

I stroked her cheek, said, "You're such a good person, Bree Stone."

My wife kissed my hand, said, "You are, too, baby. The best man I know."

Chapter 11

OUTSIDE THE FRONT ENTRANCE of the Four Seasons in Georgetown, security guards flanked Marcus Sunday as he waited for the valet to bring him his car. The maître d' coldly handed him a doggie bag containing his breakfast.

"You guys have zero sense of humor," Sunday remarked, making a show of stroking his flaming-red Abe Lincoln beard.

"Harassing our patrons and posing as a guest are not funny matters, Mr. Mulch," the maître d' seethed.

"I was checking in later today," the writer replied with great indignation. "Or thought about it, anyway. But now? No chance, gentlemen. No chance."

A two-hundred-and-fifty-thousand-dollar Bentley Continental GT Coupe convertible rolled up.

The writer went around, took the keys, and gave the valet a fifty before donning driving gloves and climbing in. He glanced over at the shocked maître d' and the guards, scratched at his fake beard with his middle finger, and drove out from under the hotel's portico onto Pennsylvania Avenue, heading east.

That had to have made an impression, Sunday thought, and felt very happy. That breakfast room had been the height of absurdity: a place of power plagued with so many rules, customs, and mores that any creativity, any resourcefulness was impossible.

But if anything, Marcus Sunday was a very, very creative and very, very resourceful man. Take the driver's license in his wallet that identified him as Thierry Mulch of Boise, Idaho. The bogus ID had cost him $145, purchased from a kid he met in Boston who catered to the underage drinking crowd at the local colleges. The fake license was flawless, like the six other Thierry Mulch driver's licenses he carried from time to time, so good that he'd used them to get past TSA agents at the airport, blue-light watermarks and all.

TSA: The Stupid Administration.

Turning north onto Rock Creek Parkway with

a triumphant grin on his face, the writer thought of the quality of those fake licenses as more evidence in support of one of his long-held theories. Sunday had heard politicians claim that corporations were people, but the writer took it a step further:

People are documents, my friends!

There was no disputing that fact, as far as he was concerned. With the right papers and the right attitude you could be anyone. Hell, you could be six or seven people at once with the correct documents.

Wasn't his life sterling proof of that? Indeed it was, and in every way.

Those ideas pleased Sunday as he pulled into the EuroMotorcars lot in Bethesda. He parked out front, noticed the subtle odor of azaleas on the breeze, and had no sooner turned off the ignition than a man with a scrubbed, boyish face hurried out the door of the dealership.

"Mr. Thierry Mulch!" he cried, fairly skipping toward the convertible. "What do you think of the Bentley?"

"Like a restaurant dedicated to lackluster cuisine," Sunday said in that whining, nasal voice, and tossed the salesman the keys. "I'm going over to Porsche, see if the Germans are still better engineers than the Brits."

He started to walk off the lot.

The salesman was first slack-jawed and then insulted. "You just can't afford it!"

The writer looked over his shoulder, said, "Thierry Mulch is a man who can afford anything he wants and do anything he wants. Remember that."

Sunday nodded with satisfaction as he strolled north toward the Landmark Theatres complex. It was true: money had not been an issue since he'd turned eighteen. Indeed, the writer rarely gave finances a thought. He just did what he wished and had accountants who paid for it all.

And yet the writer was not given to excess unless it was necessary. Excess—chic clothes, expensive cars, and the like—attracted attention, and attention, in his opinion, was only good if there was a purpose behind it, this morning being a case in point.

Sunday found the beige vacuum repair panel van right where he'd left it: behind the theater where the employees parked. He unlocked the van, slid back the side door, climbed in, closed it, and tossed the doggie bag in the front seat.

With great care, he stripped off the flaming-red wig, Abe Lincoln beard, and eyebrows, revealing close-cropped salt-and-pepper hair. Two quick movements and he'd popped out the colored contact lenses, turning his eyes from ice-blue back to light slate-gray. Out, too, came the nose rings.

He traded his outfit for jeans, a black polo shirt, and boat shoes. The purple sneakers and the rest went into a shopping bag. He traded the Mulch driver's license for another identifying Howard Moon, residence Falls Church, Virginia.

Completing his transformation with Ray-Ban aviator sunglasses and an ill-fitting Washington Nationals baseball cap, Sunday appraised himself in the rearview mirror. A sublime portrayal of a boring loser, the writer thought, nothing like the court jester who test-drove a Bentley and stunk up power breakfast at the Four Seasons.

Putting the van in gear, he drove back into the city.

It was nearly ten when Sunday parked down the street from Cross's house. Turning on all-news radio, he listened with great interest to coverage of the Mad Man Francones murders. He was fascinated by tales of men killing other men, of women killing other women, and of every variation in between.

Murder was not only Sunday's academic field, it was the story of his life, and the most sublime act of all in the human comedy, the snipping or slashing or squeezing away of existence, the end of the absurdity and meaninglessness of it all in an ecstatic fit of violence.

He'd heard of peaceful death, of course, but considered such tales fantasy and nonsense, wishful thinking of the most pitiful kind.

Sunday spotted Cross's wife, Bree, exiting the house in a warm-up suit and running shoes. Through his binoculars he watched her walking down past the Dumpster. As he watched her jog off, he nodded to himself, thinking that death was never, ever peaceful. In the writer's experience, death was always drama that rose to a wicked battle and a brutal, brutal end.

Chapter 12

BREE WAS GETTING READY for the department's annual fitness test and left for the gym around ten. On the way downstairs, I peeked inside my daughter's room. Jannie was two years younger than Ava but already the lanky adolescent, still sleeping because it was an in-service day for teachers.

My seven-year-old, Ali, was up, however, lying on the couch in the family room watching a DVD. A guy with a cowboy hat was running and shooting at . . .

"What are you watching?" I asked.

"*The Walking Dead,*" Ali replied. "It's a TV show. Really good. There are, like, zombies everywhere and these are some of the last people left alive."

"What happened to Cartoon Network?"

"It closed down after the zombies showed up," Ali said, and gave me a grin that revealed the gap where he'd lost a tooth the week before.

Someone on the screen shot a zombie. Someone else put an axe blade in its head. "That's the best way you can kill them," Ali explained. "Destroy their brains."

"I told him to turn that nonsense off," Nana Mama chided as she walked into the room. "I don't like him watching those zombie things."

I wasn't a big fan of the idea, either, but Ali groaned, "It's good, Nana. It's not about zombies, 'cause they don't talk, you know? It's more about the people who are fighting them."

My grandmother looked at me, and I shrugged. Annoyed at my lack of resolve, she said, "Well, I'll be long gone before that bird comes to roost. Your breakfast is ready. Then we'll get the last things packed and moved to the basement."

Packed and moved to the basement? I felt that squeezing sensation again when I remembered I'd promised my grandmother that I'd help her pack up the kitchen before the remodelers showed up to start. How long was that going to take? Whatever. It had to be done.

I gave her a kiss on the cheek before I went

into the kitchen and found my favorite breakfast waiting: bacon, sunny-side-up eggs, toasted
Portuguese bread, fried green tomatoes, and grits.

One bite and I was ten again, and feeling safe
because my grandmother had rescued me and
brought me to live with her in Washington instead
of an orphanage down in North Carolina. That's
the power of a home-cooked meal. You don't get
that at IHOP or McDonald's, no matter how hard
they try to sell it.

"Alex, what time did the contractor say he was
going to come?" Nana Mama asked as I broke up a
piece of toast, stabbed a chunk of it with a fork,
and dipped it in the egg yolk.

"Around noon," I replied. "And our contractor
has a name: Billy DuPris."

My grandmother used to be an inner-city high
school vice principal, and even at ninety-plus she
usually has a bemused, seen-it-all air about her.
But that morning she looked stressed in the way
she worried her hands with her apron and glanced
all around the kitchen as if trying to figure out
what to do next.

I put down my fork. "You okay?"

"I'm fine, Alex," she said, hesitated. "I just don't
know where to start."

"I said I'd help you, and I will, just as soon as I finish eating."

Distracted, she swallowed, looked all around again, nodded.

"Something *is* bothering you," I said.

"It's nothing," Nana Mama replied. "Just a foolish old woman who can't abide change is all."

I saw it then, understood the source of her anxiety. From the moment I set foot in this house more than thirty years ago, my grandmother's kitchen had been just that, *her* kitchen, this domain that she ruled with skill, humor, and unquestioned authority, with a place for everything and everything in its place.

I got up, went to her, and put my arms around her, amazed at how tiny she felt. "You said you wanted a new kitchen," I said. "A fancy six-burner stove with a built-in griddle. The new stainless fridge. All of it."

"I know," she said, pressing her head into my chest. "I just get sentimental. That's all. Nothing will ever be the same, Alex."

I released her, put my finger under her chin. "Weren't you the one who taught me that every minute of life is a change?"

"Doesn't make it easier," she said.

"You want me to call Mr. DuPris, pull the plug?"

She bit at her lip a second and then shook her head. "No. I'll just have to make do. What's that they always say, 'Evolve or die'?"

"Seems to me I've heard that somewhere," I said.

There was an awkward silence between us before she said, "You go on back, and when you finish with your breakfast we'll start with the cookbooks, the spices, and everything I want in the fancy new pantry I'm—"

My cell phone rang. Captain Quintus. I didn't want to answer but did.

"Cross," I said.

"Where are you?" the homicide captain barked. "All hell is breaking loose down here. The chief wants answers. The mayor wants answers. The Francones killing has become a symbol of the murder rate, Alex. All hell is breaking loose."

"And I've got a contractor coming in to tear my house apart in less than two hours," I replied. "I promise you I'll be there as soon as I can."

Quintus's voice turned heated. "Goddamn it, Alex, find someone else to do it and get your ass in here."

I clicked off the phone without giving him an answer.

Chapter 13

EARLIER THAT SAME FRIDAY morning and several blocks south of the Takoma Metro station, Kelli Adams, a blond woman wearing heavy makeup and a conservative blue suit, watched a sleek black Audi A5 roll up in front of Child's Play day care center.

A tall, rail-thin guy in a Brooks Brothers suit came flying out of the Audi, ran around the other side.

He yanked open the passenger-side door, fumbled around inside, and soon came out with an eight-month-old baby girl and a blue diaper bag. He hurried through the gate and up the steps, then disappeared inside.

"Father of the year," Adams muttered under her breath. "It's time your little girl got to know her mother."

The father of the year exited Child's Play, ran down the stairs, jumped into his Audi, and sped off.

That's enough of that, Adams thought righteously, and started across the street. Giving the front door a quick double rap with her knuckles to indicate she meant business, Adams entered Child's Play and found herself in the center hallway facing a counter staffed by a cheery-looking young woman whose nameplate said SUSAN.

"Hi," Susan said. "Can I help you?"

"I'd like to see Marylyn Green," Adams replied. "She does run this facility?"

"Yes. And you are?"

Adams pulled out a billfold and showed Susan an ID card from the city's Office of the Deputy Mayor for Health and Human Services. She worked as an investigator with the office's agency for child and family services.

Susan stood up. "I'll get Ms. Green."

"Why don't you take me to her."

"What's this about?" Susan asked.

Adams gave her a cold stare. Susan pushed a button behind the counter. There was a buzzing noise. The door to her right came unlocked. They entered a hallway that smelled of children and babies and echoed with their laughs and cries.

They exited into a large room where toddlers were playing.

"Ms. Green," Susan called to a tall redheaded woman with a kind face. "Someone to see you."

Adams showed her ID again, said, "I'd like to see Joss Branson. She is in your care, correct?"

"Yes. Joss? What's wrong?"

"What isn't?" Adams said.

The day care owner led the way into a nursery. There were four cribs in the room. Three were occupied by sleeping babies. A fourth lay on her back, squalling while a tired-looking woman in her fifties changed her diapers.

"Eliza, Ms. Adams is an investigator with DC Child and Family Services," Marylyn Green said, looking confused. "She wishes to see Joss."

Eliza pressed the last diaper tape into place and said, "You're looking at her."

Adams crossed to the changing table and picked up the wailing child.

"What's wrong?" Marylyn Green asked again.

"Is she often agitated like this?" Adams demanded.

Eliza looked uncertain. "We call this the crying hour, usually right after they all come in. But they settle down. I guess Joss a little less easily."

71

"It's probably the meth."

"*What!*" Green said.

"No," Eliza said. "Mr. Branson is a scientist at the Smithsonian, and his wife, Crystal, has cancer. Why would they—"

"Mr. Branson is a chemist, and you're right, she does have cancer. We believe it's like that television show *Breaking Bad*. DEA tells us they cook it in the basement. Explains the Audi, doesn't it?"

Marylyn Green's hand went to her mouth. "My God, we had no—"

"Why would you?" Adams snapped. "In any case, I am here because we are concerned that Joss has been exposed to a multitude of toxins. Because of an ongoing federal investigation, we are not free to step in and take Joss, but I have a writ that allows me to take her to have her blood, skin, and clothing tested so we have a clear idea of her level of exposure. I am assuming you can keep this confidential? As I said, there is an ongoing FBI investigation of her parents. And I won't be long. We'll go to Bethesda."

"Yes, of course, my God, whatever is best for Joss."

"Should I get her things?" Eliza asked.

"That would be much appreciated," Adams

said, bouncing Joss in her arms. "The sooner I can get her to the lab, the sooner I can have her back."

"Oh, you've got time," the day care owner said. "Mr. Branson is rarely here before five to get her."

For the first time, Adams smiled. "That makes things a little easier."

Chapter 14

AROUND FOUR THAT AFTERNOON, Cynthia Wu slowly peeled back the Mad Man's scalp, revealing a nasty splintered hole where the .40-caliber hollow-point bullet had entered the back of his head, and finally the shattered cheekbone where the bullet had exited.

"How far was the shot?" John Sampson asked.

"Ten? Fifteen feet?" the medical examiner replied.

"Like you said, John, looks like a pro," I commented.

"Either that or obsessed," Sampson replied, gesturing across the room, where another medical examiner was working on Kim Ho, one of the dead Korean women from the massage parlor. "Everyone in the spa except our boy here was shot at close range. I'm thinking the shooter likes to see their faces, their reactions just before he pulls the trigger, but he got intimidated when he saw Francones's size."

It was possible, I supposed, another variation in the catalog of strange fetishes we'd seen over the years in association with mass and serial murderers.

"Sometimes close-range shots like this are meant to disfigure as well as kill," I said. "But that's usually the case in murders provoked by the infidelity of one partner or another."

"Far as I can tell, the Mad Man was all about infidelity," Sampson replied. "But you believe the gossip, he somehow managed to get along with all of them, you know, like Charlie Sheen in *Two and a Half Men*."

"Charlie disgusted most of the women he slept with eventually. Didn't you see the one where he dies and they have the funeral?"

"No, I must have missed that one," Sampson said.

"Any clue where Mad Man's girlfriends were at the time of death?"

"I don't have a complete inventory of his harem, but according to *People Magazine*, he's been seen in public quite a bit with Mandy Bell Lee, the country-western singer. They met after a Titans game in Nashville last year."

"Where's she?"

"I can find out."

"Mad Man must have had an agent, lawyer, some kind of business manager. Those people might know about enemies or financial grudges. Maybe about coke use, too. Anything else?"

"Quintus and the DA have filed for a warrant in Virginia so we can search his place out in McLean. Until it comes through, the sheriff over there has the estate blocked off."

I was about to ask when the warrant was likely to come through when my phone beeped, alerting me to an e-mail. I stepped aside and opened it, seeing documents attached courtesy of Captain Quintus.

I scanned them. A Delaware real estate trust had bought the building that housed the Superior Spa the year before. The massage parlor was a DBA of Relax LLC, a Falls Church, Virginia, company with a post office box address and a Trenton Wiggs named as president.

One more piece of the puzzle, I thought, and considered what I'd been able to dig up after moving the last of the kitchen into boxes and the basement and watching the horror in my grandmother's face when Billy DuPris entered the house with crowbars and rolls of plastic sheeting.

Donald Blunt, the dead night manager of the massage parlor, had been working on his doctorate in molecular biology at the University of Maryland. I'd tracked down his two roommates at their apartment in College Park.

One roommate said Blunt took the job at the spa because it "paid like twenty bucks an hour, was light duty that allowed him time to study, and he got his rocks off, like, anytime he wanted." The other roommate said Blunt had no enemies that he knew of. And neither roommate could come up with a scenario that would have a cold-blooded killer targeting their friend.

In the two hours I'd had before the scheduled autopsies, I'd tried to work on the chain of circumstances that had led the two dead Korean women to the United States, to Washington, and to the Superior Spa. I started by putting in a request with USCIS to see their temporary work visa applications but was told it would take several days to fulfill the request.

On the way to the morgue, I made a depressing inch of headway on Cam Nguyen, the missing third prostitute. Other detectives had been to her place that morning and found it empty. Once the forensics team finished at the Superior Spa, they would move to her place.

I kept that from Cam Nguyen's parents in Garden Grove, California. I'd called them from my car. They said they had not spoken with their daughter in nearly a week. The mom went hysterical in Vietnamese and left the phone when I explained that Cam was missing and wanted for questioning in connection with murders at a massage parlor where she was reputed to work.

Cam's father had turned furious, accused me of dragging Cam's name through the mud, but then broke down when I told him I was only giving him the facts as I knew them.

"Cam such a smart girl," her father had sobbed. "Cam supposed to follow American dream, make us proud."

Standing there in the morgue, surrounded by the massage parlor dead, I couldn't help thinking of my daughter, Jannie, and imagining the dimensions of Mr. Nguyen's heartache.

"Alex?" Cynthia Wu called, breaking me out of my thoughts.

I turned. Francones's chest had been sawed

open. His heart lay in a pan. But the medical examiner was holding a piece of paper. "Preliminary tox screen is positive for cocaine. Lots of it."

Then she pointed at the football great's heart. "It's enlarged, outsize even for him. And I found signs of a deviated septum from chronic use."

" 'Say hello to my little friend,' " Sampson said, doing a pretty good imitation of Al Pacino in *Scarface*.

I nodded. "Cocaine smugglers and bloodbaths go hand in hand."

My phone rang. Bree.

"Hey," I said. "Don't tell me there's already a problem with the renovation."

"I haven't been home, so not that I know of," she replied. "But I'm heading to Takoma and I think I'm going to be late."

"What's up?"

"Somebody posing as a city investigator walked into a day care and walked out with a baby who hasn't been seen since."

Chapter 15

"YOU GAVE OUR BABY away to a fucking stranger!" a man yelled. "What did you expect me to do? Act happy? Sing 'Here We Go Round the Mulberry Bush'?"

Okay, Detective Bree Stone thought. She swallowed hard, climbed the steps of Child's Play. Three satellite TV trucks were already parked down the street. A crowd had gathered at the police lines.

Cross's wife went through the front door and entered chaos.

"We're shutting you down!" screamed a sick-looking woman wearing a silk head scarf and stabbing her finger at Eliza and Marylyn Green. A young Metro patrol officer stood behind her.

"She said she was an investigator with Child Services," Eliza moaned.

"She showed me a badge, an identification card, and a writ from Judge Banner in Family Court that commanded us to turn Joss over," Marylyn Green said, crying. "She said you were like that guy in the show *Breaking Bad*."

"You mean a meth maker?" the missing baby's father said, first in disbelief and then anger. "That is complete bullshit!"

"I'm going to be sick," Joss's mother croaked.

"Okay, that's enough," Bree said firmly, taking charge. "I want everyone to take it down a notch. My name is Detective Bree Stone, and I'm here to help. Officer, please help the lady to a bathroom."

The young patrolman nodded and helped the poor woman from the room.

Bree pointed at Branson. "I gather you're the father?"

"I gather you're not a rocket scientist," he replied.

"Name?" Bree said, ignoring the jab.

"Theodore Branson," he replied. "My wife's Crystal."

"I need a photograph of your daughter, Mr. Branson," Bree said. "I'll also need a description of what she was wearing. I need the footprints they took of your daughter at birth. I also need any identifying features, mole, birthmark, eye color, number of teeth, anything that says Joss."

At that Branson straightened, stowed the anger, and said, "I have a picture right here on my phone. I took it this morning at breakfast. Crystal was feeling sick from chemo and I was feeding Joss. She just looked so cute, I . . ." He looked lost suddenly and began to cry. "My little Miss Muffin is gone."

"We'll get her back, Mr. Branson," Bree said, softening her tone.

"How?" Branson asked, his voice thin and weak.

"I'm going to trigger an AMBER Alert to start. Get your daughter's face in front of every law enforcement officer within five hundred miles of here."

Chapter 16

AROUND THAT SAME TIME, Marcus Sunday slipped back into the apartment in Kalorama, finding the music off and Acadia Le Duc waiting for him, wearing a simple cotton dress with an Indian pattern, no shoes, and fresh daisies in her hair. The dress was faded and threadbare and left little to the imagination, certainly not the fact that she wore nothing much beneath.

"Ready for your present, sugar?" she asked with a coy grin.

"It's all I could think about the entire day," he replied.

"Me, too," she said, and started toward the hallway and the storage room.

As the writer followed, he was once again thinking that when it came to Acadia Le Duc, anything *was* possible.

She was a photographer by training, a good one. They'd met by chance two years before at a bar on Bourbon Street in New Orleans. There'd been this mutual, explosive, reckless attraction between them, the kind Warren Beatty and Faye Dunaway had in that old movie *Bonnie and Clyde*. At least that was the way Sunday saw it.

Acadia was definitely crazy and bold enough to play Bonnie Parker, he thought, stopping in the storage room doorway to watch as she touched the computer genius's shoulder just so.

Preston Elliot startled, ripped off the head-phones, and whirled around, smiling. He *was* roughly Sunday's size. He even sort of looked like Sunday at a quick glance.

"Huh-huh-hi, Acadia," Preston said, stuttering painfully.

Acadia stroked the stutterer's upper arm with the fingernails of one hand, played with her curly blond hair with the other. Preston looked mes-merized until she said, "This is my friend I told you about, sugar. He wants to see your invention at work."

The stutterer spotted Sunday, sobered, nodded awkwardly, and acted like he wanted to speak, but didn't. He turned to a laptop, gave it a command.

The screens on the wall displayed what looked at first glance like a collage of images.

At center was a photograph Acadia had recently taken of Alex Cross's house from across Fifth Street. Dotted lines traveled from various windows in the house out to pictures of Dr. Alex, his wife, his grandmother, his daughter, and his younger son. Set off to one side was a framed picture of Damon, Alex Cross's older son, seventeen and a student at a prep school in western Massachusetts.

Digital lines went out from each portrait, linked to images of schools, police stations, churches, grocery stores, and various friends. There were also lines connecting each member of Cross's family to calendar and clock icons.

"He uses mind-mapping software and an Xbox 360 with Kinect to make it work," Acadia explained. "It's interactive, Marcus. Just stand in front of the camera and point to what you want."

Intrigued now, Sunday stepped in front of the screens and the Kinect camera. He pointed at the photograph of Cross. The screen instantly jumped to a virtual diary of the detective's recent life, everything from photographs of Bree Stone, to his kids, to his white Chevy sedan and his best friend, John Sampson, and Sampson's wife, Billie.

Sunday pointed at the calendar, and the screens showed a chronological account of everything he had seen Cross do in the prior month. He gestured at the photograph of the house, and the screen reverted to the original collage. Interested to see just how far they had taken the data, he gestured at the photograph of Damon, Cross's older son.

The screen mutated yet again, showing a collage dominated by a color map of the campus at the prep school Damon attended, but there was little detail about the young man's day-to-day life there.

Sunday decided he would have to beef up that portion of his research. Then he turned to Acadia and Preston. "It's brilliant."

"Mo-mo-more," Preston stuttered.

"The best part, in fact," Acadia said. "Put the helmet on, sugar."

Sunday hesitated but then saw that a cable linked the helmet to the server. He put the helmet on, lowered the visor, and gasped. He was now looking at a 3-D image of Cross's house.

It hovered there in front of him like a hologram.

"Touch the front door," Acadia said through speakers in the helmet. "Your hands guide you."

Chapter 17

SUNDAY REACHED TOWARD THE door. It swung open and he moved inside a digital model of Cross's house, not quite architectural rendering, not quite photograph. He was in the front hallway. He moved his right hand and was quickly peering into the front room. He moved his left hand and a closet opened.

"The entire place like this?" he said.

"Top to bottom," Acadia said. "You can see the house as it is now, and as it will be during and after the construction."

Fascinated now, the writer climbed the virtual staircase and found Alex Cross's bedroom. He looked at the bed, thought of Bree Stone in those jeans she'd been wearing. Despite that pleasurable image, he did not linger.

There was one place in particular he very much

wanted to see. He navigated out of the bedroom
and climbed a second, narrower staircase to the
attic and Cross's home office, which was depicted
with near-photorealism.

The writer was ecstatic. This was where Dr.
Alex did some of his best work, at least according
to a fawning profile of him that had run a few years
back in the *Post*'s Sunday magazine. The piece had
included the photograph of the attic that Preston
had somehow melded into the cyber-rendering.

Sunday panned about, seeing the desk, the
chair, the filing cabinets, even the snapshots of the
victims of unsolved murders and various news
clips regarding those cases thumbtacked to the
wall. He spotted two and almost gasped.

Could it be? Cross was still obsessed with the
Perfect Criminal cases?

Sunday pointed at one clip. To his delight, it
was enlarged, and he scanned a story from the
Austin American-Statesman about the Monahan
murders, pausing on a picture of Alice, the young
mother and wife. In Sunday's mind he saw her as
he always did: naked in the bathroom, screaming
before the razor cut her throat.

But rather than dwell on that, he pointed at the
second clip, a story from the *Omaha World-Herald*

describing the brutal slayings of the Daley family. He lingered on the wife and mother, Bea. She was older than Alice Monahan by nearly twenty years. In his mind he saw her naked, too, and begging for mercy before the razor slashed her—

"Love it, sugar?" Acadia asked over the headset, breaking his attention.

"I do."

There was no doubt about that. Through his clever invention, young Preston Elliot had made Sunday invisible, free to roam Cross's house at will, free to become familiar with every inch of the place so that someday soon he could creep into it in the dark for real.

That would be exciting. Wouldn't every cell in his body buzz?

Yes. Oh, yes, it would. But there was more than that. Looking around the cyberversion of the office, Sunday felt as if he'd already violated Dr. Alex's privacy, slipped inside the detective's sanctuary, and made himself right at home. What could be better?

What could make things better?

Nothing!

Feeling untouchable now, Sunday tore off the helmet and smiled at Preston. "Acadia said you were a genius, my friend. She's right."

Preston glanced at Acadia, blushed, and squirmed in his seat.

"No one knows you've done this work for us, correct?" Sunday asked.

"Ju-ju-just me," Preston said. "Like A-A-Acadia asked."

Sunday looked at her. "And you know how to enter future data?"

"Preston's a very good teacher," Acadia said, rubbing the young man's shoulders sensually.

"Pay him," Sunday said, heading toward the door.

"My great pleasure," Acadia said.

As he walked through the apartment to the front door, Sunday felt the building thrill of anticipation pulse through him again. He opened the door, shut it again, and slipped off his shoes and thin belt. He stood there inside the door, listening.

Acadia laughed seductively and said, "Come to my room, sugar? See what a good old Louisiana girl can do between the sheets?"

A few moments later Sunday heard a door open, and soft music begin to play. He flashed on the image of himself at eighteen with the shovel in his hands, slipping up behind that figure, starting to swing.

Feeling insanely alive now, beyond all laws, all rules, beyond any sense of moral order, the writer crept down the hall toward the bedroom. He was embracing freedom, true freedom, and it left him panting.

Sunday stood in the hallway, listening to Preston grunting and Acadia urging him on. It was over in less than a minute. Probably a sophomore.

Five minutes later, Acadia said, "Something more exotic, more erotic, sugar?"

"P-p-please," Preston said.

"Get off the bed and onto your knees, then, *chéri*," Acadia ordered. "I want you to orally worship me this time before we join."

Preston gave a pleasurable sigh. Sunday moved to the open door. The stutterer was indeed on his knees, his back to the writer. Acadia was stunningly naked, gently writhing her sex in front of the computer genius's face.

Preston's attention never wavered from her. But Acadia's did when Sunday looped the belt around the programmer's neck and began to throttle him.

The entire time the stutterer struggled toward death, she stared into Sunday's eyes with a reckless desire that matched his own.

Chapter 18

I HUNG UP THE phone in my office around six thirty that Friday evening, exasperated that we were having trouble getting copies of the feed from the closed-circuit television cameras mounted at intersections in the blocks around the Superior Spa.

The guys over in the IT department said some kind of programming glitch or bug or something had corrupted the files. They weren't gone, but they weren't opening, either. The IT guys were feeling the strain of the high murder rate and the Francones case as much as we were. It might take several days before a tech could debug the relevant files.

Earlier, I had tracked down Francones's agent and business manager, or figured out who they were, anyway. But the two of them were currently in a private jet en route from Los Angeles to DC to help arrange memorial services for the Hall of Famer. Their secretaries said they'd be free to meet with us in the morning.

Trenton Wiggs, the named owner of the massage parlor, was not in any of the metro-area phone books I looked at. I ran the name through Google, found ten different men of that name in various locales around the country, but nothing that pegged any of them as a sleaze merchant. Then again, who advertised that kind of thing?

In the meantime, Francones's murder had become the hottest news story of the moment. Nearly every cable and network news show had led with the case, almost all of the coverage slanted at the Mad Man's bloody demise in a massage parlor in what they were calling the Murder Capital of the World.

"I'm going home, see how the renovation is going," I told Sampson. He was feeling the stress as much as anybody. "You should go home to Billie. We were up late and up early."

"Reading my mind," he said, yawned. "Beer?"

"Nah, not tonight," I said, and left.

Twenty minutes later, I drove past my house, seeing that the Dumpster in the front yard was almost full of construction debris. I almost parked, but then drove on by, heading over to Anacostia, one of the toughest neighborhoods in the city and the reigning champion when it came to murders per capita.

Ava Williams had lived on the streets in Anacostia before Nana had rescued her. I went to some of the places she'd told us about: a convenience store in Congress Heights, the ER at St. Elizabeths Hospital, the woods east of Mississippi Avenue, Fort Stanton Park. I showed her picture to groups of young people hanging in all those places, and to every homeless person I could find. Not one of them recognized her.

Frustrated, I finally drove to the abandoned factory building where we'd discovered the burned body. There was a police seal on the place, but it had been broken already. I got a flashlight and went inside, climbed down the near stairs to the basement room where the burning had been done, found where the cement floor was charred with death.

I stared at it for a long time and then flashed my light around. The basement had been gone over by a forensics team and was still fairly clean. Then I felt a sudden breeze, coming from back toward the second set of stairs, as if some window or door had been opened.

I went back out there, trying to find where the draft was coming from. I shined the light into a room beyond those stairs.

He came at me wild-eyed and insane, swinging a Louisville Slugger that caught me flush in the stomach, knocked all the wind out of me, and drove me to my knees.

Part Two

KILLING TIME

Chapter 19

AROUND MIDNIGHT I WAS icing my stomach in the dining room while Bree heated up leftover chicken stew on the portable electric double burner I'd bought to get us through the remodel. Heavy plastic sheeting closed off the kitchen area, which looked like a bomb had gone off inside.

"The guy was long gone by the time I could stand up," I said.

"You get a good look at him?" Bree asked, spooning stew into bowls.

"Some dirty, crazy homeless guy with wild, frizzy hair," I replied. "Probably lives in that room. I found a mattress, ratty blankets, fresh McDonald's wrappers, and three bags of clothes, including something you're not going to want to see."

Bree set the bowl of steaming chicken stew in front of me. "What?"

I reached down, groaned at the ache in my stomach, and got the plastic grocery bag sitting beside me. I pulled out a large Ziploc evidence bag that contained a teal-blue sweater with distinctive little brass buttons.

"That's Ava's!" Bree cried, her hands going to her mouth.

"Her Christmas present from Nana Mama."

"What are you going to do?"

"Have it analyzed, give the loony who hit me a couple of days to settle back into his nest, and then go back in there after him."

"I'm going with you next time," Bree said.

"Probably a good idea," I said, reached out and squeezed her hand.

She held on to it while we ate, and when she finished, said, "Do you know how lucky we are, Alex?"

"Of course," I said, rubbing her knuckles with my thumb. "We've got our health, each other, the kids, the jobs, a house. I'm grateful."

"So am I," she replied. "Sometimes I forget, but then I see people like the Bransons losing their baby daughter, and . . ."

Tears began to drip down her cheeks.

"Any ransom note?" I asked.

"No," Bree said, frustrated. "And she was smart, the kidnapper. She didn't seem to touch anything in that day care other than Joss. Just in, out, vanish."

"Woman that age, could be the ticking clock drove her to it."

"I thought of that," Bree said. "No ransom note will be coming, in that case, and we've got way too little to go on. I don't know how I'm going to tell the Bransons that tomorrow."

"You'll get her back for them," I said, standing up to hug her.

But as I moved into her arms I found myself looking over my wife's shoulder at Ava's sweater and wondering if that was true.

Chapter 20

AT TWO THAT SATURDAY morning, Marcus Sunday checked to make sure that the sperm from Preston's used condom was triple-wrapped in Baggies and hidden in a cold cuts drawer in the fridge. Then he tied a rope around the computer genius's ankles.

Lights off in the apartment, he and Acadia pushed the corpse out the window and lowered it until the head was about three feet shy of the alley pavement. Sunday tied the rope off around a heating pipe and went down the back stairs to the alley. He backed up the van, got out, and opened the rear door.

Getting hold of the dead programmer's torso, he made a meowing sound and soon felt the rope slacken. He had the body inside and under a carpet in less than a minute. Before he moved on, he changed the magnetic signs on the sides of the van. It now belonged to the Ralston Feed Company.

That was the thing about embracing an existential lifestyle, Sunday mused as he shut the doors and started to drive. With an existential lifestyle you ascribe no meaning to anything, even your identity, so you can be anyone you want, at any moment you want.

A corollary of this philosophy was that the writer did not believe in good or evil. Nor did he believe in justice. Like crime, justice was an abstract, something cooked up by men. It wasn't intrinsic to the universe. Life just was. It happened, sometimes meagerly, sometimes abundantly, sometimes in violent excess. There was no right or wrong about any of it.

As far as Sunday was concerned, there was no recipe that ensured a good life, and virtue was a joke. So was Karma. Life slapped down the righteous and the spiritual just as easily as the wicked and the free. The trick was to embrace this reality wholeheartedly. In so doing the smart man, the perfect man, the free man could act without fear of consequences.

Bolstered by these thoughts, Sunday drove to Purcellville, Virginia. It took him an hour. He drove another fifteen minutes toward Berryville before he took a side road south through farm country.

As the writer drove the Berryville Road, he kept thinking back to Acadia and how wild she'd become sexually after they'd let the computer genius's body crumple to the floor between them, as if murder was her aphrodisiac, which of course it was. It was Sunday's aphrodisiac, too. Once you were free, killing became a turn-on, the strongest he'd ever known.

Reaching the four-mile marker, Sunday pulled into a grassy lane on the right and drove into the woods far enough not to be seen. He put on a headlamp, turned on the red light, and got out, aware of a familiar, terrible smell almost immediately. Cutting Preston Elliot's body free of the garbage bags, he turned off his headlamp and got the corpse up on his shoulders in a fireman's carry. He set off into the wind toward the stench.

With a half-moon to guide him, Sunday soon reached the edge of a clearing. He peered out at a farmhouse a solid half-mile away and down the hill. A farmyard light shone, but no other, and he knew there likely would not be any real activity for another hour, maybe longer. It was only three thirty, after all.

Turning his attention toward the long, low-roofed building in front of him, Sunday hurried to a door, dropped Preston's body, and pushed the door open. He heard only a few muffled grunts as he dragged the corpse up onto a narrow catwalk with rails and low steel mesh fencing on either side.

The smell inside was ungodly. Closing off his nasal passages with practiced ease, Sunday pulled the programmer's body a solid twenty-five feet across the catwalk. Sweating, he turned on the red headlamp again and saw more than a thousand young pigs crammed wall to wall below him.

Most of the shoats in the feedlot were lying all over each other, less than a hundred pounds each, covered in crap and sleeping. But then a few of the pigs that were awake saw his light and began grunting noisily, waking others.

As Sunday struggled to lift the programmer's body up onto the catwalk rail, he flashed again on himself at eighteen, fighting to get another body over into the pigsty on the farm where he grew up in West Virginia. Both bodies tipped and fell over the side.

The stutterer's corpse landed on pigs that screamed and squealed in alarm. But other young hogs sensed a meal and began to crowd in.

Sunday remembered how the pigs his father fed for years had attacked the old man's dead body with similar enthusiasm. Pigs will eat you— clothes, skin, meat, and bones—if you give enough of them enough time. Not even a piranha will do that.

It's the endless story, he thought, turning off his headlamp. *One life takes another, consuming it, ending it. There's nothing good or bad about that at all.*

Creeping from the building, Sunday listened as the squealing and grunting behind him built into a blind bloody riot that seized the pigsty from one end to the other. But he crossed back to the forest relatively unconcerned, knowing from personal experience that the farmers would not come out to investigate.

This kind of feeding frenzy went on all the time inside commercial hog operations, especially when one pig died and the others turned cannibal.

Chapter 21

THE PROBLEM WITH CASES like the Mad Man Murders, as the New York tabloids were now calling the killings, is that there are too many angles, too many potential avenues of investigation to run down in that critical first forty-eight hours, especially if there is only a team of two working full-time.

Which is why I was at work early Saturday morning with Sampson, waiting for Captain Quintus to arrive.

"Tell me something good, Alex," Quintus said by way of greeting.

"We need help," I said.

"Still bucking for that slot on Letterman?"

Sampson grimaced, said, "Guess you're ready to take the heat, explain why the killing of Pete Francones doesn't merit more manpower?"

"It's the damn murder rate," Quintus fumed. "If I put more people on him, I'll have relatives of every victim we got in here ready to wring my neck!"

"You don't get it," I said. "The Francones murder *is* the murder rate, at least to everyone else in the world. You give us the legs, we'll close the case. And everyone will think you're acting boldly."

Quintus studied me. "Comedian and master strategist?"

I smiled. "A man of many dimensions."

The homicide captain sighed. "I'll give you two more men part-time, in their spare time."

"Cap," Sampson started to complain.

"It's the best I can do."

"You'll be able to claim a task force is on the case," I said. "Thanks."

"Close this, Cross," Quintus said.

"Fast as we can, Captain," I assured him.

Sampson and I made a list of what we wanted the other detectives to run down, including the location of Trenton Wiggs, the massage parlor owner, and Cam Nguyen, who was now officially a missing person. Just after two that afternoon, we got good news: a Virginia judge had given us a warrant to search the Mad Man's home in McLean.

On the way there we stopped for a meeting with the Mad Man's agent and business manager at the Willard Hotel.

"Maybe these guys will give us someone who wanted Francones dead," I said before we entered the lobby.

"Maybe," Sampson said. "Unless it was just random, some crazy fucker, and the Mad Man just got unlucky."

"In which case, every victim was the target, and our shooter is a psychotic," I said. "But until we determine that, we need to focus on Francones."

"Best way to keep the heat off us," Sampson agreed as we went in.

We found Alan Snyder, the Mad Man's agent, and J. Barrett Timmons, his business manager, waiting for us in the lobby, a grand, elegant space. Snyder, a short, intense man who was constantly checking his phone, suggested we have coffee in the restaurant.

But Timmons, a puckered sort in his fifties, shook his head.

"I'd rather we did this privately," he said. "The press has been hounding me nonstop. They're not above trying to eavesdrop in a public restaurant."

Sampson spoke with the head of security, an

old friend, and within ten minutes we were locked inside an unused office with a full pot of coffee and a plate of pastries.

"I wish to say that I'm pleased you two are on the case," said Snyder, the agent. "We've heard of you, Dr. Cross. And you, Detective Sampson."

"Flattering," I said. "Tell me why Mad Man would be in a place like the Superior Spa, and why he would be the primary target of a mass murderer."

Timmons frowned and shook his head as if he still could not believe the circumstances of his client's death.

"I can't square it any way I look at it," Snyder said. "The Pete Francones I represented the last fifteen years is not the person who died in that massage parlor. And the primary target? No, I can't believe that. What could possibly be the motive?"

"Money problems?"

"Hardly," Snyder snorted. "He had plenty. Thirty million."

"Death beneficiary?" I asked.

Timmons's eyes crinkled up. "Two nephews, his sister's sons, are provided for in well-endowed trusts. Otherwise, all money is to be divided among the various charities Mad Man tirelessly championed."

I figured it was time to drop the bomb. "Tell us about his cocaine use."

"You've lost your mind if you think Pete Francones used drugs of any kind," Snyder snapped at me without hesitation. "He was the cleanest guy I knew. Had his head on straight. That high? It was life, Detective."

Francones's manager nodded softly, but there was something in his posture that made me say, "That your assessment, Mr. Timmons?"

Timmons hesitated, cleared his throat, and said, "I have no personal knowledge of drug use."

"I hear a 'but' coming," Sampson said.

Timmons struggled until I said, "You didn't hear it from us, but Mad Man died with three grams of high-grade blow in his pocket, and a gram at least up his nose. According to our medical examiner, the condition of his upper respiratory tract indicates he was a chronic user. And the size of his heart said he wasn't going to last long because of the coke use."

The agent looked stunned, bewildered by all this, but the manager sat forward, cupped his face in his hand. "For Christ's sake. It's one of those things you choose to look away from."

"Tell us," Sampson said.

Timmons described Francones's "slush fund." It was the Mad Man's mad money, which amounted to quite a lot: ten thousand a month, which bumped to twenty grand a month in his latter years as a player, and bumped again to thirty K a month after he landed the gig with *Monday Night Football*.

"Even if he spent twenty percent of that, it's a lot of blow," I said.

"Yes, but that's not what I'm . . ." The manager stopped, then said, "Beginning shortly before Christmas, Mad Man started burning through money and asking for supplements. Ten, sometimes twenty thousand."

"In cash?" I asked.

"Transferred to his cash accounts, yes," Timmons said.

"He a gambler?" Sampson asked.

"Well, before today I would have told you not a chance," said Snyder, shrugging. "But now? Who knows?"

"Gambling wasn't the issue, in my opinion," the manager said, glancing at Snyder. "Mandy was the—"

On the table in front of him, his cell phone rang. He sat forward, frowned. "I'm sorry, this must be an emergency of some kind. I asked them not to call unless it was."

Timmons picked the phone up, answered.

"He was talking about Mandy Bell Lee?" Sampson said to Snyder.

The agent's face soured, but before he could reply, Timmons roared, "That conniving bitch!"

He slammed his phone down, his face beet red. "Mandy Bell's holding a live press conference out at the house. She's claiming that she and the Mad Man were married secretly last month, and that she plans to contest the will!"

Chapter 22

WE GOT TO THE gates of Francones's sprawling manor in McLean, Virginia, around four p.m. Satellite TV trucks were parked up and down the road, with reporters gushing into cameras about the latest turn of events.

A Fairfax County deputy sheriff sat in a patrol car to the left of the gate, facing the road. She climbed out when we pulled up and showed her our badges.

"She's in there, waiting for you," the deputy said. "Mandy Bell."

"Wait, you let her in?" I demanded.

"Not like it's a crime scene," she replied defensively. "And she has a marriage license that's clear: she was the Mad Man's wife, which means she has a right to be in her home."

Sampson said, "What, did she give you an

autograph, or promise you concert tickets?"

The deputy reddened, then said, "She's a widow, Detective. I tried to show her some respect in her grief."

I sighed. I didn't like the fact that Francones's alleged wife had had access to the house, but it was water under the bridge. "Let us in, please."

The deputy nodded, walked to the right side of the gate, and pressed a button. The gate swung back. We drove up a winding driveway to a house Tony Soprano would have loved. I half expected to see Carmela opening the front door. Instead, a long, lanky man answered. He wore a dark suit, no tie, and black cowboy boots, and sported a jaw that looked straight out of central casting.

"Tim Jackson," he said in a Tennessee twang, extending his hand. "I'm Ms. Lee's attorney. How can I help you, Officers?"

"We're running the investigation into Mr. Francones's death," Sampson said. "We'd like to ask Ms. Lee some questions."

"Is Ms. Lee a suspect?"

"She claims to be the deceased's wife," I said.

"She *is* the deceased's wife," the attorney said, bristling. "We've got documents, witnesses. It's iron-clad."

"All the more reason for us to want to talk to her," Sampson said.

"As you might imagine, this has been a terrible blow, having to keep the depth of their relationship secret, and then to have him die, well, she's devastated and exhausted. Could we—?"

"She wasn't too devastated and exhausted to hold a press conference," I observed. "In any case, it's not your call, Counselor."

Sampson reached into his jacket, pulled out the search warrant, and handed it to the attorney. I pushed by him into the house, which was not at all like its exterior. Either the decorator or Francones had a strong interest in modern art, because there were pieces of it in every room except the library, which was a shrine to the Mad Man, with all his trophies, framed photographs, game balls, and other sports memorabilia.

In there we found Mandy Bell Lee, curled up on a leather couch and drinking bourbon neat, and not quite three sheets to the wind.

Chapter 23

MANDY BELL LEE WAS, as Sampson later described her, built for speed.

Tall, curvy, and busty, Mandy Bell had a hairdo that screamed Texas, but her face looked straight out of *Vogue*. Her skintight jumpsuit in mourning black looked ready to pop every time she moved, which was often. And the diamond engagement ring on her right hand was, well, huge. Her attorney moved to her side, saying, "Mandy, these detectives would like to talk to you. I would advise against doing that in your present condition."

She blinked blurry eyes at us. She'd clearly been crying. "You investigating my M&M's death?" she asked in a soft, soulful voice.

"We are," I said, identified myself, and introduced Sampson.

"How can I help y'all?"

"Mandy—" her attorney began.

"I got nothing to hide, Timmy," she snapped, and then tried to refocus on us. "Whaddya wanna know?"

"When did you and Mad Man get married?" Sampson asked.

"She already covered that in the press conference," Jackson complained.

"Unthinkable, I know, but we missed it," I said.

"Last month, March twelfth, in Playa Del Carmen," Mandy Bell said dully.

"A spur-of-the-moment kind of thing," her attorney explained, handing me a wedding certificate and several photographs of a simple service by the sea at sunset. "Their families didn't even know."

"You both look happy," I said.

"Isn't that what you look like on your wedding day?" she asked as if I'd implied something, and began to cry.

"I was saying it out of compassion, Mrs. Francones," I said.

"Oh," she said, dabbing at the corners of her eyes with a balled-up Kleenex. "I'm sorry. I just never lost somebody I loved like this."

"Newlywed and all," the attorney said. "Not even used to being called Mrs. Francones."

Over the next half hour, the Widow Francones explained that she'd met the Mad Man by chance at a bar in Nashville where she was singing. Despite their twenty-year age difference, there'd been a strong, immediate attraction.

"We've heard he had that effect on women," Sampson said.

Mandy Bell thought that was funny. "He did. And I know what you're thinking, 'bout all those girls in his past. Tell you the truth, at the beginning I figured I'd just be one more gal to him, and decided to have some fun. He was a fun guy. That's what I'll miss most about him. M&M lived like his hair was on fire."

"Whose idea was it to get married?"

"His," she replied firmly. "We were down in Cancún, drinking a little tequila, and he just looked over at me and said that he hadn't been happy like this ever and he wanted to marry me. So we did."

"Why not just announce it?" Sampson asked.

"It would of broke my mama's heart she didn't get to have a big wedding for me," Mandy Bell said, glancing at her attorney. "We just figured to marry twice, you know, before football started up and he had to go on the road."

"What about where he died?" I asked.

"You don't have to answer that," her attorney said.

"Why not, Timmy? He's dead," she said, and took a long sip of the bourbon. "If you're asking if I knew M&M went to places like that, the answer is no. But I can understand why he did."

"Why?"

"He was a sex addict," she said. "Told me so himself."

Chapter 24

MANDY BELL LEE UNCOILED off the couch in the Mad Man's library, crossed to an open bottle of Maker's Mark, and poured herself another two fingers. She had something about her, star quality, I guess. You couldn't take your eyes off her.

Sampson cleared his throat. "Sex addict, huh? How'd you react to that?"

She sighed as she came back to the couch, sat with one leg pulled up under her. "I appreciated his honesty because he promised he was gonna change, be a one-woman man." Her face rippled with pain. "Guess not."

"Tell us about his cocaine use."

Mandy Bell's eyes shot to her attorney, who said, "She only recently discovered that."

"I flew up from Nashville the other day to surprise him and caught him snorting lines right on that table there," she said, gesturing with her chin. "He said he used it like that Sherlock Holmes did."

"And how was that?" I asked.

"M&M said he thought better when he did small amounts. I didn't know what to think about that. Still don't. Why?"

"He was high at the time of death, and we found several grams in his pockets," I said.

Mandy Bell took a deep breath, shrugged. "I don't know what to say."

"His business manager said he was spending a lot of cash in the past few months," Sampson said.

She drank and shrugged again. "Probably on me. He liked going out with lots of money and blowing it. Big tips. Anything we wanted."

"Where were you Thursday night?"

She shook her head. "Nashville. I called Timmy the second I heard and we flew up last night."

"And called a press conference?" I asked, not understanding that fully.

"That was Timmy's idea," she said.

Her attorney looked uncomfortable but said, "I felt we needed to state her claim right away. That seemed the best way to do it. Get it out in the open."

"And how long have you known Timmy?" I asked Mandy Bell.

"Fifteen years," she said. "We went to the same high school. He was a senior when I was a freshman."

"You two an item back then?" Sampson asked, wagging his finger between them.

Mandy Bell blushed, said softly, "That was a long time ago, Detective. I called him because these days he's the best attorney in Nashville."

"Sure," I said, smiling at them both. "Makes sense. But now I'm going to have to ask you both to vacate the premises for the time being."

"But the house is hers," Jackson protested.

"I've got an evidence team on the way, Counselor, and for the sake of finding out who killed Mr. Francones, I'd prefer you not be here."

The attorney looked ready to argue, but Mandy Bell drained her glass, said, "It's okay, Timmy. We'll just go get rooms at a hotel. Good one. Four stars. Five stars. Why not?"

Chapter 25

AT A QUARTER TO seven that evening, Marcus Sunday watched Mandy Bell Lee and her attorney spill out of a taxi in front of the new Mandarin Oriental Hotel overlooking the Tidal Basin.

She must be a handful between the sheets, the writer thought, *maybe as crazy as Acadia.* He had been following the pair since they left Francones's house, not quite sure why, relying on instinct rather than clear purpose in his decision to abandon his surveillance of Cross in favor of these two.

He had the valet take his van.

"Checking in, sir?" the doorman asked.

"Going to the bar," Sunday replied. "Heard it's nice."

"Yes, sir. Empress Lounge, top of the stairs."

Given her wobbly state exiting the taxi, he

figured the lobby bar as the most likely place to spot the pair, and he was right, or at least half right. While the attorney was checking in, Mandy Bell Lee was causing quite the stir in the sunken lounge area. She had every guy in the place gaping as she sashayed up to the bar, leaned over, and placed an order with one hip cocked provocatively.

Sunday glanced back in the attorney's direction and wondered for a moment about the connection. Were those two monkeying around? Did it matter?

And right then he understood why his instincts had driven him here: it would matter to *Alex Cross* whether or not the singer and her lawyer were involved, because a love triangle is a proven motive for murder.

But that's nonsense, Sunday thought, taking a seat where he could see the entire bar. At least, in this case it seemed obvious to him from the news coverage that Francones should not be the focus of the Superior Spa investigation. Yes, the Mad Man was a celebrity, a lady-killer, a football god and all that. But those were just pegs for the news guys to hang on to, things they could worry to death for the sake of ratings.

Everything he'd read about the slayings said "freak" to Sunday, even the way the killer had taken the hard drive that recorded the feeds from the interior security cameras. The *Post* story this morning had described that as "the shooter covering his tracks." Nonsense again.

This killer was not perfect. He believed in something—in this case, himself. In Sunday's mind the murderer became a narcissist who wanted to see himself in action, wanted to relive every moment of mayhem again and again. At some level, the writer understood that compulsion, but he also realized that it was a terrible flaw, one that could easily get the killer caught and convicted.

Watching Mandy Bell Lee eagerly tossing back a shot that set her body swaying to the lounge music, Sunday realized there was something else he knew about the killer in light of the missing surveillance tapes.

The Superior Spa was not a one-time deal, the writer thought. *He's done this before!* He could feel it: somewhere, somehow, this imperfect killer had left carnage and evidence behind him. He was also sure that Cross, blinded by the Mad Man's celebrity, was not considering this angle.

That got Sunday excited intellectually. He fervently believed he understood murder, crime, and violent chaos at a much deeper level than Alex Cross ever could. What did Cross know, really, about cold-blooded killing? The lust that rose in an active murderer? The addictive desire to end lives?

He was certain that Dr. Alex had all sorts of half-baked theories, while he, Marcus Sunday, had insight, true insight into what made men kill.

Then he had a thought, a delicious thought. Wouldn't it be enjoyable to see Cross one-upped before he was destroyed? Wouldn't it be satisfying to see him groveling in failure just as his life began to disintegrate?

Yes. Yes, it would. And in a flash, an impromptu plan developed quite organically in Sunday's fertile mind. *That's it,* he thought after several moments' reflection, *that would do it.*

Mandy Bell Lee's attorney returned to the bar, spotting the country-western star ready to toss back another shot of Maker's Mark. Jackson crossed to his client. They had an intense conversation. The attorney signaled to the bartender that she was cut off.

He led her by her elbow out of the bar. The whole place was watching the scene. As they passed Sunday, who was acting interested in the drink menu, the singer said in a slurred voice,

"You're an asshole, Timmy. You always were. I don't know why I called you. I must have been out of my mind to think you were my friend."

"I'm your lawyer, dear," Jackson said. "There's a big, big difference."

As the pair disappeared toward the elevators, Sunday nodded with satisfaction at a new thought, a new plan, risky, reckless, but overwhelmingly attractive.

This will completely throw Cross, the writer thought, fighting against a smile. *He'll never, ever see this one coming.*

Chapter 26

I FINALLY GOT HOME around nine forty that Saturday evening. Ali was already asleep, but Jannie was still up, eating strawberry ice cream and watching *The Colbert Report*, her favorite show, on TiVo.

"Hey, stranger," I said, and kissed her on the forehead.

"Hi, Daddy," she said. "Don't you think Stephen Colbert is the fastest thinker ever?"

"He's lightning quick with the comebacks," I agreed. "But a guy named Johnny Carson could have given him a run for his money."

"Who's Johnny Carson?"

"Poor girl," I said, feeling older by the minute.

"I got an A on my history paper," she boasted. "And Coach says my times are really dropping in the four hundred."

I bumped knuckles with her and said, "See? Good things do happen to people who work hard."

She rolled her head to one side as if she didn't want to agree, but she nodded, said, "I'm going to do that with all my classes and sports now."

"Excellent move," I said.

Jannie was a freshman and the transition into high school life at Benjamin Banneker had been a little rough at first. She hadn't known how to handle the workload. It was nice to hear she'd figured out that working harder might help.

"Bree home yet?" I asked.

"Taking a shower," Jannie replied.

"Ali and Nana?"

"Gone to sleep. Dad?"

"Yeah," I said, going to one of the coolers that we were now using instead of a refrigerator and getting a beer.

"Did you notice that Nana Mama seems sad these days? I thought she'd be happy about the new kitchen and the addition. But today when she found out they were going to cut out the back wall in a few days, I thought she was going to start crying."

"I think she will be happy once it's all done, but this kind of thing, living in a construction site, and everything new and chaotic, it's tough for a lady her age."

"I don't like other people walking around in our house."

"Necessary evil," I said, hearing Bree coming down the stairs.

The Colbert Report came back on, seizing Jannie's attention, and I went to my wife and wrapped her up in my arms.

"You smell so good," I said.

"And you smell so bad," she replied, giving me a peck on the lips and then pulling back to head into the dining room.

"I'll take a shower before bed," I said, following. "Good day?"

"Tough day," she allowed, getting herself a beer. "But we made progress."

"You got hits on the AMBER alert?"

"No, nothing that positive, unfortunately. But we've got an artist's sketch of the woman based on the descriptions the two women at the day care center gave us."

"Got it with you?"

"I do," she said, crossing to her purse and pulling out a folded composite drawing of a woman I figured must be in her early thirties.

"She's got soft features in some ways, but her eyes and lips are hard-looking," I observed.

"I guess you'd have to have hard-looking eyes or lips to be brazen enough to steal a baby out of a day care center," Bree replied before sighing. "Anyway, am I wrong to feel guilty about not going out to look for Ava tonight?"

"I told you, we've got something solid with her sweater and the guy who hit me. Let's give it another night for him to come back."

She made a puffing noise but then shrugged and nodded before gesturing at the plastic sheeting the contractors had put up to seal off the construction site. "Do we dare look?"

"Why not?" I said, grabbed a second beer.

Bree had already peeled back enough duct tape to slip through and turn on the lights. I followed her and got an immediate sense of why my grandmother was so upset.

The appliances and fixtures were long gone. The linoleum had been torn out. The Sheetrock was gone, too, leaving only the skeleton of the load-bearing walls. Red chalk marked the area where the back wall would be cut out to accommodate the addition.

"They'll be kicking us out of our room before you know it," I said.

"Not tonight," Bree said. "I've got plans." I arched an eyebrow. "That right?"

She smiled. "I've been thinking about you all day, baby. So why don't you get upstairs and take that shower already?"

I saluted her, did an about-face, and headed quickly back into the house.

Chapter 27

NEARING MIDNIGHT, MARCUS SUNDAY roamed the bars of Old Town Alexandria, across the Potomac from DC. After a quick trip to the apartment, where Acadia was already asleep, he'd retrieved Preston Elliot's chilled condom and come here, where single young professionals gathered in search of anonymous hookups on Saturday night.

The writer had spotted several likely candidates, all of them in their late twenties, early thirties. But when he'd slipped past them and sniffed the trailing air, he'd failed to catch the specific aroma he was seeking.

Sunday was about to give up and return to the apartment for a few hours, when he spotted a prospect leaving Bilbo Baggins pub on Queen Street. Long, willowy, with pale skin and sandy hair that hung well down her back, she wore a tight black skirt and was laughing and hanging on to one of those long-jawed, sculpted-haircut types who seemed to populate the DC area.

The writer walked at them, head down, a man with places to be, as she said, "Let's walk to my place, Richie. It's not that far."

Sunday went past without eye contact and caught her scent. It smelled of sweat, lilacs, and fertility. In an instant, he knew she was the one. Walking on twenty more yards, he jogged across the street and ambled in the other direction, watching the couple take a right off the main drag onto North Lee Street.

Tailing them six blocks to a brick-faced town house with steep stairs that climbed off a sidewalk shadowed by old oak trees, Sunday timed his approach almost perfectly.

As she fumbled for her keys, her hookup nuzzled her ear, causing her to giggle and say, "Give me a chance, Richie."

Sunday bounded up the stairs, drawing a small Colt pistol, which he jammed against the back of the young man's head.

"If either of you so much as thinks of turning to look at me, I'm going to blow poor little Richie's head off," he growled in a thick accent.

"Rich?" the woman cried softly.

"Claudia, please," Richie said, shaking now. "Do what he says."

"Go inside, now, Claudia," the writer ordered.

Claudia pulled open the front door.

Keeping the brim of his cap and his face pointed at the floor in case there were cameras, Sunday pushed them inside a small vestibule with three mailboxes and three buzzers.

That makes things more manageable, Sunday thought. *Unless . . .*

"Roommates?" he demanded as Claudia put her key into the second door.

"What? N-no," she stammered as she pushed the door open. "I live alone."

"Where?"

"Right here," Richie said, nodding at the door at the bottom of the stairs.

"Go inside," the writer ordered.

"What are you going to do?" Claudia whimpered.

"It's a surprise," Sunday said.

Trembling now, the woman opened her apartment door, stepped in, and flipped on a light switch.

The writer pushed Richie forward and then hit

him hard behind the ear with the butt of his pistol, watched his knees go to quicksand as he buckled to the floor. The writer turned off the light. He could see the woman's silhouette starting to turn, held up the gun, and said, "Freeze."

She did. Sunday stepped up directly behind her and set the gun to the back of her head.

"Please," she said.

"I am pleased," Sunday said, and he moved her toward a couch. "Very Mulch pleased at how you smell tonight, Claudia."

"Oh, God," she whined.

"So you understand you are ovulating," he said appreciatively as he kicked her feet apart and wrenched up her skirt. "There's only one thing you can't deny about the absurdity of life—it's meant to go on and on."

"Please," Claudia sobbed softly.

"Don't worry, Mr. Mulch won't hurt you," Sunday soothed as he got out Preston's used condom and turned it inside out. Unzipping his pants, he slid the open end of the condom over his penis, leaving the stutterer's DNA exposed.

"Mulch will steal something from you so you don't have to tell Richie what we've done. But afterward, Mulch will know what's in your womb, Claudia, because he will be watching you."

She was choking and weeping now.

"And because Mulch will be watching you, knowing what we share, you're not going to the police. No, you're going to love our little future life. You hear that, Claudia? You are going to love our future life."

Sunday thrust a little way into her and moaned and shuddered as if in immediate climax. Then he hit her, knocked her out, and left her there, skirt up over her hips, sprawled over the back of the couch.

Excellent, the writer thought, peeling the condom off and gingerly returning it to the Baggie. *I think that will do the trick rather nicely.*

Chapter 28

"ALEX? WAKE UP."

I felt Bree shake me and opened my eyes groggily to find the lights blazing in our bedroom. It felt like I'd only just drifted off.

"Time is it?" I asked blearily. "What day is it?"

"Nearly five," she said. "Sunday morning."

"Five? C'mon, Bree. I need a few more hours of—"

"I can't wait anymore," my wife insisted. "I'm going to that building with or without you. Now."

"Bree, I told you—"

"You said give him another night," Bree said. "We gave him one. He could be in there sleeping as we speak."

I was hopelessly awake by then and I could see by the way she held her jaw slightly to the right that it was useless to argue anymore.

"Okay, okay," I grumbled. "We'll go, but then I'm coming back for a nap."

"I wouldn't have it any other way," she said, jumped out of bed, and started to dress.

I moved a little more slowly, but within fifteen minutes we were driving through the back streets of Southeast and then heading across the river into Anacostia. Dawn was still just a shade of gray when I stopped at a coffee shack.

"Do we have time for this?" Bree demanded.

"I don't want to go prowling around in there until I can at least see a little," I replied. "That old building is his home. He can walk around it in the dark easy. I can't. And neither can you. And if we go in with our flashlights, he'll probably just spook out of there, and at that point he might be gone forever."

She looked at me a long moment before saying, "Hazelnut latte. Double shot of espresso."

By the time I parked us down the street from the abandoned factory building, it was cracking light and the caffeine had done its work. I was alert and on edge when I climbed out of the car.

I described the layout to Bree, including the room where the burned body had been found, the other room where the homeless guy was camped, and the escape route I thought he'd taken up the stairs and out a rear window. Then I told her what I wanted her to do.

"Sure you want to go in there alone?" she asked.

"I think I can handle it. You?"

She smiled. "You just flush him. I'll take care of the rest."

We split up as we approached the building. Bree looped around the back. I went in the same way I had two nights before, through the front door, making no effort at all to be quiet. Instead, I kicked cans and made small bursts of racket as I looked for the near staircase to the basement.

It was almost full light outside, but in the old condemned building it was still twilight. Then again, I didn't need to see the homeless guy run anyway.

I heard him go when I was almost to the bottom of the stairs, right by the room where Jane Doe's body had been burned.

He pounded up the far stairs. I ran after him at a more leisurely pace, giving him time to make his preferred exit.

By the time I reached the broken window and looked out, he was cursing at the fact that Bree had him facedown, a knee on his back and zip-ties going around his wrists. The Louisville Slugger lay on the ground behind her.

Chapter 29

"THAT'S QUITE THE SWING you've got there," I said to the homeless guy, whom Bree had dragged back into the building along with the baseball bat.

He said nothing as we returned him to his nest and set him down on his filthy mattress. In the light of day he bore more than a passing resemblance to Ted Kaczynski, the Unabomber, with that wild tangle of hair and beard, and pale-blue eyes that tracked out of sync.

"Name?" I asked, noticing small twigs and bits of leaf in his beard.

"You cops?"

"As a matter of fact, we are," I said, showing him my badge and ID.

"I need a lawyer?" he asked.

"I could arrest you for criminal trespass and

assaulting a police officer," I said. "Or you can answer our questions."

He studied us with those weird eyes for several moments before saying, "Everett Prough."

"Where are you from, Everett?" I asked.

"You're looking at it," he said.

"This where you've always lived?" Bree asked in a kind tone.

"Does it matter how I got here?" he asked.

"Not really," I said. "How long've you lived here?"

"I dunno, off and on. What do you want, I mean for real?"

I held out Ava's blue sweater in the plastic evidence bag. Everett Prough blinked, looked at it for several seconds and then at me, feigning a lack of interest. "So?"

"I took it from your grocery cart the night before last, right after you hit me."

"Yeah. That sounds right. Thief."

"Where did you get it, Everett? This sweater."

The homeless man squirmed as if something had crawled up his pant leg, said, "Don't remember."

"Sure you do," Bree said. "Do you know who that sweater belongs to?"

Prough cringed, looked at the floor as if it contained secrets that only he could decipher, and then nodded. "I know her anywhere."

I felt a terrible sensation suddenly in my gut, a hollow feeling like no other. What was this guy to Ava? What had he done to her?

"Who does the sweater belong to?" Bree pressed.

Prough squinted and set his jaw as if he were being forced to relive some best-forgotten horror.

"Belongs to the girl," he said. "The girl who killed that other girl and lit her body on fire."

Chapter 30

TWO HOURS EARLIER, AND pulsing again with the thrill of anticipation, Sunday sat in the van parked down the street from the service entrance of the Mandarin Oriental Hotel, drinking yet another can of Red Bull to stay fully awake. He'd been there ever since his escapade in Alexandria.

The writer figured to make his move around a quarter to five. To pass the time, he stuffed cotton into his cheeks, put in brown contact lenses, and pulled on a dark-brown pompadour wig and a pair of flesh-colored latex gloves. He used the gloves to smear self-tanning liquid all over his face and then wiped them dry with Kleenex.

Four forty-five went by, and nothing.

So did four fifty.

Sunday began to doubt his instincts, a rare event. But then he spotted a late-model Toyota sedan driving by the service entrance, passing his van, and parking down the street. A man climbed out wearing black slacks, black shoes, a white shirt, and a tie. He carried a white server's jacket. The first breakfast waiter was arriving for work.

Without hesitation, Sunday got out of his van. He, too, wore black slacks and black shoes, a white shirt, and a tie.

Sunday crossed the street, angling at the waiter: late twenties, looking barely awake.

"'Scuse me, mate," the writer called in a decent Australian accent. "First day on the job."

"Follow me," the waiter said dully as he passed.

"Right you are," Sunday said, and hit the back of the waiter's skull hard with a sap.

The waiter pitched forward, but the writer caught him by the back of his shirt before he could face-plant on the sidewalk. Dragging him behind one of the hotel's Dumpsters, Sunday rifled through his pockets, found his hotel ID. He stuck it in his pocket and put on the jacket. Not a bad fit.

He hit the waiter again and hard enough that he wouldn't move for hours. Then he threw trash on the man, went directly to the service entrance, and used the ID in the electronic security box. He grinned when it opened.

Entering the empty service hall in the basement at the rear of the hotel, Sunday smelled bread baking, bacon frying, and coffee brewing. Fighting off the nausea the smell of bacon provoked, he grabbed one of three room service carts parked to one side of the hall, pushed it into a less well-lit part of the hallway. He threw his gym bag on the cart's lower shelf. He found a white tablecloth and then several plates. He tossed on a napkin and silverware, a steak knife, two drinking glasses, and an empty coffee carafe.

"Java's almost up," a woman commented.

The writer turned, smiling in welcome. Fifteen feet down the hall, in her early fifties, wearing a flour-dusted apron, she shook a cigarette from a pack.

"Excellent," Sunday said agreeably.

"New?" she asked, squinting as if she couldn't see him very well.

"I am," he said. "A temporary gig, but could turn permanent. Happy here?"

Her laugh became a smoker's cough. "Happy as you can be slaving at a four-hundred-degree oven at four a.m. on Sunday morning. Good luck. Gotta have a cig."

"Enjoy."

The service door opened and shut. Sunday waited and then went to the doorway where the woman had appeared. He found a staging area outside the already bustling main kitchen, which was visible through a pass-through window. Three coffeemakers were bubbling to the right of the pass-through. He grabbed a carafe, walked over, and was filling it when a man called from the kitchen, "Denver omelet, bacon, and no potatoes up."

The writer filled the carafe three-quarters full and waited for the chef to leave before grabbing the breakfast plate and hustling back to the hall. He set the plate under the stainless cover and hurried ahead, looking for a service elevator.

He found one around the corner, got in, and pushed the button for the fourteenth floor, keeping his head down. When the doors closed, he squatted, got the gym bag, and unzipped it, hoping he had the correct room.

Shortly after leaving the hotel the evening before, he'd used a throwaway phone to call the Mandarin Oriental and ask to be connected to Timothy Jackson's room. Jackson had answered and Sunday had affected a British accent, saying, "This is Mr. Mulch with the front desk. We've been getting reports of loud noise and music in room 604, next door to you, sir, and wanted to—"

"You're way off, Mulch. I'm in 1401," Jackson said, irritated. "But while I've got you on the line, I want breakfast at six forty-five. I'll hang the order on the door."

"Very good sir," Sunday had said, and rung off.

From the gym bag, the writer removed a white 120-milliliter bottle with a label that read:

QZT VAPES
92.2% TASTELESS NICOTINE LIQUID
EXTRACTED FROM THE FINEST SOUTH CAROLINA
FLUE-CURED LEAVES

Seeing that the elevator had already passed the seventh floor, Sunday quickly opened the bottle. Happy again for the latex gloves he was wearing, he poured several ounces into the coffee.

Ding! The elevator doors opened. The four-teenth floor.

The writer glanced at his watch. It was 5:25 when he set off. He felt no fear, had no thought of capture, only pure intent. He spotted the security camera high up on the first corner, pulled a small can of Pam out of the gym bag, and sprayed the lens with vegetable oil as he passed.

He did the same with the three other cameras on the floor before going to room 1401, where he knocked sharply.

As Sunday half expected, he got no answer the first time, so he knocked even more loudly and said in a Hispanic accent, "Room service."

He heard cursing inside and then someone coming to the door. The writer smiled at the peephole with total confidence. The bolt threw, the door opened. A pissed-off Timothy Jackson looked out at him.

"I said six forty-five," Jackson complained. "It's five twenty-five."

Sunday acted flustered. "Oh," he said. "Sorry. They write down wrong?"

"So much for the five-star rating," Jackson snapped.

"You want I should come back?" the writer asked.

Jackson took a deep breath, then shook his head. "No, I'm up already. Bring it in. It's not your fault."

"Yes, sir," Sunday said, acting the deferential servant as he wheeled the cart into the room, one of those executive affairs with a king-size bed, a sofa, and a desk for the traveling businessman.

Jackson walked behind him, letting the door shut. The writer parked the cart by the sofa, said, "This good?"

"Yeah, sure, whatever," the attorney replied, and yawned. Sunday knelt as if to lock the cart's wheels while swiping the exterior and interior of Preston Elliot's used condom on the leg of Jackson's suit pants, which were lying on a chair. Pocketing the condom, the writer stood, picked up the coffee carafe.

"That's not decaf, is it?" Jackson asked.

"French roast, sir," Sunday said.

"Good, that's what I—" The attorney had lifted the cover over the omelet. "What the fuck? I asked for three eggs sunny side up, bacon, and wheat toast."

Sunday did his best to grovel. "I am so sorry, sir. I take and get you right away the right breakfast."

"What?" the attorney groused. "Yes, please do that. This isn't what I ordered at all."

"I leave you coffee, though, and be right back."

"Sugar and milk, too. And get me a copy of the *Washington Post*."

Sunday bowed and set the cup, saucer, carafe,

milk, and sugar bowl on the table. "I apologize again, sir. There will be no charge for breakfast."

"Well," Jackson said as Sunday wheeled the cart away. "That's good."

"It's the least the Mandarin Oriental could do," the writer replied, and let the door shut behind him.

Chapter 31

BREE AND I LEFT the old factory building shaken and depressed, with Everett Prough following us in a slow homeless-person shuffle.

"I can't believe it," Bree said in a low pained voice.

"His story's plausible," I replied, not liking the sour taste of it any better.

"But convincing?"

I struggled to answer. We'd shown the homeless man a photograph of Ava, and he'd fingered her as a killer and a mutilator. Prough said Ava was one of six or seven runaway girls he'd encountered squatting and using drugs in the old factory over the past few months. He moved his nest often, rotating among several places so as not to attract attention. When he returned to the factory around dusk the night of the murder, it had been a month since he'd last slept in the basement.

Approaching the abandoned building, Prough claimed he heard girls arguing over money and meth. They were high on something for sure. Prough said he snuck in and watched from the shadows as Ava and another girl with Goth black hair got into a screaming match that became a hair-pulling catfight.

"She tripped the other girl and then hit her like this with her elbow," Prough told us, holding his wrist and driving the elbow of that same arm sharply to the side and behind him in a move I sadly recognized.

I'd taught it to Ava. I'd taught it to all my kids.

Prough said the Goth girl had fallen hard at the blow. Her head had struck a post. She never moved again.

"The one who hit her started crying once she realized what she'd done," Prough said. "Then she got a can of gasoline and poured it over the Goth girl, and lit a cigarette and threw it on the gas."

Prough said Ava had a blue backpack when she ran from the factory. Not wanting to be around when the body was found, he said he followed Ava several minutes later and found the sweater lying in her escape path.

Several things had bothered me about the story. "Where'd the gas come from?" I asked.

Prough shrugged. "She had it in there for some reason."

"That would mean premeditation if she brought it with her," Bree said.

Prough was puzzled by that but then shrugged again. "I don't know."

"How many times had you seen her before that night?"

"More than once," Prough said.

"She talk to you?" Bree asked.

"She didn't know I was there, ever," Prough said. "I don't like people."

"But you spy on them?"

"Sometimes," he admitted.

"You're willing to testify to what you saw?" I asked. He hesitated, nodded, said, "If that's what it takes."

I had recorded most of our conversation. But we were taking Prough downtown to make a sworn statement. We put him in the backseat and had to roll the windows down, he smelled so bad. I started the car, feeling numbed by the idea that the shy girl who'd lived under our roof for so long might have run away, gotten caught up in the world of street drugs, murdered another girl, and then desecrated her body.

My cell rang before I'd driven a block. Sampson. I answered, said, "John?"

"Alex, Timmy Jackson was just found dead at the Mandarin Oriental."

Chapter 32

MANDY LEE FRANCONES'S ATTORNEY lay sprawled at the foot of the king-size bed. A coffee cup was spilled beside him. The attorney's eyes were severely bloodshot and looked buggy. His mouth was open as if gasping.

"First glance, I'd say a massive heart attack, Detectives," said Tony Bracket, the ME on the scene.

"This guy's like thirty-four," Sampson said. "And he's built like a bull."

"Bulls need bull hearts," Bracket said. "He under a lot of stress?"

"You could say that," I replied. I'd left Bree to take Prough in to make his statement and had taken a cab straight to the hotel.

I scanned the room now. Coffee carafe on the table. Ripped and empty raw sugar packet. Used creamers. The pants and jacket of the suit we'd seen the attorney wearing. Using latex gloves, I picked up the pieces of the suit, saw the smear of something on the leg right away.

"That's fresh," I said, handing it to a tech for bagging.

Then I picked up the creamer containers and the sugar packet. I tasted them. Nothing. When I twisted the carafe open and sniffed the contents, I smelled only coffee. I almost stuck my finger in it, but the sudden racing of my heart stopped me.

Dizzy, I set the carafe down and had to hold on to the table a moment before my heart slowed and that upended feeling went away.

"Sorry, Doc," I said to Bracket, who was taking the corpse's temperature. "We're treating this as a murder until proved otherwise."

"Why?" asked Sampson, who was going through the closets.

I gestured at the coffee carafe. "I'm not going near that again without a gas mask, but either I just had a coincidental heart arrhythmia or the coffee was laced with something mucho bad."

"Where'd he get the coffee?" Sampson asked, coming over and looking at the carafe as if it smelled gross.

"Exactly," I said.

From digital records provided by the security staff at the Mandarin Oriental, we knew almost immediately that Jackson's hotel room door was opened at 5:25 a.m., and again at 5:29, about an hour and eighteen minutes before room service discovered the body.

We also found that someone had sprayed some kind of goo on the security camera lenses a few minutes before the door to Jackson's room was opened, leaving the feed a blur. Was that what was on the attorney's pants?

In any case, while the crime scene techs worked and the hotel security staff made copies of all closed-circuit feeds for the last five hours, Sampson and I went to find Mandy Bell Lee Francones. The country-western star was in her room two floors below Jackson's, wearing the same clothes we'd seen her in the night before, sitting up against the headboard with her feet drawn up under her. She was tear-streaked, mascara-streaked, nursing a hangover, in shock and grieving.

"People dying all around me," she said in a trembling voice.

"We wondered about that," Sampson said.

"Someone said it was a heart attack?" she asked.

"We don't know exactly," I said. "When was the last time you saw Mr. Jackson?"

"I don't know. Nine? Ten? I'd had a lot to drink."

"Here the entire night?" Sampson asked.

"Yes, I . . ." Mandy Bell stared at her lap, looking lost. "I passed out in my clothes, woke up when security came knocking."

Knowing that the electronic records backed up her timeline, I said, "For the moment, let's say it wasn't a heart attack. I'm not saying it wasn't, but I have to ask in any case. Do you have any stalkers? Someone who'd want Mad Man and Mr. Jackson out of your life?"

The country-western star began to weep softly. "Two or three. I got restraining orders on all of . . . Timmy had a son, you know? From before the divorce? Garth's only two and now he's never gonna know his daddy. And I . . ."

That last thought seemed to crush the spirit out of her and she started to sob. "'Scuse me," she said, got up and went to the bathroom, and shut the door.

She returned several moments later, having cleaned the makeup off her face and looking pale and bedraggled.

"Can you give us the names of the stalkers?" Sampson asked.

She nodded numbly, sat on the bed again, said, "I hate them."

"You got someone you want us to call?" I asked.

"You mean like another lawyer?" She sniffled.

"Like someone who could be with you," Sampson offered. "This is kind of a lot to deal with, don't you think?"

"My parents are dead," she said dully. "Got a sister in Omaha. Cindy Bell."

"Give me Cindy Bell's number," I said.

Ten minutes later, I hung up, said, "She's catching the next—"

There was a knock at the hotel room door. I went and opened it to see the hotel's security chief, a small man named Waters.

"One of our waiters just staggered in here bleeding from the head," Waters said. "He says a guy who looked like Elvis knocked him out."

We found Carl Raynor being attended to by EMTs in a locker room off the hotel kitchen. Raynor told us it was still dark out when Elvis came up claiming that he was arriving for his first day of work.

"Next thing I know," Raynor said, "I come to in the bushes, my head feels like World War Three . . . and my ID's gone."

Now we had an even better time frame, and using electronic records and the cameras in and around the security entrance, we were able to get several looks at the man we believed had killed Mandy Bell Lee's childhood sweetheart.

Elvis was smart, though. Like the suspect we'd seen in street camera footage near the Superior Spa, he walked hunched over, seemingly aware of the lenses trying to capture his image. We saw him wheeling a food cart and heading to Jackson's floor. We saw him leave through the service entrance fifteen minutes later. But we never got a solid look at his face.

One of the hotel's bakers came forward, said she'd come face to face with the killer, talked to him even, and gave us a much better sense of his features after looking at still shots of him from the surveillance cameras.

"He seemed like a nice guy," she said. "Cheerful, you know?"

Sampson nodded sadly. "We've been investigating murders a long time, ma'am, and I'm sorry to say that you almost never hear someone say they met someone who turned out to be a killer and they just knew from the get-go that he was an out-and-out psychopath."

Chapter 33

AROUND A QUARTER TO eight the next morning, Kelli Adams blinked at the dregs of a migraine, checked her makeup, and then walked confidently to the door of a luxury row house in Georgetown, near Foggy Bottom. Gone was her conservative blue suit. Today she was dressed as a recent graduate of Catholic University, at least according to her Windbreaker.

Adams pulled her right hand into the sleeve of the jacket and used her knuckle through the fabric to press the doorbell. She heard a man shouting almost immediately. No one came. She rang again and this time heard feet stomping before the door swung wide, revealing a harried-looking professional woman in her thirties, carrying an eight-month-old baby boy in her arms.

"Kelli?" the woman asked.

"Hi," Adams said brightly. "Dr. Lancaster?"

"Ellen," Dr. Lancaster replied, extending her hand. "Come in?"

"Yes, please," Adams said, shaking her hand, stepping across the threshold, and winking at the boy, who took to sucking furiously on his thumb.

"This is Evan," Dr. Lancaster said. "He's fallen in love with his thumb."

Adams tickled the boy, said, "Hi, Evan. We're going to be great friends."

Evan giggled and ducked his head shyly.

"This is good," his mother said. "We've tried a couple of other nannies before this. It's difficult for him to attach at first, but he seems to like you."

"That's what you mentioned," Adams said. "But we'll do fine."

"So good of you to be available on short notice," Dr. Lancaster said, handing over her son. "The last one gave us no warning she was quitting."

Adams began to rock the baby expertly in her arms. "I saw the ad go up on the jobs board and called you immediately."

"Well, I'm glad you did. Your references gave you rave reviews."

"Both families were wonderful to babysit for, but I am looking for full-time work now."

Dr. Lancaster's hand covered her heart as if she were saying the Pledge of Allegiance. "Perfect. You don't know what a hassle it is finding someone to—"

"Got to go, gonna be late!" cried a man in a business suit, crisp white shirt, and rep tie, who was hustling down the stairs while looking at his iPhone.

"Bill, this is Kelli," Dr. Lancaster began.

"Charmed, but I'm due in Senator McCord's office in twenty minutes," her husband said, charging past and out the door.

Dr. Lancaster glanced after her husband, said, "Say good-bye to Daddy, Evan. And I have to hurry, too. Don't want anyone dying of a broken heart, do we?"

"What time should I expect you?" Adams asked.

"I've left you a list on the kitchen table, my phone numbers, my husband's numbers, Evan's likes and dislikes, his routine. I pumped enough milk for the day. It's in the fridge. Oh, and there's medicine for the earache he's been fighting. The rest is self-explanatory."

"I'm sure," Adams said.

Dr. Lancaster blew her son a kiss. "Mommy's only working until two."

She went out the door and Adams followed, cradling little Evan, holding his forearm, which she waved at his mother's retreating figure.

Softly, she whispered in the baby's ear, "Say bye-bye, Evan. Say bye-bye to Mommy."

Chapter 34

I GOT TO MY desk late that Monday morning to find two reports from Detective Paul Brefka, one of the part-time detectives Captain Quintus had promised us.

Brefka was obviously an efficient and intuitive investigator. Given the name of the holding company that owned the Superior Spa—Relax LLC—he followed a hunch and searched for other limited-liability corporations with the word *relax* in their name. He found nineteen, all registered in Delaware.

Trenton Wiggs—the listed owner of the Superior Spa—was not named in connection with any of those companies. But a Harold Trenton and a Charles Wiggs were. According to the papers, the men were partners in Total Relaxation Ventures, with offices in Reston, Virginia. It sounded to

Brefka and it sounded to me as if one person was using at least three identities to control a massage parlor empire. I jotted a note: *Pay a visit to Total Relaxation.*

Detective Brefka's second report focused on Cam Nguyen.

Using the texts and recent phone calls on her iPhone, he identified and talked to many of her friends and fellow students, all of whom claimed to be dumbfounded when they learned she'd been working as a prostitute. So did her boyfriend, a GW student who'd been washing dishes at the Froggy Bottom Pub the night of the killings. He and the rest of Cam Nguyen's friends had not heard from her since.

A check of her bank account showed she had nearly fifteen thousand dollars in savings. According to her debit card records, the missing girl had a history of spending freely, a history that had come to a screeching halt the night of the murders.

"Are they connected?" Captain Quintus asked, startling me as I stared at the reports. "The shooting of Francones and the poisoning of Jackson?"

"Got to be a hell of a lot more than a coincidence."

"Security tapes?" the homicide supervisor said, moving to take a seat.

"Elvis was good," I replied. "Real good. Never gave us a decent look at his face, and he must have been wearing gloves because he left nothing in Jackson's hotel room. At least so far."

"Who would want Francones and his widow's lawyer dead?"

"Maybe the Mad Man's widow, though I doubt it," said Sampson, coming in with coffee. "Or maybe one of the three creeps who've been stalking Mandy Bell. Or Francones's agent and manager."

"Snyder and Timmons," I said, nodding. "They did have a strong reaction when they found out Mandy had married Mad Man."

"They trying to control her in some way, killing Jackson?" Quintus asked.

"Seems heavy-handed," Sampson replied. "I mean, their future earnings were tied to Mad Man, not her."

"Check it," Quintus said. "Check all of it."

I smiled wearily. "We always do, Captain."

Chapter 35

WHILE SAMPSON TRIED TO reconnect with Mad Man Francones's agent and manager, I got a car and drove toward the Fourteenth Street Bridge, bound for the offices of Total Relaxation Ventures in Reston, Virginia.

Until my cell phone rang. It was Bree.

"Hey, you," I said. "Finish with Prough's statement?"

"Yes, but I haven't turned it in, and I still feel shitty about letting Prough go yesterday."

"No reason to hold him," I said.

There was a pause. "Hold on a second."

There was silence for several moments, and then she came back on the line with urgency in her voice. "Where are you?"

"Heading toward Reston. What's wrong?"

"There's been another kidnapping," she replied.

"And this time it's high-profile. He's the baby boy of a cardiologist at GW and a big-time lobbyist on the Hill. I need you on this."

"I'm working four capital cases as it is, and I'm getting nowhere on all of them," I said in a strained voice.

"Just the initial interviews," Bree insisted. "I believe this could be a serial kidnapper now. Isn't that one of your areas of expertise?"

"I've dealt with one other," I said. "Doesn't make me exactly an expert."

"More expert than I am," Bree said. "The kidnapped boy is only eight months old, Alex. He's their only child."

I sighed, checked my watch, saw it was nearly three, and said, "Give me the address."

When I called Quintus and told him I was going to Georgetown to help for two hours maximum, he reluctantly agreed and said he'd send Detective Brefka to pay the massage parlor tycoons a visit.

I got turned around, heading back toward Georgetown, thinking, *Eight months old?* In turn, I flashed on each of my children at that age: Ali, Jannie, and Damon, wide-eyed, full of contradictions, delighted one minute and hysterical the next. What if one of mine had been taken at that age?

A pit soured in my stomach. I had the sudden urge to hear my kids' voices, especially Damon's. We hadn't spoken in a week. Midterms, he'd said.

I pulled out my phone and punched in his number.

The phone rang and rang and rang. I called him six times, and six times I got voice mail. Parking and getting out down the street from the yellow tape that surrounded the town house, I couldn't help thinking how annoying the whole cell phone and teenager thing was. You buy them a phone. You pay for a national plan so they can keep in touch, and they've never got the damn thing on. Then again, midterms were coming up and—

"Dr. Cross?" someone called as I got near the tape.

I looked to my right and recognized the eager babyfaced patrolman who'd so smartly sealed off the Superior Spa when he'd seen the bodies.

"Officer Carney, right?" I said.

"Yes, sir," the patrolman said, beaming. "I thought you worked homicide?"

"I do," I replied, ducking under the tape. "Just doing a colleague a favor."

"Sounds like they'll need the help," Carney said, glancing over at the house. "Scary, isn't it?"

"What's that?"

"You know, some psycho stealing babies?"

"You're right, Carney. It is scary. Something no parent should go through."

"But they'll catch her, right? The nanny?"

"Sure going to try," I said. "Hold down the fort."

"Yes, sir," Carney said, and I moved on.

Another patrolman stood at the door, opened it to let me in.

Even from the foyer, I could hear a woman sobbing.

Chapter 36

ON THE KRAFT SCHOOL campus in the Berkshires of western Massachusetts, Damon Cross ignored the phone whining in his pocket and gestured at an ivy-covered building. "This will be our first stop. Commons, where all students eat."

Damon was leading the final campus tour of the day for seven prospective students and their parents. He enjoyed being a tour guide. He'd been doing it since sophomore year.

He held the door to the school dining hall open as his group filed inside and was about to follow them when he heard a woman cry in a southern accent, "Hold that door, sugar. Am I too late to join the tour?"

Damon looked back over his shoulder and saw a seriously attractive woman with wild blond hair and the kind of body that . . . well, the black stirrup pants and the white turtleneck clung to her beneath a smart leather jacket and sunglasses. She was hurrying across the quad toward him.

"It's not too late," he said. "We're just starting."

"So good," she said, clapping her hands and coming right up to him. She smelled faintly of perfume. "You are a tall one, aren't you?"

"Yes, ma'am," Damon said, embarrassed. "I'm on the basketball team."

" 'Ma'am'?" she drawled, sounding offended. "You make me sound like some old crone. I'm only twenty-six. You?"

Damon glanced inside the Commons door, where one of the dads was eyeing him and the woman. "I'll be eighteen in January."

"Almost a man," she said.

"Right," he said, feeling his cheeks flush. "We should go in."

"Of course," she said gaily, and started through the door. "What is your name, tall boy tour guide?"

"Damon," he said, following her. "Damon Cross."

"I'm Karla Mepps. Don't you forget my name now, Damon. Karla Mepps," she drawled, and sidled into the dining hall, leaving the light scent of perfume in her wake. Damon followed, fascinated. He'd never had anyone like Karla Mepps on a campus tour before. He'd never *smelled* anyone like her before.

But instead of engaging her in further conversation, he returned to the task at hand, describing the meal plans and the times of day when Commons was open. After answering several questions about lactose intolerance and the availability of gluten-free items, he ushered his group outside again, heading toward the library.

"You do this a long time?" Karla Mepps asked, sliding alongside him.

"Two years," Damon said, feeling flushed again. "It's fun."

"You are very good at it," she replied. "You make me want to tell my nephew to come to school here."

"Nephew?"

"My sister's son, Jack, who's fourteen," she explained. "They live in New Orleans, but they knew I was in the area and asked me to come have a look."

"We have students from all over," he said. "Sorry, I've got to—"

"No, no," Karla Mepps said, smiling warmly at

him. "You go ahead, finish. I'm enjoying your presentation."

Damon got in front of the tour group and began delivering his usual spiel about the library, the number of volumes, the databases, Internet access, hours of operation, and the like. Then he led them through one of the dorms, showed them a typical room for underclassmen, before a trip through the sports complex.

Karla Mepps didn't talk to him at all the rest of the tour, but Damon kept looking her way to find her gazing at him with a knowing little smile, as if she found him funny, amusing. He lost sight of her after he'd returned the group to the admissions office and started talking about the interview process and what they could expect on the application.

Where had she gone? Damon wondered, then shrugged it off.

Ten minutes later, after signing out with the tour coordinator, Damon went outside. It was almost four, and a chilly breeze was blowing. He'd go to the gym for an hour or so, eat, and then hit the books. He always studied better after working out and he had a tough test coming up in—

"Oh, there you are, Damon!" Karla Mepps cried.

The boy turned to see her coming toward him with that knowing little smile again. "Sorry, I had to use the ladies' toilet, but I have some more questions. Can I buy you a cup of coffee, sugar?"

He hesitated.

"Oh," she said, crestfallen. "You have somewhere important to go?"

"No," Damon said. "No, nothing like that. Of course we can go get coffee. There's a shop just off campus, across the street."

"You are such a good tour guide," Karla Mepps said, falling in beside him. "Tell me, how is the social life here at Kraft?"

"It's mostly class, books, and athletics for me," he replied. "But we have dances with our sister school, Beech Glen, outside Tanglewood."

"You have a girlfriend there at Beech Glen?"

"Me?" Damon said, feeling his phone buzz in his pocket again. "Uh, no."

"But you are so handsome, how is this possible?" she cried softly, while smoothly taking his arm. "Come, you must tell Karla everything."

Chapter 37

WHEN I FOUND THE kitchen, Bree was consoling Dr. Lancaster, who was sobbing from the depths of her soul. Her husband's expression was one I recognized. I'd seen variations of it on the faces of the survivors fighting the zombies on that show Ali liked so much.

"Mr. Lancaster, I'm Alex Cross," I said, reaching out to shake his hand.

A lobbyist, Lancaster shook hands for a living, but now he gave my hand the faintest of squeezes, looked at me with yearning, and said, "Can you find her?"

A familiar male voice behind me said, "We can and we will, Bill."

I looked over my shoulder. Special Agent Ned Mahoney, an old and dear friend and colleague from my days at the FBI, was coming into the kitchen.

"Ned?"

"Bill's my cousin, Alex," Mahoney said, patting me on the shoulder and then going around me to hug Lancaster. "I promise you we will do everything possible to get Evan back."

The missing boy's father lost that yearning look. His lower lip trembled. "Ned, I've been so goddamned busy lately. I hardly know him."

I glanced at his wife, who looked at the floor as if it held answers.

Gently patting Dr. Lancaster's back, Bree said, "With the three of us working the case, it's only a matter of time before we find him."

"Unless she's killed him already," Dr. Lancaster moaned.

"That's highly unlikely," I said. "Young women who do this sort of thing are more often than not motivated by their inability to conceive. They are so desperate for a baby, they'll steal one."

"He's right," Mahoney said.

"Could you look at the drawing again?" Bree asked. "Tell us if that's Kelli Adams?"

"I barely saw her on my way out to work," Lancaster said.

But his wife wiped her eyes, picked the sketch off the counter, and studied it carefully before saying in a thick voice, "Could be. She wore a lot of makeup. The eyes are the right shape but the wrong color. The hair's different, and her cheeks were not so full as this. My God, she had references. I spoke to them myself."

"We'll need those names and phone numbers," Mahoney said.

Dr. Lancaster nodded and reached for her phone.

"Did she touch anything?" I asked.

The missing boy's mother looked up at me with that dazed expression I'd seen only moments before on her husband's face.

"She was only here a few minutes and yet she's touched everything," Dr. Lancaster replied, beginning to cry again. "That woman's touched and ruined everything in my entire home!"

Chapter 38

"SO, NO GIRLS?" KARLA Mepps asked, setting a coffee in front of Damon. "I'm sorry, but the former LSU cheerleader in me is saying, 'How is that possible?' "

Damon smiled, glanced over at some other boys from the school who were staring at him dumbly, and squirmed a little. He'd never had a girl, much less a beautiful woman, talk to him like this. "I dunno," he said. "Just too busy, I guess."

Karla Mepps took off her leather jacket, revealing just how tightly the long-sleeved white turtleneck clung to her breasts. She cocked her head coyly, as if she'd caught him looking, and said, "But you like girls, right?"

"Well, yeah. Sure," he said, feeling his cheeks burn and happening to glance at the back of her left hand where the sleeve had pulled back. She had some kind of tattoo there, like the tail of some animal.

"Well, yeah, sure," she said, and laughed. "Good. The other way would have been such a tragic waste to womanhood."

Damon didn't understand at first, but then did, and his ears burned, too. He couldn't look at her and instead turned his gaze back to that tattoo of a tail slinking out from under her sleeve. What kind of tail? He wondered what the rest of the tattoo looked like.

"You wanted to ask more about the school?" he said finally.

"I do," Karla Mepps said.

And for the next half hour, she kept the conversation squarely on school life, asking first about housing. He explained that the annual housing lottery was at the end of the school year, with seniors having first draw. He'd picked tenth and gotten one of the nicest rooms on campus, a single with a fireplace on the first floor of North Dorm, looking toward the woods, where he often saw deer in the morning.

"Can you show me this North Dorm on the map?" she asked, getting the school's brochure out of her jacket pocket.

Damon did and then said, "We didn't get over there on the tour. Here's a picture of North, though."

He pushed the brochure back to her and tapped a photograph of a granite-faced building that looked more than a hundred years old. "That's my room there on the far left corner."

"Yes?" she said, and studied it carefully. "Very lucky."

"I was. Yes."

When Karla Mepps asked about the quality of the teaching at the school, Damon replied that every teacher he'd had at Kraft was tough but seemed to care about him, and that the teachers were almost always available.

"Your parents?" she asked. "They're happy, too?"

Damon hadn't really thought about it before, but he nodded. "I think they would say so. My dad says I've grown up a lot the past couple of years."

"You see them often?"

"Every six or seven weeks," Damon replied. "Either they come up here for a long weekend, or I go home on vacations. And summers, of course."

"How many vacations do students get?"

Damon had to think about that. "Four—three long, one short at Thanksgiving. Then three weeks at Christmas, and like ten days at Easter."

Karla Mepps found that interesting. "So you have a vacation soon?"

"I leave a week from Friday morning," he replied, nodding.

"And how will you get home to . . . ?"

"Washington?" Damon said. "I usually get a jitney in town that takes me over to Albany to catch the train."

"Amtrak?"

He nodded. "Takes five or six hours."

"That's not bad," she allowed. "But I wonder if my sister will want my nephew to fly all that way alone back to Louisiana on breaks."

"They have, like, escorts and stuff for that," Damon offered. "Some of the younger kids get them."

She smiled again as she stood. "Well, thank you, Damon Cross. I must go. It's getting dark and I have a long way to drive."

"Oh, sure," he said, struggling to get up. "Hope I've helped."

"More than you know," Karla Mepps replied, gazing at him, making a show of putting on her jacket. "C'mon. You walk me to my car? I'd feel safer."

"Oh," he said. "Oh, sure."

Ignoring the gapes of the other boys in the coffee shop, Damon led her outside. The wind had picked up. Twice during the short walk to the visitors' lot, she seemed to stumble against him and he had to hold her up.

"So strong," she said the first time.

"So fast," she said the second time.

When they reached the car, a blue Honda sedan, Karla Mepps pressed the unlock button, turned to him. "I very much liked meeting you, Damon."

"Uh, yeah, me, too, Ms. Mepps."

She reached out to shake his hand and held on to it a second too long, whispering, "Here's a little something to keep you awake. Some night—who knows when?—Karla just might come out of the woods behind your dorm and climb in your window. So leave it unlocked and open."

Damon blinked, pulled back his hand. She chuckled like a cat purring, climbed into the car, and started it.

Then Karla Mepps drove off into the gathering night.

Chapter 39

I WATCHED A CRIME scene tech dusting the Lancasters' doorbell for fingerprints. Little Evan aside, it was the only thing we knew for sure that the kidnapper had touched. Other techs were inside the foyer, working. Ned Mahoney was triggering an AMBER alert across Maryland, Virginia, Delaware, and Pennsylvania. Bree was with the Lancasters, going through the house, trying to determine whether the nanny had taken anything of note besides their only child.

I was about to join them when my cell phone buzzed in my pocket. Tugging it out, I saw the caller ID: Damon.

"Your phone does work," I answered, walking away from the front stoop. Television camera trucks were already camped out beyond the police tape, no doubt having come from outside the apartment building of Joss Branson's parents. The only thing that will draw the media off a missing child case these days is another missing child.

"Well, sure my phone works," Damon said.

"You don't answer it much."

"I'm sorry, Dad, I was leading a late tour and there was someone—a woman, the aunt of some kid from Louisiana who's interested in applying. She stayed behind and, I don't know, asked a lot of questions."

I'd forgotten he was working as a campus tour guide.

"No problem," I said.

"What did you call about? You didn't leave a message."

"Hate leaving messages," I said.

"You could have sent a text."

"I like hearing the sound of your voice in real time, is that okay?"

"Is that why you called six times?"

"As a matter of fact, yes."

"Oh," he said, and paused. "Well, what do you want me to say?"

"The alphabet."

"Really?"

"No, I just . . . how was your day, kiddo?"

"Good. Real good."

"Anything exciting or new happen?"

There was a pause longer than I expected before he said, "No, not really. Just that lady on the tour." He hesitated. "And a lot of studying to do. I've got a big physics test tomorrow. First midterm."

"Okay," I sighed. "I won't keep you. Just want to say I love you."

"Love you, too," Damon said. "Dad?"

"Yes?"

"Have you ever—"

"Alex!" Bree called to me. "They've found a few things."

"Sorry, son," I said. "Got to go. We'll talk later, okay?"

I hung up before Damon could answer.

Chapter 40

AS I HEADED TOWARD my wife where she stood on the stoop of the Lancasters' town house, my cell phone rang again. It was the medical examiner's office. Exasperated, I held up a finger to Bree and answered, "Cross."

It was Cynthia Wu from the ME's office. She said, "Alex, that coffee from the Jackson crime scene you asked to have analyzed?"

"Yes?"

"Someone dumped nearly pure liquid nicotine into it, enough to give a horse a heart attack."

"Liquid nicotine?" I said, puzzled. "Wait, wouldn't you taste something like that? Wet cigarettes aren't exactly appetizing. Smell gross, too."

"Because they're made from tobacco," Wu replied. "This is extracted nicotine, the kind that people use in those electronic cigarettes, though that stuff is a hundred times more diluted than this was."

"Any idea where you'd get something that pure?" I asked.

"Gotta be brokers somewhere," Wu said.

"Anything else?"

"Preliminary report on that smear on the attorney's suit pants," she said. "Vaginal secretions. Some semen, too."

I thought about that, came up with the most likely conclusion. "Order tests on the female DNA against the samples we got from Mandy Bell Lee and confirm the semen is Jackson's."

"Might take a while."

"A while I've got," I said. "And thanks, Cynthia, I owe you one."

"Anytime, Alex," she said, and hung up.

As soon as I entered the Lancasters' foyer again, Bree pointed at the stairs. "They found synthetic hair on that second step. Cheap wig, I figure, which means Kelli's changing her look, which means that sketch we put out of her had to have been close."

"Maybe," I said. "Or maybe it's just part of a disguise. What else?"

"She took a diaper bag and a stack of diapers with her," Bree replied.

"So she's caring for Evan."

My wife squinted. "You mean, the way a barren woman might?"

"Could be. Or maybe she just wants to care for him long enough to sell him to some couple desperate to have a—"

I caught movement out of the corner of my eye, looked at the top of the staircase, and saw Dr. Lancaster staring at us with a horrified expression. "Sell?" she said. "Sell my baby?"

Chapter 41

IT TOOK US ALMOST an hour to get the Lancasters to calm down after they'd overheard my frankly stupid remark. There was a chance that Kelli Adams had stolen the babies in order to sell them, but I should have had the good sense not to say so inside their house.

"The first scenario is much more likely," I kept telling them. "This is probably a woman who has a history of psychiatric problems and infertility."

"That's right," Mahoney said, and Bree nodded.

But the damage had been done. When my wife and I left around seven thirty that evening, I could see that both parents were still chewing on the idea that their baby boy was about to be sold to the highest bidder.

Mahoney stayed behind, repairing the damage.

I followed Bree back to police headquarters. I

thought about going upstairs to get some more work done, letting her have my car and taking a cab home, but after parking, Bree climbed in the passenger side with me and said, "Let's go find Ava."

My wife had that look about her that indicated this was not a negotiable idea, so I nodded and said, "I'm going to need something to eat first."

"Henry's?" she said.

"That'll do it," I replied, and set off.

Ten minutes later we pulled up outside Henry's Soul Café at Seventeenth and U Street. All the food's good at Henry's, but the fried chicken and sweet potato pie are the best in DC. And there's something about the smell of the place and the good vibe of the people who work there that reminds me of a similar joint back in Winston-Salem, where I spent the first nine years of my life.

Bree covered my shirt in paper napkins and handed me pieces of fried chicken and an ice-cold Coke as we headed toward Anacostia. We were crossing the bridge when my phone rang.

"Are you purposely avoiding me, Alex?" Nana Mama said in greeting.

"Me? Never."

"I haven't seen you in days."

"Late nights," I said.

"Tonight?"

I glanced at Bree and replied, "About an hour or so."

"I'll wait up for you," Nana Mama said. "I want you to see what they've done to the kitchen floor."

"Who did what to the kitchen floor?"

"The workmen," she said. "They ripped up the old floorboards today. It's all gone!"

"Oh," I said. "Uh, that was supposed to be a secret."

"What?" she cried.

"I'll explain when I get there, Nana," I said, and hung up.

Bree said, "Told you not telling her was a bad idea."

"I wanted to surprise her."

"One thing I've figured out about your grandmother?"

"What's that?"

"She doesn't like surprises."

Over the course of the next hour we drove once again past all the places Ava had mentioned during the time she lived with us. We talked to kids her age and showed them her picture. But as before, none of them said they'd seen her.

We were about to go home when I decided to

swing past Owens Road Park. I'd never heard her talk about Owens Road, but I knew it was a hangout for kids as much as Seward Square was. As we drove past the park, I spotted a girl about Ava's age sitting on a park bench and pulled over immediately, saying, "I know her. She came to the house to visit Ava once."

Chapter 42

I SEARCHED MY BRAIN for the girl's name and came up with it.

"Yolanda?" I called to her after getting out.

She looked at me, puzzled, until I got closer. Then her face clouded.

"You remember me?"

Yolanda nodded. "You're the Man, right? After Ava?"

"Yes. But I'm looking for Ava as her friend. Not as the Man."

She chewed the inside of her cheek before replying, "Lot of people looking for Ava, I hear."

"Why?" asked Bree, who'd come up behind me.

Yolanda looked at her suspiciously, then said, "She owe people money."

"Drug people?" I asked.

"Them, too," she said.

"You know where we can find her?" Bree asked.

Yolanda pursed her lips, shook her head. "I ain't seen that girl in two weeks. Last time she was dirty and smelled bad, like smoke. She was strung out, too, acting all paranoid, said somebody tried to kill her, and he still trying. I figured she was just in need of an oxy. But I gave her twenty bucks and told her to run."

"So she was doing oxycodone?"

"And Percocet. Anything painkilling."

"You see her, you give her a message," Bree said in a strained voice. "You tell her Bree and Alex just want to talk to her. No judgments. No matter what time it is, she can call us. Okay?"

Yolanda shrugged. "Way I figure it, way I hope it, that girl is long gone, way out to California by now and got that monkey off her back. I know that's how it would be I had that many people chasing my ass."

Back in the car, heading home, I waited several minutes before I said, "Two weeks ago she was dirty and smelled like bad smoke."

Bree closed her eyes and started rubbing her temples. "I know. Right about the time Jane Doe was set on fire."

"I've got to tell the captain about this tomorrow. Show him Prough's statement."

My wife said nothing but nodded. We drove the rest of the way in silence.

It was nearly nine when I followed Bree up onto the porch, carrying the sweet potato pie from Henry's. Nana Mama makes a mean sweet potato pie herself, but she loves Henry's version. I figured to use it as a peace offering.

Bree said, "I'm going to take a shower."

She opened the door and I watched her climb the stairs as if she had an anvil strapped to her shoulders. I felt similarly when I turned toward the front room, where the television was on.

My ninety-something grandmother, former English teacher and vice principal, was sitting on the couch in her pajamas and bathrobe, watching a bunch of zombies attack a family. I couldn't help smiling.

"*You're* watching *The Walking Dead*?" I asked incredulously.

Nana Mama acted as if she'd just noticed me, said, "Hush now, this is bad stuff going down."

Two zombies had cornered the mother when the episode ended.

I looked at Nana Mama, still amused.

Nana Mama raised her chin defiantly, said, "Ali made me sit down and watch the first episode with him on DVD. He's right. It's not really about zombies. They're sort of interchangeable. It's the people who are running from the zombies who are interesting."

"Right," I said, and handed her the bag from Henry's. "Your favorite."

She didn't take the bag. "What's this secret?"

I sighed. "Remember that Italian tile you loved that I said we couldn't afford?"

"Yes?"

"I figured out a way to afford it."

That surprised her, and she softened. "Really?"

"I thought they weren't going to rip up the old wood flooring until just before the appliances went in," I said.

My grandmother got up. She's a tiny woman. She reached up and stroked my cheek and said, "You are a good man, Alex."

"Still friends, Nana?"

"Of course. Now let me get a plate so I can have some of Henry's pie."

We ate and talked until her eyelids started to droop. Then I went around and shut off the lights and helped her up the stairs. After she'd gone into her bedroom, I said good night to Jannie, who was still up studying, and looked in on Ali, fast asleep.

So was Bree when I climbed into our bed. My mind still swirled with all that had happened that day. I recalled my brief phone conversation with Damon, and how I'd had to cut him off in the middle of a question.

That kind of thing had happened too often in his life, and I felt a pang of guilt. *Watch over him, God*, I prayed as I drowsed into sleep. *Keep my boy safe.*

Chapter 43

THE MOON WAS HIGH overhead around one that Tuesday morning. The wind was picking up, and the air smelled like coming rain when Acadia Le Duc prowled like a jaguar through branches and vines in the leafless woods between the county highway and the Kraft School campus.

Acadia often thought of herself as one kind of animal or another. She'd grown up in rural Louisiana surrounded by bayous and dense forests, with deer, ducks, goats, sheep, dogs, a monkey, and a cockatoo. Her father even kept several alligators in a penned backwater down the far bank from their home.

But Acadia was not a gator. She was a jaguar, a panther. She was always a big cat at moments like this, hunting for that darkest part of herself. She checked the compass app on her phone every few minutes to stay on a steady northward course over blown-down trees and through boggy bottoms until she hit an old two-track path she'd seen on Google Earth.

Following the path in the direction of the school, she could not help flashing on deep, dark secrets. In Acadia's memories, cicadas thrummed in a terrible heated night. There were lightning, far-off thunder, and the patter of rain. Her mother screamed for mercy. Her drunken father's fists gave none.

Acadia remembered it all as if it had been yesterday, but she roused from the memory when she passed several stacks of freshly cut wood before the way bent hard to the right beneath a giant spruce tree. She couldn't be more than a quarter-mile from the North Dorm now.

She almost laughed. It all felt so delicious. How did Marcus describe this feeling? Free from restraint? Free enough to be authentic?

Whatever you called it, Acadia truly loved feeling like this, an outlaw of the body and the mind. The half-pint of vodka and the joint smoked in the car hadn't hurt, either, and she flashed once again on that steaming night long ago when the lightning cracked over the bayou and the thunder almost drowned out the slamming of the porch door.

Acadia spotted three lights through the trees and soon saw that they were mounted on the roof of North Dorm, aiming down at the rear lawn.

Damon's window was at the far end of the building.

Sticking to the dark shadows right next to the woods, she was soon opposite his room, which was dark. To her delight, she could see that his window was raised several inches above the sash.

A spotlight shone down brightly from above the window, revealing a metal pipe jutting out of the ground beside the dorm wall. She could climb up onto that pipe and be almost at chest height to the window sash. She'd push the window up, climb through, and rock that boy's . . .

Intoxicated by the idea now, Acadia was nevertheless aware that she would be exposed as she moved across the lawn and when climbing through the window. She would have to be quick and precise. Noticing clouds smothering the moon, she took one last look around before bursting from her hiding place and racing across the lit-up lawn in less than ten seconds.

Acadia reached the pipe below Damon's

window and stepped up onto it, so focused on keeping her balance as she reached for the window sash that she didn't notice the flashlight beam in the distance.

A man far to her left yelled, "Hey! What do you think you're doing?"

Chapter 44

ACADIA SPUN AT THE shout, launched herself off the pipe, and hit the ground running. She used fear as a whip that drove her across the lawn, into the shadows, sprinting toward that two-track path she'd come in on.

Ten yards shy of where she figured the path would be, she glanced over her shoulder and saw to her astonishment that the security guard was racing right down the middle of the lawn, holding the flashlight like some goddamned Olympic track star's baton and gaining ground on her by the second.

Terrified that she might get caught, she felt adrenaline spike through her. She dodged onto the two-track, found a higher gear, and accelerated into the woods.

But without the moon, the forest was much

darker than before. Roots grabbed at her shoes and threw her off-balance several times in the first hundred yards. Behind her she heard a stick crack and heard the guard yell, "Hey, lady, stop!"

Acadia wasn't stopping for anything or anybody. But she was a very, very smart woman, with a keen sense of logic and strategy; and it was instantly apparent to her that the guard was going to run her down. She flashed on the image of the hunting cat she'd carried in her mind earlier.

She felt the jaguar come up in her the same way it had the first time, when she was sixteen and her father had come out of the house through the door of the screened porch, his wife's blood on his knuckles as he stumbled toward the bayou and the fenced-in pool where he kept his gators.

In the woods behind Damon's dorm, Acadia spotted the looming shape of the huge spruce tree on the two-track and remembered that the way bent left beneath it, not far from where she'd left the deep woods.

Acting instinctually, before she'd even consciously devised her plan, Acadia sprinted around the tight curve in the road and cut hard left toward the dim shape of the stacked logs and limbs.

She snatched up a stout chunk of tree branch

about six inches around and two feet long. It felt familiar and weighty in her hands when she darted behind the spruce tree and jammed her back against the trunk, already hearing the pounding of the guard's footfalls, already seeing the slashing of his flashlight.

Seeing that cutting beam, Acadia remembered the lightning that long-ago night when she snuck up behind her father as he aimed his flashlight down the bank into the pool, calling his reptiles by name and laughing drunkenly. The hatchet she'd carried that night was almost the same weight as the chunk of wood in her hands now.

The guard had slowed to a trot. Acadia heard the patter of the first raindrops falling and tightened her grip when the flashlight beam played on the track right in front of her.

Acadia coiled her muscles, became the jaguar. The guard was walking and gasping for air now.

He took a step into her field of view and was swinging the light her way when Acadia uncoiled and whipped the primitive club as if it had a steel cutting edge. There was a dull cracking noise when it hit the guard square on his forehead. He went down in a heap, dropping his light.

Her heart pounding wildly, Acadia picked the

light up and shined it on the guard. She'd opened up a nasty gash that gushed blood. His eyes were partly closed and rolled up in his head. He was wracked with twitches and spasms.

She crouched over him a few moments and watched, as fascinated as she'd been when she'd seen the first alligator attack her father and heard how he screamed for help and found none.

The skies opened up over the Berkshires. Rain poured down on the woods. Acadia stood and set off with the flashlight and her club, not giving the guard another look. He'd been in the way. He'd had to be removed. And for a few moments there, she'd been treated to those death throes. They'd made her legs grow weak and spawned a warm feeling that traveled in her lower tummy.

Acadia got out her phone, checked the compass heading, and turned into the deep forest. Even in the pouring rain, she'd be at her car in ten minutes.

In twenty, she'd be at the motel, gathering her things.

With luck she'd be back in bed with Marcus Sunday by dawn.

Chapter 45

HELMET ON, FACING THE Kinect camera in the apartment's storage room, Sunday moved ultra-slowly as he crept into Alex Cross's virtual home, trying to take in everything, studying the dimensions and quirks of the old house, imagining the rooms filled with furniture and people.

The writer moved as a ghost might, out through the kitchen under construction into the backyard, where the foundation for the addition was already curing. He saw the blueprint in his mind and realized that this would be the part of the house Cross would know least. That could matter, he reasoned, and he made a mental note to have Acadia advance the software the next time so he might experience the addition half done and then complete.

Sunday returned to the bottom of the virtual staircase. He practiced slipping up the stairs, seeing every riser, imagined himself silent, lethal. He moved from room to room, conjuring up Cross's grandmother asleep, and his son and daughter, too.

Lingering in the great detective's bedroom, Sunday fantasized Bree Stone in his mind so vividly that he swore he could smell her. But once again, he was drawn to the third floor and the detective's home office.

He stayed up there for a long time, altering his perspective by inches, examining every bit of the space, especially the articles about the mass killings outside Omaha and Fort Worth. When Sunday saw his own name and the quotes he'd given the journalist, he could not help smiling.

Your doom is right here, Cross, and you have no clue.

Reluctantly, the writer turned from the office and went to stand in the doorway. Then he took off, bounding down the virtual staircases and landings and bursting out the front door. When he removed the helmet, he was sweaty, exhilarated, and disoriented. The virtual model was so real he felt like he'd just escaped the place.

Outside, the sun was rising. He shut the Kinect down, went to the fridge in his own kitchen, and found cold Ethiopian takeout food. Acadia's, no doubt. She loved that kind of stuff. Anything strange.

But why hadn't he heard from her since she'd gone to the Berkshires on a scouting assignment? Sunday had tried her cell several times and had gotten nothing but voice mail. He popped the food into the microwave, thinking that this silence wasn't that unusual. Acadia often fell out of touch. Hell, he did, too.

But for a moment, thinking about her, Sunday remembered how electric it felt when he was with her, how it had been that way right from that first night. They'd wandered the French Quarter drinking, listening to music, and telling each other their life stories.

Around two in the morning, back in his hotel after they'd made passionate love for the first time, Acadia had asked him what his deepest, darkest secret was. Looking into her fathomless eyes, Sunday had felt compelled to tell her something he'd never told anyone else. He'd killed his father with a shovel. He'd fed the body to his father's hogs.

When the writer had finished his story, Acadia had looked at him in wonder and said, "I think we were meant to be together, Marcus, to meet tonight."

After hearing her explain how she'd killed her

wife-beating father and destroyed the evidence by feeding her father to his pet alligators, Sunday had believed the same thing. He didn't believe in souls or Kismet or Karma, but he did believe their meeting was destined somehow.

"How did you feel after you hit him?" he'd asked. "Your father."

"Same way I do now," she'd said, and rolled on top of him hungrily. "You?"

"Exactly the same way."

The microwave dinged in the kitchen, waking him from his memories.

Sunday ate the leftover Ethiopian beef dish and got his mind off Acadia by thinking about Cross. He wondered whether he was moving too slowly, not putting enough pressure on the man. As he finished his meal, he ticked through the basic strategy once again.

After several minutes of detached analysis, he decided the overall plan still worked. It still did the job. He wasn't going to try to short-circuit the process.

But perhaps there *was* more to be done in the short term.

The writer thought over everything he'd discovered about the Superior Spa killings in the last twenty-four hours. Could he use that information now? And then he saw how it might work, how it might dovetail nicely with his recent monkey business at the Mandarin Oriental.

Returning to the storage room, he sat at Preston Elliot's laptop and called up Microsoft Word. He started futzing with the fonts, changing them every few words, until he had a letter that looked sufficiently bizarre but read rather well.

The writer considered it a moment and decided one more thing was needed. He put on leather gloves, fed his printer new paper. After printing the letter, he took the page into the living room, where he turned on the television and found a pen.

Sunday watched CNN as he doodled in the margins and along the top and bottom of the—

"Washington Metro police are treating the death of Mandy Bell Lee's attorney as a murder," the reporter on the television screen said, tearing Sunday away from his artwork.

He stared when a sketch appeared on the screen and the reporter said, "Police sources tell us they believe this man posed as a room service waiter and brought in coffee laced with pure liquid nicotine, which caused Jackson to suffer a massive heart attack."

Sunday was unmoved by this news and by the police sketch of the suspected killer, which prominently featured the pompadour hairdo.

"Doesn't look a thing like me," he sniffed.

Another image appeared. A pretty young Vietnamese girl.

"Police are also looking for Cam Nguyen, a missing George Washington University student, in connection with the murder of Mad Man Francones at a notorious District massage parlor earlier this week."

That interested Sunday, and he kept listening as he got an envelope, addressed it, and stuffed the letter inside. He wet the glue and the stamp with a sponge and decided to mail it straightaway.

But it was raining outside, and before he could get his coat on, he heard keys in the lock. The front door swung open.

Acadia came in all wired, like she'd been up all night partying on speed or cocaine. She carried a flashlight and a stout cut branch. When she saw Sunday, her nostrils flared and she kicked shut the door with the heel of her shoe.

She tossed the length of wood and the flashlight on the sofa and came at him, feverishly unbuttoning her blouse. He smelled her as she attacked him and knew all too well that particular odor oozing from her pores.

Acadia had killed again.

He knew it as surely as if he'd done the deed himself.

Part Three

APRIL *IS* THE CRUELEST MONTH

Chapter 46

I LEFT WORK AROUND six that Tuesday evening with little to show for ten hours of work. It was as if we'd come to a standstill on every case on our desk. At least there had been no new murders in DC that day, and I gave weary thanks for that as I got into my car to head home.

My cell rang halfway down Pennsylvania Avenue. A miracle. Damon was calling in for the second day in a row.

"Dad?" Damon said in an agitated voice.

"Hey, kiddo. What's up?"

"One of the school security guards, Dad, he got killed out in the woods behind my dorm last night."

"Killed?" I said, shocked. The Kraft School was an idyllic place in the middle of nowhere. It was part of why we'd sent him to school there, far away from the street influences that can take a boy down before he's even started. "How?"

"I don't know," Damon said. "Some of the cross-country kids found his body. They said his head was, like, bashed in."

"Police there?"

"All sorts of them. They're talking to everyone in the dorm, you know, asking did we hear or see anything."

"Did you?"

There was a pause before he replied, "Not really. I mean, I thought I heard, like, someone yelling 'Hey, D-top,' but I thought it was in my dreams."

"Hey, D-top?" I said.

"I don't know," Damon said, sounding miserable.

"Male? Female?"

He thought about that. "Male, I guess. I just woke up for a bit."

A murder on the Kraft campus and my son might or might not have heard a male yell "Hey, D-top." My initial impulse was to go straight there, but I couldn't. I had no jurisdiction, and my own murder caseload was overwhelming.

I said, "You want me to put in a call to the police up there?"

"No. It's not like that or anything. It's just that . . ."

"What, son?"

"I dunno, Dad, I guess I'm not that used to people dying around me, like you are."

I sighed, said, "I'm sorry it happened. You knew the guard?"

"Carter. Everyone knew him. Carter was a good guy."

"That makes it worse," I said sympathetically, and despite my concern, or maybe because of it, tried to change the subject. "How'd the calculus test go?"

"It was physics, and it went fine," he said, distracted now. "Listen, I gotta go. Dinnertime."

"Looking forward to seeing you next week."

"I am, too, Dad," he said, and hung up.

I drove the rest of the way home in silence, feeling my skin prickle with worry, wondering why in God's name someone would want to bash in the head of a security guard at my son's school.

And what the hell did "Hey, D-top" mean?

Chapter 47

THE FOLLOWING DAY, a Wednesday, I was drinking coffee and scanning the newspapers when Sampson tossed an envelope on the desk that looked like a lunatic had written it.

Postmarked the day before, addressed to me, no return address, and the fonts on the envelope were random, the letters multicolored. The same was true of the letter inside, which made the words hard to decipher at first sweeping glance. The margins were covered in strange and troubling cartoonish doodles.

One lurid caricature appeared to depict me holding a magnifying glass to my eye like Sherlock Holmes, and possessing an enormous penis on which birds were perched. Feeling rightfully disturbed by that, I was about to toss the letter and chalk it up to being in the public view from time to time and therefore a target of ridicule by the mentally ill. But there was something about it. Forcing myself to deal with the strange font sizes, styles, and colors, I read the letter.

Dear Dr. Bungler Cross,

You have no clue, no vision, and you are barking up the wrong tree.

In my considered opinion, the killings at the Superior Spa had nothing to do with Mad Man Francones. He just happened to be a sex addict who got in the way. The media jumped all over it because of his celebrity. So you, a man of little imagination, jumped all over it because of Francones's celebrity.

Dog wanna bone?

If you'd done your homework, you'd have discovered that there have been other incidents like the killings at the Superior Spa. Look in Tampa, two years ago. Look in Albuquerque, four years ago. It will penetrate your thick skull eventually, and you'll see what you've really got on your hands.

No regards,
Thierry Mulch

I read it twice more, seeing things like that phrase: "In my considered opinion . . ." That's the kind of language an expert testifying at a murder trial might use in response to an attorney's question. So Mr. Mulch was smart, well educated, and—if the stuff about similar mass killings proved true—an amateur sleuth who knew what he was doing.

But why the crazy typefaces? Why draw me like that?

Was Mulch the killer? I'd had serial murderers taunt me over the years, but in those cases the killer was up-front, making it a game of him against me. In this case, however, Mr. Mulch was calling me an idiot from the sidelines.

Or was he? There was clearly something way off about the guy, as if he had a chip on his shoulder, calling me Bungler and talking about my thick skull. And the penis?

Who are you, Mr. Mulch?

Turning to my computer, I ran the name Thierry Mulch through Google. I got fifteen hits.

The first lived in Santa Clara, California, and appeared to be some kind of social media entrepreneur. Another Thierry Mulch was a regional sales manager for Kirby vacuums based in

Nebraska. A third was involved in the feed, seed, and fertilizer business in southern Kentucky. The closest any of them got to Washington, DC, was Thierry Mulch of Covington, West Virginia, but according to a brief obituary in the local paper, he'd died in a car crash sixteen years ago at the age of eighteen.

The others were spread from Maine to Arizona, a cross-section of men who did not stand out and scream "smart crazy bastard" in any way whatsoever. I ran the name through Facebook and found much the same list. There didn't seem to be that many Thierry Mulches in the world.

I put on latex gloves, got an evidence sleeve, and slid in the letter and the envelope. My fingerprints were on the letter, but maybe Mr. Mulch's prints were there as well. It was certainly worth a shot, anyway.

Sampson returned from the cafeteria with two cups of coffee. I showed him the letter. He scanned it, looked at me, and said, "That supposed to be you with the big, uh, physicality?"

"Evidently."

"So he understand something about you I don't?" Sampson said, laughing.

"Read the letter, wise guy," I said, turned away,

and started searching for killings in massage parlors in Tampa and Albuquerque.

It didn't take long to find them.

Chapter 48

TWO APRILS BEFORE, a hooded killer had attacked Sensu Massage in Tampa, killing two Korean women, a male customer, and the guy working security at the front desk. All were shot at relatively close range. Bullet placement—head and chest—had in all cases ensured a quick but violent death.

I soon reached Steven Hall, one of the Tampa detectives charged with investigating the slayings. Hall said that the killer in Tampa had left little if any evidence, though he'd neglected to take the security tapes with him.

"You never see his face," Hall said. "Very smart about it. But you see him taking the third girl."

"Third girl?"

"Esmeralda Felix, twenty-year-old Cuban-American coed at Florida State, working her way through school."

"This sounds like the same guy," I replied. "We've got a missing Vietnamese female from George Washington University who worked in the spa."

"Hope she doesn't turn out like Esmeralda," the Tampa detective said before explaining that the student's body had turned up on a remote beach south of Naples, Florida, sixteen days after the massage parlor killings in Tampa. "She'd been dead for three days, strangled with a strip of green terry cloth. Before the sicko throttled her he cut off her nipples with pinking shears."

I tasted something foul at the back of my mouth, asked Hall to e-mail the file to me in the morning, and told him we'd be in touch if we got any significant leads.

Arlene Lavitt, the detective overseeing the massage parlor killing in Albuquerque, was less forthcoming when I reached her at her desk. Then I told her I used to work FBI behavioral science with Gabriel Rodriguez, the current chief of the Albuquerque police department.

"I'm sorry," Detective Lavitt said. "We're just swamped here."

"You haven't heard about the murder rate in DC?" I asked.

She sighed. "I can't even imagine."

"Just tell me what I need to know and I'll be out of your hair."

Detective Lavitt was all business then, and shared the following with me: Four Aprils prior, a hooded male opened fire in the Empress Spa on a desolate stretch of Highway 85 south of Albuquerque. A Korean girl working there was shot in the head. So was an older woman at the front desk. A third female was shot in the chest in the locker room. A fourth was kidnapped.

"Let me guess," I said. "She turned up dead, mutilated?"

"Strangled but not mutilated," the detective replied. "Fifteen days after she disappeared, a hiker found her body up on US Forest Service land east of the city. She'd been dead two days."

"Pick up any terry-cloth fibers on the body?"

"As a matter of fact. Green terry cloth."

I considered the two cases. "Some of his ritual appears set and some of it is evolving, Detective."

"You're saying you think he's a serial killer?"

"A mass serial killer. Albuquerque might have been his first go. Certainly the first one we know of, anyway. I'll have the Tampa files sent to you."

She promised to send me a copy of the file on

her case as well. I hung up and told Sampson everything I'd learned.

The big man looked sober, sipped his coffee, but then shook his head slowly as if swallowing a bitter pill. "He's evolving. He doesn't torture the girl in Albuquerque before strangling her. But two years later he mutilates the student in Tampa before he takes her out. Hate to say it, but makes me wonder what sick new ritual he's got planned for Cam if we don't find her first."

My stomach soured completely, and I put my coffee down. Nodding grimly, I picked up the bizarre letter that had begun my day. "But somehow I keep coming back to Thierry Mulch. Who is this guy?"

Chapter 49

THE FOLLOWING MORNING, MARCUS Sunday smiled at the woman at the front desk at Sojourner Truth School on Franklin Street. But she was looking suspiciously at his flaming-red Abe Lincoln beard, white pants, white shirt, purple shoes, and violet suspenders.

"Thierry Mulch, here to see the principal," he said, handing her a flawless forgery of a California driver's license that featured a photo from Preston Elliot's school ID doctored up with a red wig, red eyebrows, and the Lincoln beard.

The woman took the fake ID and ran it under a lamp to check the blue-light watermark, which was right where it was supposed to be. She handed it to him without any change in expression and gestured over his shoulder, saying, "Ms. Dawson's waiting for you down the hall there. First double doors on your right."

"Love it," he said, winking at her. "And thank you."

Sunday turned and strolled down the hallway, enjoying the reflections of himself he caught in the glass cases that lined one wall. With this getup, he was one step shy of a cartoon character. Just about perfect for his intended audience.

The writer sniffed. What was *that* smell? Burgers frying in the school lunchroom? Had to be. Was there anything more elementary school than that?

He neared the double doors and heard the excited chatter of children. A tall African American woman dressed in a blue business suit came out. She beamed at him, said, "Mr. Mulch?"

Sunday reacted as if overjoyed. "Principal Dawson?"

She grabbed his hand, pumped it, said, "You don't know how much your offer to come speak to our children means to me."

"Giving back," Sunday said modestly. "It's the least I can do."

"Well, I know they'll appreciate it."

"Not as much as I will."

She opened the door and let him pass inside.

The auditorium was packed with second and third graders, who erupted into cheers and laughter when Sunday started grinning and waving with wild exaggeration, as if he were some escapee from Ringling Brothers.

The writer responded to their amusement by punching at the sky and skipping sideways up onto the stage, where he stopped and looked about brightly, searching for someone in particular.

The principal followed uncertainly and went to a podium. Waving her hands to calm the churning crowd of seven- and eight-year-olds, Ms. Dawson called into the microphone, "Quiet down, now. As fun as Mr. Mulch seems to be, I hope you listen closely to what he has to say."

She paused, waiting for the last goofballs and whisperers to stop their squirming antics and fall silent.

"Thank you," she said. "Mr. Mulch is the founder of a website like Facebook that is going live later in the year and is dedicated to kids your age. He'd like to tell you a little about himself, his life, and the site. Mr. Mulch?"

Sunday didn't respond at first. Amid the clapping children, he'd spotted the one he was looking for, over there, third row, at the end on the right.

"Mr. Mulch?" the principal said again.

The writer cocked his head, shifting his focus off his quarry and smiling at the principal. "Glad to be here, Ms. Dawson."

Sunday stepped to the podium, let his eyes roam over the kids looking up at him with the sort of immediate attention given to a man well over six feet tall with a shock of flaming-red hair.

"You'll hear this again in your lives," he began. "But Mr. Mulch is here to tell you that you can do anything you want, be anybody you want to be. When I was a little boy about your age, I lived on a pig farm. And now look at me."

Chapter 50

SUNDAY TWISTED HIS FACE until he had the boys laughing, and most of the girls, except for a few who were crinkling their noses and whispering, "Eeeuuw, like a real pig farm?"

Perfect, he thought, glancing at the one he'd come to see, sitting forward, watching, waiting.

"We lived in central Appalachia, up a holler in West Virginia," the writer went on, laying on a little southern charm. "I tell you, children, we were as poor as poor can be. Raising pigs was the only way my mama and daddy knew to make money, so it's what they did."

Sunday paused, seeing he still had most of them but determined to have all of them. "My house stank," he said, doing his best to look revolted. "My yard smelled worse, especially in the summer when it was hot. Them pigs would poop everywhere and lay in it and just grunt and grunt. All happy and such."

The children started to giggle and clap their hands over their mouths. He'd known they would, and glanced over at Ms. Dawson, who was frowning.

"I had to feed the pigs," the writer went on. "Sometimes I had to wash them and shovel out their sty."

That simultaneously grossed out the children and glued their attention on him. "I hated it," Sunday continued. "Just hated it."

He paused dramatically before adding, "I used that hate to drive myself at school so I wouldn't have to live on that pig farm anymore."

Sunday went on in this vein, now telling a largely fabricated story about studying until late at night so he could win a scholarship to college, where he majored in computer engineering and learned to write code.

He told them how he'd worked for a computer game company for a while before he'd come up with the idea of a website for elementary school kids.

"When I was growing up, I didn't have friends," Sunday said. "There wasn't a girl that would give me the time of day. I mean, would you be friends with a kid who smelled like pig poop?"

He waited until their laughter died, continued, "So I came up with this website idea so kids like you could have friends far away from home. Like all around the world. Doesn't that sound cool?"

Kids clapped. Others shouted, "Yes!"

Sunday pointed at his head, said, "I'll tell you more about the site in a second, but it's important that you know that I did all this by being positive. As a kid, I used to hate that pig farm, but now I kind of like the fact that I grew up there. Makes my story even more interesting, don't you think?"

Sunday saw that the one he was interested in was nodding, and he smiled right at the child, said, "I used to hate my parents, but now I actually like the fact that they were pig farmers."

The writer snatched the microphone from its stand and walked across the stage, saying, "Do you get it? You can use the things you don't like about your life to change it." He climbed down the stairs, knowing that he was beginning to lose some of them. "I'll prove it," he said, and walked straight toward the kid on the far right end of the third row.

"What's your name?" Sunday asked, and tilted the mike at him.

The boy looked embarrassed. "Me?" he said.

"Why not?"

"Ali Cross," the boy said, sniffing and curling his nose.

"Ali Cross," Sunday said as if the name were a marvelous thing. "How old did you say you are?"

"Seven."

"Second grade?"

Ali nodded, sniffed and curled his nose again.

"What do your parents do?"

"My father's a police detective," Ali said proudly. "He used to be with the FBI. He catches killers and, like, bad guys. So does my stepmom."

The writer found the answer irritating but managed to look very impressed. "Well," he said. "No pig farm and pig poop for you, then."

The other children laughed, but Ali looked serious as he shook his head.

"No," Sunday said. "Nothing you hate about your life?"

Cross's son shrugged, said, "No. Not really."

"Well, then," Sunday said. "Maybe you aren't the best example, Ali. Great life you've got, great crime-fighting mom and dad and all. But remember, life can change like that." He snapped his finger. "You understand that, don't you, Ali?"

The boy looked confused at first but then nodded. "Like someone in your family becoming a zombie or something?"

The kids around Cross's son laughed nervously.

But the writer thought about that and found the idea pleasing. "Yes," he said, patting the boy on the shoulder. "Exactly like that."

Chapter 51

I GOT HOME BEFORE Bree that night, heard voices around the back of the house first, and saw that Nana Mama was out there inspecting the day's work. The contractors had cut out the kitchen wall and covered the gaping hole with plastic sheeting. They'd started to frame up the addition as well.

"The wall was there when I went over to the school and gone when Ali came back an hour later," my grandmother said, shaking her head in wonder.

"They said it will go fast now," I replied, putting my arm around her tiny shoulders. "Before you know it, we'll have a whole new house."

She frowned. "I don't want a whole new house."

"You know what I meant."

"I guess. Let's go on in now, and I'll get you dinner."

"Kids already eat?" I asked as we walked out front.

"Nope, Ali's waiting on you. He's in there watching some cockamamie show about a dysfunctional family that makes duck calls."

"Jannie?"

"Still at track practice."

We came around the corner of the house and spotted Bree trudging up the walk past the Dumpster, looking as spent as I've ever seen her.

"Someone looks like they need a little love," Nana Mama murmured. "I'll get dinner on the table."

I nodded and went to my wife. We hugged and I rubbed her back for a while and put my nose in her hair, the scent reminding me I had so many good people in my life. "Want to tell me about it?"

"Beer first," she said, collapsing into a chair on the porch.

I went and got us both cold Brimstone beers from the fridge in the garage. I sipped mine, waiting until she unwound enough to tell me about a depressing visit to the Branson family late that afternoon.

"I went out there to tell them things would be okay," Bree said. "I knew it wasn't true."

241

"How's that?"

My wife shrugged. "Been a week since that woman took Joss."

"Hope you're not giving up on her, or the Lancaster kid, or Ava."

Her eyes flashed. "Not a chance on any of them."

"That's my lady," I said, and then told her about the letter from Thierry Mulch and the massage parlor killings in Albuquerque and Tampa. "Mulch was right. Because of Mad Man's involvement, I never looked for other mass murders at massage parlors."

Bree thought for several long moments. "You know, I haven't looked to see if there've been baby kidnappings like these in other cities, either."

I tipped my beer toward her, said, "There you go."

Jannie came home then, full of funny stories from school and practice. Banneker is known for track, and it was interesting to hear how the school approached the sport. Nana called us all in to eat pan-fried pork chops and kale stir-fried with garlic and sea salt. Of course, she apologized for serving such a simple meal, and we all told her it was fit for a king and his family.

"How was school for you today?" Bree asked Ali as he ate his ice cream.

"Pretty good," he said. "We got out of social studies to listen to some guy with really red hair. He said you can be anybody you want to be."

"The man with the really red hair is right," Nana Mama said. "Anything you can dream, you can become."

"Yeah," Ali said. "Like that."

"What was his name?" I asked.

He thought about that, his nose wrinkled, and then he shrugged. "I can't remember, but he started some website for kids."

Bree and Jannie got up and started clearing the table.

Jannie said, "I got this, Bree, you look tired."

"You want to wash them in the bathtub by yourself?"

"It's not that bad."

My wife looked at me, said, "Can I use your office for a bit?"

"Sure."

"Maybe we could go for a drive later?"

"That, too."

She smiled, got her computer bag, and disappeared upstairs.

"Dad?" Ali said. "Wanna watch the first episode of *The Walking Dead* with me? I recorded it."

Zombies weren't really my cup of tea, but given that my grandmother had succumbed to the show's charms, I agreed.

Sitting on the couch a few moments later with the DVR cued to play, Ali said, "You're gonna love this, Dad. It's based on comic books."

He said it so earnestly I had to laugh and rub his head.

Okay, I had to admit. It was good. If you haven't seen the show, it starts with Rick Grimes, a sheriff's deputy, waking up from a coma only to discover that the world has been taken over by "walkers," or zombies. The actor who plays Grimes is very convincing and you buy into the situation right away. But it wasn't until I learned that Grimes's family had survived and were living with other nonwalkers outside the city that I really got hooked, and—

"Alex?"

My wife stood in the doorway to the dining room, holding a sheaf of papers and staring at it in total disbelief.

"What's the matter?" I said, getting to my feet.

She shook her head. "You're not gonna believe what I found."

Chapter 52

CAPTAIN QUINTUS AND JOHN Sampson gazed at Bree and me skeptically around ten the next morning. A Friday. We were in the conference room. The homicide supervisor and my partner had only just arrived.

"Wait," Quintus said. "You're saying they're connected?"

"Yeah," Sampson said. "Run that one by me again."

I held both palms out toward my wife, who said, "I went on the Internet last night, searching for news stories about baby kidnappings in other cities. It's horrible to say this, but it's more common than you think."

Quintus nodded. "Every couple of years, some wacko tries to steal a kid."

"Some succeed," Bree said. "And if the parents

are from a lower socioeconomic class, the stories don't get big play."

Sampson said, "But how are the killings and the kidnappings connected?"

"The cities," Bree replied. "And the dates."

During her research, Bree had found references to the kidnapping of five-month-old Juanita Vicente and seven-month-old Albert Tinkler in Albuquerque, in April four years before. The connection didn't dawn on her until she discovered two separate abductions in Tampa, in April two years later, a boy and a girl, four months and eight months old.

"It's virtually the same time frame as the massage parlor shootings in those cities," I said.

We showed them stories from April four years prior in the *Albuquerque Journal* and others published April two years ago in the *Tampa Tribune*, which referenced the massage parlor killings, the missing prostitutes, and the baby kidnappings on the same day but not in the same articles.

"They were thought of and treated as separate crimes," Bree said. "We believe they're all part of the same series of crimes perpetrated by the same two people, a man and a woman working together."

Studying the reports intently, Quintus mumbled, "Jesus H. Christ."

"It gets worse," I said, putting the last of the stories from both papers on the captain's desk. "In Albuquerque and in Tampa, the babies were found several days after the dead prostitutes. Drowned. But here's the thing. When we compared the autopsy reports, we saw that the babies and the hookers *died* at roughly the same time."

"So let me get this straight," Captain Quintus said. "Every two years this couple hits a massage parlor, kills everyone except for one prostitute, whom they take hostage, and then they kidnap two babies, girl and boy."

"Correct," Bree said. "And then the prostitutes are strangled and the babies are drowned. And then they're dumped apart."

"They died at roughly the same time, right?" Sampson asked.

I nodded. "Give or take an hour."

"Any other timetable to this?" Captain Quintus said.

"I don't follow," Bree said.

"Parallels as far as time sequences," he replied a little testily. "I haven't had as much experience with ritualistic killings as Alex has, but here you have two years between each of the events, which always occur in April. There have to be other consistencies like that."

I agreed and started going through the files, looking at dates and times, while Bree, Sampson, and Quintus continued to analyze what we already knew, looking for more connections we might have missed. Ten minutes later, they were speculating on what could possibly have driven a man and a woman to mass murder, kidnapping, and infanticide, when I saw another parallel.

"Thirteen days and seventeen or eighteen hours," I said, interrupting them. "In both Albuquerque and Tampa, the babies and the prostitutes were murdered in the early evening thirteen days after the massage parlor was attacked."

"You're sure?" Quintus said.

"Positive," I replied. "Which means—"

"Cam Nguyen, Joss Branson, and Evan Lancaster are all dying this coming Wednesday night," Sampson said.

Chapter 53

ALMOST FORTY EXCRUCIATING HOURS passed with no significant gain in any of the investigations we were running. The entire time, I was aware of the clock ticking on the lives of the coed and the two babies. I kept thinking about my own kids, how gut-wrenching this all had to be for the Branson and Lancaster families. More than once, I bowed my head and prayed that we'd get some kind of break.

Around four thirty on Palm Sunday, we did.

I was at home, upstairs in my office after attending Mass with Nana Mama, when I got a text from Detective Brefka. It had taken almost ten days for a tech at the FBI computer lab at Quantico to debug the files from the city's closed-circuit television cameras in the blocks around the Superior Spa the night of the mass killings. Brefka had spent the weekend going through them all and sent a report on what he'd found to my departmental e-mail.

I forwarded the file to Sampson and called him at home. I got Billie, who turned testy when I said John needed to download the file and then call me back. Billie reminded me curtly that he had not had a day off in three weeks. I replied that I hadn't had a full day off in four weeks, and that it shouldn't take long.

"Alex, you really know how to handle my wife," Sampson said when he called back about twenty minutes later.

"Really?" I said.

"No," he replied.

"Got the file up?"

"Right here."

Brefka's report noted that the street camera closest to the massage parlor had been on the blink and caused most of the corruption in the data files. But street cameras to the north and south of the Superior Spa showed a few things he thought we'd want to see. He gave a URL to click on.

I did. My screen jumped, and a video began to buffer and display snatches of CCT footage along with a running time stamp.

At 5:45 the night of the killings and soon after Blossom Mai saw her, Cam Nguyen walked by a camera two blocks south of the Superior Spa, wearing a yellow Windbreaker, sweatpants, and running shoes. She carried a Prince tennis bag and was heading toward the massage parlor.

At 6:40 p.m. a businessman in his fifties passed in front of a camera a block east of the massage parlor, heading toward the spa.

At 7:02, a street camera three blocks north picked up a figure walking south. Of better-than-average height and build, the figure carried a backpack and wore baggy jeans, Nike basketball shoes, and a Redskins sweatshirt with the hood up, shielding his face but not his hands. He was Caucasian.

At 7:06, the businessman rushed past that same camera. He had a contented smile on his face.

Thirty-two minutes later, at 7:38, the figure in the Redskins sweatshirt passed a camera two blocks south of the Superior Spa. Head down, hood up, you never saw the face. But you could see Cam Nguyen clearly. She wore the same tennis outfit from earlier in the evening and walked very close to the guy in the Redskins hoodie.

"There's our killer and kidnapper," I said.

"Redskins sweatshirt?" Sampson said. "We're not dealing with a psychotically disgruntled fan, are we?"

"How would he know Mad Man was in the Superior Spa?" I asked. "No, this was about Cam and the hookers. Francones just got in the way."

"Where *is* Mad Man?" Sampson replied. "He's not on the tape at all."

I thought about that, said, "He got there by taxi? Stopped right out front where the camera was on the blink?"

"Possible."

"I say we get a still shot of Mr. Redskins and Cam Nguyen out to the media. See if anyone recognizes her or the shooter's hoodie and backpack."

"I have a better idea," I replied, rewinding the file and stopping it a few seconds later. "We'll put out video of the guy in the suit. You can see his face clearest, coming and going."

"Okay, but why that guy?"

"The Redskins fan passes the camera at seven oh two, heading south on the way to the massage parlor, and the businessman comes back the other way at seven oh six, leaving the massage parlor," I said. "Unless I'm terribly mistaken, sometime in those four minutes this happy and lucky customer of the Superior Spa came face to face with our suspect."

Chapter 54

THE FOLLOWING EVENING AROUND eight, Abigail Barnes whipped an almost-empty bottle of Chianti Classico past me and Sampson. The bottle missed her intended target—a sandy-haired fifty-something guy in an Armani suit—and shattered the face of an antique mariner's clock that hung on the living room wall. Wine spattered across the tan rug. "You pig, Harry!" Abigail Barnes raged. "You goddamned pig! Do you know what this will do to me?"

Harry Barnes gaped at his wife, turned pissed off, and shouted, "That was Grandmother's clock, Abby! What the fuck is—? Who the hell are these—?"

Abigail Barnes went ballistic. With a crazed look, she shot across the living room of their million-dollar home in Chevy Chase, screeching like a banshee, her ruby-red fingernails leading, as if she intended to scratch her husband's eyes out.

She was wearing a ruby-colored sweat suit emblazoned with the logo of the Chevy Chase Country Club. Sampson grabbed her by the nape of the jacket and stopped her before she could attack. She jerked to a halt, struggled.

"Let me go, Detective!" she screamed.

"That won't help things, Mrs. Barnes," Sampson said.

"Detective?" said her husband, who looked baffled and then worried.

"Washington DC Metro Homicide," I said, showing the man my badge.

"Murder?" Barnes said, paling. "Abby, what's—"

His wife wrenched so hard against Sampson's grip that I heard fabric tearing before she went off on Barnes again. "I saw you, you pig, on tape!" she yelled. "So pleased with yourself after God knows what debauchery!"

"Tape?" he said, genuinely confused and looking at me.

Before I could answer, Abigail screeched, "You were leaving that sleazy massage parlor on Connecticut Avenue where Mad Man Francones was murdered! They have it on tape. They're showing it everywhere! Betsy Martin saw it on the television in the bar at the club and showed me! At the club!"

She broke down weeping and sagged. Sampson caught her and walked her to a wingback chair.

Harold Barnes's skin had lost all its color. His hand sought his mouth and he staggered out of the room, choking, "My God, what have I done?"

That seemed to revive Abigail Barnes, because she interrupted her crying to start screaming after him again, "You've ruined us, that's what you've done! I'll be the laughingstock of . . . of everything!"

"Mr. Barnes?" I called, hustling after him.

But by the time I reached the hall, he'd dodged into a powder room, shut the door, and started gagging. I stood there listening to his wife crying back in the living room, and him retching, and frankly felt bad that my instincts had been correct and my idea had worked.

Right after I'd spoken with Sampson I'd called Captain Quintus and convinced him to release the footage of the man in the business suit leaving the area of the Superior Spa.

"Gonna be a shitty wake-up call for some poor bastard and his wife," Quintus had told me after agreeing to the plan.

Cross My Heart

Leaning against the hallway wall, suffering the sounds of a fracturing marriage I'd helped break, I had to agree.

Chapter 55

HAROLD BARNES WAS A successful and influential patent lawyer with an impeccable pedigree. Dartmouth. Georgetown Law. Editor of the law review. Clerked at the US District Court. Became a partner in a prestigious firm. Husband of twenty-seven years. Father of three girls.

"Thank God they're all off at school," Abigail moaned as I turned the corner back into the living room and found her slumped in the chair.

I raised an eyebrow at Sampson. "See if you can find her some coffee."

Behind me I could hear the door of the powder room opening. Barnes's wife looked toward the hall, said, "No, I want to hear everything about his filthy life."

"I'll let you two deal with that in private," I said firmly. "Right now we're hoping he can help us solve a mass murder and maybe save three lives."

Mrs. Barnes looked appalled and then incredulous, as if I'd somehow challenged the idea that the planets revolved around her and not the sun.

"Let's take a walk, Mrs. B," Sampson said, and held out his hand.

She balked and then, reluctant and wobbly, got to her feet. Barnes must have heard me talking, because he'd stalled back there in the hallway. Sampson supported the crushed socialite as they left the room by another door.

As it shut behind them, I heard her sniffle, "I never thought my life would become a cliché. Was I naïve, Detective?"

Her husband came back into the room, looking like a husk of what he'd been not ten minutes before. Broken glass crunched beneath his wingtips, but he seemed not to notice.

"My name's Alex Cross," I began.

"I know who you are, Dr. Cross," Barnes said weakly before sinking into the chair his wife had just occupied. "I read the papers."

"I'm sorry about all this, but we had no other way of finding you," I said.

Barnes made a flick of his fingers, replied,

"I debated coming forward days ago. But I kept thinking maybe it wasn't necessary."

He fell silent and then gazed at me intently. "I want you to know that I wasn't like Francones. Sex is not an addiction for me. Nor an obsession."

"Okay."

The attorney moved uncomfortably. "The truth is that my wife is more interested in her status than in sex. Or at least since she turned fifty and—"

"No offense, Mr. Barnes," I said. "I'm not particularly interested in the motivations that led you to the Superior Spa."

He knitted his brows, said, "Oh."

"Just to confirm: You did actually go into the spa?"

Barnes blinked, thought like a lawyer, and said, "So you *don't* actually have me on tape entering or leaving?"

"Does it matter?"

"It would in court."

"If you were on trial here, and you're not. But if you don't talk and it turns out we can gather evidence that places you in that massage parlor before the murders, I can and will arrest you on obstruction charges, Counselor."

Barnes rolled his lips back from his teeth, thinking, but then sighed and said, "Okay. I was there."

Once the attorney started talking, he did not hold back. He described parking well up Connecticut Avenue and then walking to the Superior Spa, corroborating the timeline we'd established from the closed-circuit tapes. He said he spent time with An Lu, the young Korean woman in the robe we'd found dead in the lobby. As Barnes was leaving, he saw Mad Man Francones going down the hallway with Cam Nguyen to the squalid little room where he lost his life.

"I was surprised, you know?" Barnes said. "Guy like that."

I wanted to say, "Guy like you," but didn't.

"He see you? Francones?"

"No, I don't think so."

"And then?"

"I got out of there, out the front door."

"See anyone?"

Barnes paused. "You mean inside or outside?"

"Outside on the sidewalk."

The patent attorney was about to shake his head but then cocked it left as if he was confronting a memory. "A guy in a red hoodie."

"Where? Standing there? Coming from what direction?"

He thought about that and replied, "Coming from the north."

I felt my pulse quicken. It matched what we'd deduced from the tapes.

"So he went by you?"

"More like we went by each other."

"You see him go into the Superior Spa?"

Barnes shook his head vigorously. "I never looked back."

"You see his face?"

He hesitated, but then nodded. "He had his hood up, but there was a streetlight there. I guess I saw him pretty good."

I wanted to pump my fist in the air but said, "You'd be willing to work with an artist?"

He nodded again.

"And you think you remember what he looked like?"

Barnes gazed into his lap, said quietly: "I don't suppose you could forget the face of the man who missed killing you by a couple of minutes."

The attorney had no sooner said those words than he got a pained expression on his face that was replaced almost immediately by one of terror.

His arm came up, traveling toward the breast pocket of his suit coat, and he looked at me and choked, "I'm . . ."

Barnes keeled forward onto the floor, gasping.

"John!" I bellowed as I threw myself down on my knees next to him. "Call 911! He's having a heart attack!"

Chapter 56

CROSS RETURNED HOME AROUND midnight. Sitting in the van down the street, Sunday and Acadia watched the detective go inside and turn off the porch light. Most of the other lights in the house were already off.

"You sure this is the night, sugar?" Acadia asked with slight worry.

"Thanks to your brilliant three-D model, yes," Sunday replied. "Besides, we need better, more up-to-date information if this is going to go like clockwork."

"You know I'm moving on if you're caught in there," she said.

He smiled at her, stroked her cheek with his finger, and said, "I wouldn't expect anything less from a girl who fed her own daddy to gators."

Acadia bit gently at his knuckle, said, "How long are you going to wait?"

The last light in Cross's house had just died.

"Couple of hours," Sunday said. "Let them all get good and deep."

"I'm going to nap until you're ready," she said, then crawled into the back of the van and a sleeping bag on a pad they'd brought along.

To pass the time, the writer reached forward, turned the radio on, and tuned to WTOP, the twenty-four-hour news station in the nation's capital. The news was all about the latest nonsense in the Middle East, the upcoming primary season, and the opening day of baseball season the following week.

But then, at 1:45 a.m., the announcer said, "In local news, the *Washington Post* is reporting in an article posted on its website that police now believe that the kidnapping of infants Joss Branson and Evan Lancaster may be linked to the unsolved killing of Mad Man Francones and several others at a local massage parlor earlier this month."

Sunday wanted to put his fist through the windshield when the announcer introduced Detective Bree Stone, who said, "We believe that this has happened before, variations of it, anyway, in Albuquerque and in Tampa. We are looking for a couple, one white male, one white female, who may be posing as the parents of the babies. They may have a Vietnamese girl about twenty with them. If you see people matching this description, please call our tip line immediately."

The story ended.

Furious that Cross and his wife had one-upped him, Sunday punched off the radio, climbed into the back, and shook Acadia awake. "It's time."

She groaned, nodded, and sat up against the van's inner wall. She got a laptop, opened it, and called up Skype. She dialed a number. Sunday heard the ring in the Bluetooth device in his ear, answered, and said, "Test."

Acadia gave him the thumbs-up, and he slipped from the van without further ado. Wearing black clothes and snug 5mm neoprene booties found in a dive shop over on S Street, he padded toward Cross's house. It was windy out, and the air smelled like a storm was coming.

Sunday had once again gone through the virtual version of the detective's home earlier in the day. As he moved into the narrow space between the real thing and the house next door, he felt supremely positive about his chances.

You stand apart from the moral universe, he told himself as he slowed and donned a black balaclava. *The laws of God and man do not bind you, Thierry Mulch. You, my friend,* are *the perfect criminal.*

Buzzing on that idea, he slipped around the back of the main house and moved to the addition. The studs of the new room were up. So were the trusses and roof boards. Visqueen sheeting had been wrapped and stapled all around the perimeter.

Sunday got a utility knife from one of his cargo pockets. With the wind blustering all around him, he slit open the plastic where it met the house. When he had a flap about three feet long, he let it go, saw the piece flapping in the wind. He got duct tape out of the backpack. He tore a piece roughly the same length as the cut and pressed it gently against the outer flap.

Then Sunday crawled through the slit onto plywood floors covered in sawdust that whirled into the breeze. He almost choked on the dust before he could draw the duct tape tight to the side of the house. Getting to his feet, he brushed off the sawdust, moved toward the space that used to be the kitchen.

It was pitch-dark, and despite his familiarity with the general layout, Sunday was finally forced to get out a small night-vision monocle he'd bought from the Cabela's catalog. He flipped it on and pressed the electronic spyglass to his right eye.

Cross's inner sanctum now appeared in a soft green glow, making it more like the virtual version of the home, which suited Sunday. In seconds he found the plastic sheeting that separated the construction space from the rest of the house. As quietly as he could, the writer separated the Velcro fastener and stepped into Cross's dining room.

He scanned it, seeing the table and the portable double burner and fridge. A few more moments' study and Sunday had his spots picked out. He climbed up onto the table, got out a listening bug, activated it, and fixed it to the chain above the modest chandelier. Then he set a tiny motion-activated fiber-optic bug, transmitter, and nine-volt lithium battery in a spider plant in the corner, fish-eye lens aimed toward the table.

"Strong signals from both," Acadia said in his ear.

Sunday made a light clucking noise with his tongue to tell her he'd heard and headed to the front room, where he placed an audio bug behind the sofa and a second optical bug in the bristles of the fireplace broom, aimed up at the couch and chairs. Then he went to the staircase and climbed as slowly and methodically as he'd practiced, keeping his weight well to the edges of the risers so they would not squeak.

Reaching the landing right beside Cross's bedroom, Sunday grinned insanely at his audacity. If he wanted, he could open the door and shoot them both, or shoot Cross and take Bree. Anything he wanted. Everything was possible in an existential world.

Be patient, he thought. *This will be so much better if you let it all play out.*

Chapter 57

SUNDAY CLIMBED UP THE second staircase to the attic and Cross's fortress of solitude. When he reached the detective's private office his heart was pounding. Was this what Raskolnikov felt as he planned the pawnbroker's death?

Of course he did, the writer thought giddily. *This sensation is classic, timeless, and shared by everyone on the face of the earth. Humans love causing destruction, especially of another human, especially those who have climbed highest. We just like to see them fall.* It was just the way things worked.

He crossed to the gable window and drew down the shade. Then he pocketed the night-vision scope, turned on the desk lamp, and gazed around the room with great pleasure, thinking, *How does that old song go?*

Ain't nothing like the real thing, baby?

For several minutes, he hummed the tune, letting his happy attention dance over the shelves and the walls, the photographs, the mementos, the framed accolades and diplomas, and comparing it all to the photograph Acadia's young computer genius had used in the virtual house.

Incredibly close, he thought. *A book moved here. A picture there. But all in all it's the same. Cross doesn't like change, especially not in his sanctuary.*

A weakness, he decided, one that he should exploit somehow.

Sunday set that idea aside for the moment and set about bugging the office, putting a keystroke repeater between the cable connected to the desktop computer and the wall socket that fed the Internet. Anything that Cross typed would be recorded and a transcript would immediately be sent to an anonymous website that Acadia had set up.

On the credenza behind the desk, Sunday taped an audio bug to the underside of the leg of a picture frame that held a photograph of Dr. Alex and his bride on their wedding day.

What about the last optical bug? Sunday looked around and spotted the perfect place. On the top shelf of a bookshelf opposite the desk, he fitted the tiny camera, transmitter, and nine-volt lithium battery between and behind two books on homicide investigation.

When he was satisfied the bug would not be seen unless Cross took down one of the books— an unlikely move—he went to sit in the detective's chair, smiled at the camera, and murmured, "Test."

"Anyone ever tell you that you look great in black?" Acadia said. "The mask especially is an improvement."

He shot her the finger, checked his watch. It was 2:27 a.m.

Sunday was about to call it good and leave when he noticed tacked to the wall behind the desk the article about the mass murders that formed the basis of his book, *The Perfect Criminal*. Unable to help himself, he thumbed through the pages, looking for the places where the journalist had quoted him.

To his surprise, he saw that they'd been underlined. Cross had written something in the margin. Sunday had to turn the pages to see it.

"Grandstander in general, but this seems smart," it read. "What else does he know?"

Grandstander? I know more than you, Cross. So much more than you.

Biting his lower lip, he considered the article

another moment and then forced his attention to roam and come to rest on a penholder made from a tin can wrapped in red construction paper and decorated with little green Christmas trees, a present from one of Cross's children, no doubt.

The penholder stood on the desk next to the phone. It had been right there in the picture the *Post* ran of Cross's office three years before. It had probably never moved. Sunday picked it up and put it at the far end of the credenza.

The move was small. It was subtle. But if Sunday was right, it would serve to rattle Cross at some level. At least, that was what he hoped.

"I'm leaving," Sunday muttered to Acadia.

He got up from the chair, careful to position it exactly where he'd found it, retrieved the monocle, and flipped off the desk light. In green night vision he crossed to the door and eased it open without a sound. Creeping down the staircase, he reached the second-floor landing and slipped toward the lower stairs and Cross's bedroom.

Sunday was right there, about to take that first step down the next flight, when he heard a latch lift. A door opened behind and to his left.

The writer froze and slowly looked over his shoulder, seeing little Ali Cross rubbing one eye.

Chapter 58

IT WAS ONLY A second, maybe two, but time seemed to stand still while the obvious option seized Sunday's mind: *Kill him! Now!*

In two steps he could have the boy, break his neck, and—

Ali dropped his hand and staggered toward the bathroom door as if he'd never seen Sunday. He pushed the door open and went inside. A motion-detector night-light went on.

Sunday danced down three stairs and froze, hearing the sound of the boy peeing. Eight more stairs, and he reached the front hall and froze again. The toilet flushed.

Small feet moved. A door opened.

There was a pause and then the boy cried out, "Zombie! There's a zombie in the house!"

Sunday fled on tiptoes down the hall, into the

dining room, and through the Visqueen into the construction area. He paused to close the Velcro strips, then got out the pistol and headed toward the slit he'd cut in the plastic sheeting that surrounded the new addition.

He felt the duct tape come free and the wind rushed in, swirling sawdust all around him again.

Sunday got outside, and despite the fact that the boy was still yelling and now other voices were adding to the mix, he calmly and deliberately pressed the tape neatly over the cut against the wall, sealing the new addition off once more.

"Lights in Cross's room and the grandmother's," Acadia said through the earpiece.

Sunday was already running. When he reached the front of Cross's house, he muttered, "Good?"

"Stick to the shadows and go!" she said.

Out of the corner of the writer's right eye he saw lights go on, figured they were over the staircase and lower hall. Cross or his wife was coming.

Sunday bolted down the short slope of the lawn and vaulted over the low fence, landing on the sidewalk. He ducked down and sprinted away from the house and was well down the street before crossing. Keeping in a crouch behind parked cars, he snuck back toward the van, seeing more lights come on in the first-floor windows of Cross's house.

But the porch lights didn't come on until Sunday had opened the van's rear door, climbed inside, and scrambled forward next to Acadia to peer over the front seats and through the windshield. Cross came out on the porch, wearing a robe and carrying a flashlight, which he played about the front yard and over the Dumpster for a few moments before going back inside.

"Dining room bug!" Sunday said.

Acadia spun around, picked up the laptop, and turned up the volume.

At first they heard nothing but static, and then Cross's voice became audible: "Anything?"

"I don't know," Bree said. "There are a few marks in the dust out in the addition that could be footprints. But nothing new."

"I'll go up and sleep with him," Cross replied. "But I think we should be changing the rules about him watching so many zombie shows."

"Agreed," said Bree. "A rationing of zombie shows."

Footsteps. The lights began to go out. Sunday collapsed against the far wall of the van, laughed, and said, "That's how a perfect criminal does things."

Acadia began to laugh, too, and crawled over to him hungrily.

Chapter 59

I FELT SOMEONE SHAKING my shoulder, startled awake, and found my younger son's earnest face about seven inches from my own.

"I know there was a zombie, Dad," he said in a forceful whisper. "When I went in to take a pee, he was there, and when I came out he was gone."

Sighing, I glanced at the clock: 7:30 a.m. Bree shifted in bed next to me, still fast asleep. Gesturing out the bedroom door with my finger, I slid out from under the sheets, grabbed my robe off the hook, and went out after Ali.

As soon as I shut the door, Ali insisted in a whisper, "He was right where you were standing. It wasn't a dream or a nightmare like you said."

I glanced down at the carpet where it met the staircase and saw bits of sawdust. We had all vowed to be careful to remove our shoes inside the house during the construction, but there was sawdust here and there all over the house. Some could easily have come in on someone's pant legs, my pant legs.

Downstairs I could hear the rumor of Nana Mama talking to Jannie, but I made out nothing distinct other than my daughter's using the phrase "never home." Noticing a bit more sawdust here, a bit more sawdust there, I went down the stairs.

When I reached the lower landing, Ali was right behind me and said in a loud voice, "Dad, why don't you believe me?"

Irritated by lack of sleep, I glared at him and said, "Keep it down. Bree is trying to sleep. And why don't I believe you? Because you say you saw him when you were half asleep, and when you came out later, more awake, he was gone. Doesn't that sound wrong to you?"

"No, that's one of the reasons I know it was a zombie."

A headache began to throb. Confused by this seven-year-old logic, I said, "What was the other reason?"

"I smelled him," he said earnestly.

Rubbing at my temple, too tired to be having this conversation, I said, "So you smelled something dead in the house? Don't you think I would have smelled something like that? Or Bree?"

He appeared puzzled, and I took that as a chance to give him a wink and head toward the dining room.

"No, he didn't smell like something dead," Ali called after me. "But it wasn't a smell we have here in the house. It was like—"

"Quit while you're ahead, son," I said, and turned into the dining room to find Nana Mama pouring coffee from an old metal percolator and Jannie eating Raisin Bran with a sullen expression.

"You look happy this morning," I said to her as I sat at the table and my grandmother handed me the cup of coffee.

"What do you care?" Jannie asked, not meeting my eyes.

"Okay?" I said. "What's up?"

Jannie said nothing, just fumed.

"She's upset and she has a right to be," Nana Mama announced.

"Over?"

"Jannie made the varsity track team at Benjamin Banneker yesterday, the youngest in the school to do it, the only freshman, and the coach thinks she has a great future in the sport. She tried to wait up to tell you, but it was after midnight and you hadn't come home."

Once again I was reminded how much I was missing in the day-to-day life of my children, something I'd vowed to end too many times to count. Too many times I'd used the excuse of having to work, but this wasn't one of them.

"I was with a guy who had a heart attack," I said. "I had to get him to a hospital. That's why I wasn't home until after midnight."

My daughter was unmoved. In fact, my answer seemed to make her even angrier. At last she turned to look at me with tears in her eyes and said, "Did you ever notice that there's always someone who needs you more than we do, Dad?"

My mouth hung open, and then I bowed my head. "You could have called or texted me—"

Crying now, she got up and said, "I wanted to see your face, Dad. Can you understand that? *Your face?*"

"Oh, God, Jannie, I—"

She stormed away, pushed her brother aside where he was still standing in the door, and pounded up the stairs.

"Dad!" Ali complained, rubbing his shoulder.

I started to get up to follow Jannie but felt my

grandmother's hand on my elbow. "You leave her be a bit," she said quietly. "Some of that's just hormones."

That served to churn my emotions even more. I'd always thought of Jannie as my little girl, but here she was the youngest in the school to make varsity track and now she was surging with hormones?

I put my head on my forearms, desperate to go back to sleep.

"What's hormones, Nana?" Ali said.

A pause. "Ask your father."

My son replied, "He doesn't want to talk to me because he doesn't believe I smelled a zombie last night."

I raised my head, shot my grandmother an I-give-up look, and said, "I think I've given Jannie enough time."

Nana Mama looked ready to argue but then shrugged and looked at Ali. "Cereal or eggs, young man?"

"Sunny side up," Ali replied as I headed toward the hall, then called after me, "Dad, will you walk me to school?"

I checked my watch, realizing that if the killer and kidnapper kept to their ritualistic timetable, in less than thirty-six hours Cam Nguyen and those kids were going to die.

"Can't, son," I yelled. "I have a meeting."

"Dad, please," he insisted.

"Tomorrow," I called back down the stairs. "No ifs, ands, or buts."

Outside Jannie's bedroom door, I raised my hand to knock but then heard Bree's voice already inside.

"It's my fault," she was saying. "I could tell you wanted to tell your dad something, but I didn't pick up on what a big thing you'd done."

There was a long pause before Jannie said in a quiet tone, "I should have told you, but I wanted it to be a surprise. You know?"

"I do," Bree said.

I knocked and opened the door, finding my wife hugging my daughter.

"Group hug for the greatest freshman quarter mile runner in Washington, DC?" I asked, throwing my hands wide in a comical gesture.

Jannie smiled and nodded. I went over and wrapped my arms around her, saying, "We *are* very, very proud of you."

She snuggled her head into my chest and said, "Promise me you'll both come to my first meet?

It's Friday afternoon. They're putting me in the invitational."

"Good Friday," Bree said. "Of course we'll be there."

I added, "Wild horses couldn't drag us away."

Chapter 60

HAROLD BARNES CAME OUT of recovery at Holy Cross Hospital in Silver Spring around three that Tuesday afternoon. He'd had a stent placed earlier in the day, and the nurse I'd been in touch with said he'd probably be alert enough to work with a police artist that evening.

I kept looking at the clock in our office, knowing that every second that passed gave us less of a chance of finding Cam Nguyen, Joss Branson, and Evan Lancaster alive. Part of me wanted to go straight out to Holy Cross, pour cold water on the attorney's face, and get him to work. But the more rational side of me wanted Barnes to have the clearest possible mind when he started describing what the man in the Redskins hoodie had looked like the night of the Superior Spa slayings. If Barnes was at all foggy, a defense attorney could shred him in court.

Bree called around six and in a stressed voice said, "What do we have now? Twenty-four hours?"

"Give or take," I said.

"The Lancasters and the Bransons keep calling. I have nothing to tell them, nothing I *can* tell them. That's the worst part. Knowing what I know about the timetable and having to keep it from them."

I felt for her, I really did. I said, "Stay positive. I'm going to head out to Silver Spring in about an hour, watch Barnes work with the artist. I'll call you the second we have something."

At a quarter to seven, I was gathering up my things to head home when Captain Quintus came rushing down the hall with that expression on his face.

Sampson saw it, too, waved his mitt of a hand and said, "No. No more."

"Four known dead at a high-class brothel in Georgetown," Quintus said. "They were all shot at close range sometime late this afternoon. This could be your guy."

"No way," Sampson said.

I shook my head, too. "Our guy targets sleazy massage parlors once every two years."

"Weren't you the one who said he could be evolving?"

Sampson drove us to Georgetown. Along the way I texted Bree to let her know about the shootings, and that it was going to be another late night.

She called as we parked south of the scene off Wisconsin near Book Hill Park. Dusk was falling. Blue lights were flashing. A perimeter had already been set up. Luckily, the word had not yet spread to the media. There were only a couple of freelance television guys. But a crowd was forming.

Sampson got out, headed toward the crime scene while I took the call.

"Is this connected?" Bree asked.

"Quintus thinks so," I replied.

"Should I come over?"

"I'll let you know once I've taken a look."

"You sound beat."

"You know that candle that burns at both ends? I'm feeling like they're almost one flame right about now."

"I know the feeling," she said. "But I promised myself I'd take a look for Ava before heading home."

"Maybe that girl was right and Ava's long gone for the Left Coast."

"Well, I'm going to give it a try, anyway."

"Another reason I love you," I said, and hung up.

I skirted the growing mob of looky-lous and reporters by walking up the west side of the street until I reached the tape.

Showing the patrolwoman on duty my badge, I ducked under and started toward the apartment building. As I did, I happened to look back into the crowd, catching a glimpse of a man I almost recognized in a Georgetown sweatshirt. I slowed, trying to get a better look.

"Alex?"

I shot my attention to Sampson. The big man stood in the open doorway with that grim expression he gets when something has rocked his world.

"Bad?" I asked, moving toward him.

"Worse," Sampson replied. "And you can forget that original body count."

Chapter 61

SOME CRIME SCENES BECOME etched in your mind, unerasable. I knew from the second I walked in that this was one of them. The smell hit you before the scene did, not citrus cleaner but Pine-Sol.

You could see from the front door down a hall past two closed doors on your left and the gourmet kitchen on your right into a luxuriously appointed main room. Blood was visible, streaked and spattered across the butter-colored carpet and up the sides of the mouse-gray drapes, couches, and chairs.

The room held four bodies. A sharply dressed man in his early twenties had been shot in the right eye at close range. He lay sprawled closest to the entry. The others were women, all beautiful, all in their late twenties, early thirties, all in lingerie and negligees. Two of them had died on the couch, shot through their heads and chests. The third was belly-down near a hallway. She'd been shot through the back of her neck. Amber splotches of Pine-Sol showed in and around the bodies. And there were 9mm casings scattered, too, ten of them by my count.

"There's three more victims down the hall in the bedrooms," Sampson said. "Two men, one woman."

Before going back there, I spoke with a shaken Officer Andrea Sprouls, who'd been first on the scene. Sprouls said she'd responded to a noise complaint—loud music and people yelling—from the elderly woman who lived in the condo upstairs. When she arrived, the angry tenant buzzed her in. Sprouls had heard the throbbing hip-hop music immediately.

Officer Sprouls had pounded on the door of the apartment, had gotten no answer, and had tried the handle. The door had been unlocked.

"I called it in based on what I could see from the entryway," said Sprouls. "Which was more than enough. I . . . I've never seen anything like that."

"It's hard every time," I said sympathetically. "Touch anything?"

"Yes," she said. "Besides the doorknob, I used my handkerchief to unplug the stereo and upstairs, to check the bedrooms. Then I backed out and waited."

"You talk to the old woman?" Sampson asked.

The officer nodded. "Mrs. Fields. She didn't think anybody lived here full-time because they were always so quiet. Which made the loud music strange."

"Good job," I said. "Officer, could you wait for the crime unit and show them everything you touched, including the outer door? They'll need your boots, too."

She nodded, looked relieved, and left. I followed Sampson down the hall toward the bedrooms. There were three bedrooms, all well appointed. The first one was empty. The second held two victims, a man and a woman, both naked. He lay on his side with a single wound to the side of his head, and she appeared to have tried to scramble forward, only to die from a bullet to the back of the skull. Their blood soaked the silk sheets, and the wooden floor was sticky with drying Pine-Sol.

The third bedroom held a single male corpse, crumpled on his side below a wide-open window. This victim's feet were bare, as was his chest. He wore pants, but the zipper was down and the belt unbuckled. The killer had shot him three times, twice in the back, once through the throat.

A man's shirt, tie, and jacket hung from a stand, shoes and socks below. A black lace negligee was draped over a rocking chair in the near right corner. A shred of black lace about the size of a thumbnail hung from the bottom of the raised window.

"Tell me what happened, Alex," Sampson said.

I paused, reflecting on what I'd observed so far, then said, "He enters through the front door, so he's expected, which means he contacted someone, a booker, maybe the dead guy in the main room, or one of the women out there."

My partner nodded.

"So he comes armed, but not in a way that triggers alarm in whoever lets him in," I continued. "A lineup of the available women, in this case three, is called. They file into the outer room. The killer stands near the stereo. He twists up the volume. The guy maybe tells him to turn it down. The killer shoots him at close range, then the two women nearest to him. He has to be quick and shoot across the room to get the third woman before she reaches the hallway."

Sampson thought about that. "Why turn up the

stereo?" he asked. "He probably had a suppressor."

I shrugged. "Maybe he wanted to drown out any screams. In any case, given how the couple in the other room died, we can assume that all they heard was loud music until the killer came in. He shoots that john first, then the girl."

Sampson gestured at the body in front of us. "And this?"

I chewed my lip a second, letting scenarios play out. "He hears something, or maybe the lady with him hears something, a scream. Whatever. They're trying to get out through the window. Though she snags and tears her nightgown, she makes it. He doesn't."

"I could see that," Sampson said. "But what if he comes in, shoots the guy trying to get out the window, and takes her like Cam Nguyen?"

"One or the other," I said. "We'll know more once Forensics gets in here."

"I'll start figuring out who's who."

"I'll be along," I said, and then stepped over the victim, stuck my head out the open window, and used my flashlight to look around.

There was a small backyard that featured a brick terrace, raised flower beds, brick walls about five feet high, and a few pieces of wrought-iron furniture. A low set of stairs climbed to French doors far to my right, probably behind those closed drapes in the main room.

The overgrown beds, the moldering leaves, dead branches on the brick, and an old Styrofoam coffee cup told me that those French doors and this terrace had rarely been used of late. I was about to draw my head back in when my flashlight beam caught something I'd missed on the first pass.

Below and to my left there was a cement stairwell littered with broken beer bottles. I leaned out farther, angled the flashlight, and saw liquid in the curve of some of the shards.

That didn't make sense. Except for the matted leaves, there didn't appear to be anything wet in the backyard, and it hadn't rained in days. I wriggled out just a little farther and saw a steel door at the bottom of the stairs. A basement?

Wanting to get a closer look at those broken bottles and that liquid, I retreated, stepped back across the victim, and went out to the main room, where crime scene techs were beginning to photograph and otherwise document the scene. Sampson was in the kitchen, going through purses and wallets.

Rather than interrupt him, I went over to the

drapes, drew them back, found the handles to the French doors. They were locked with a Master Lock that required a key, and I had no key.

Heading toward the kitchen, meaning to search the drawers and the pocketbooks for key rings, I noticed the closed doors in the hallway. The one nearest to me was a utility closet. The one nearest to the entry was locked.

Irritated, I looked up and saw the barest hint of brass sticking over the lip of the door sash. I smiled and reached up for the key. It fit the lock. It probably fit the locks on the French doors as well, but I opened the door nearest to the entry and found a steep staircase that dropped into darkness.

The air coming up from the basement was musty, a welcome break from the smell of Pine-Sol. The building was old, built back when people were smaller, and I had to duck while climbing down the stairs. And when I reached the dirty basement floor I still had to stoop to protect my head.

Slicing the flashlight beam around, I spotted eight pieces of new luggage lined up along the wall closer to me, stacks of old boxes, and garden tools covered in dust and cobwebs over by the furnace and oil tank. To the left of the furnace my flashlight found the other side of the steel door to the backyard.

I went toward it. When I passed the furnace I was digging in my pocket for the key, and my light was focused on the door. Finally getting the key out, I unlocked the door and pushed it open, getting a much better look at the broken beer bottles and the liquid in the curved shards and drying on the cement pad.

It was blood.

Not huge swaths of it like upstairs. More like spurts flaring in many directions, almost as if someone had run across the glass barefoot and . . .

I shined the flashlight down at the door's threshold, seeing smeared blood there. Taking a step back, I spotted what I'd missed in my hurry to unlock the door: bloody footprints in the dust, leading—

Silk rustled against the floor before she screamed in what sounded like a Russian accent: "I kill you, motherfucker!"

I cocked the light up, catching a big, crazed woman in a black lace nightgown coming at me with a pitchfork.

Chapter 62

MAYBE IT WAS THE fact that recently a homeless man had sprung from the darkness to hit me in the stomach with a baseball bat.

I don't know.

But seeing the sharp tines of that pitchfork arc toward my face caused me to throw myself to the side and away from her. One tine caught my ear and cut me.

I hit the cement floor hard but rolled and clawed for the pistol in the shoulder holster beneath my jacket. I kept rolling, heard the steel tines ping off the cement right behind my back, and turned over once more, flashlight in one hand, service pistol in the other.

She had lifted the pitchfork high with both hands, ready to take another downward stab at me. But the light was blinding her.

"Police!" I shouted at her. "Drop your weapon or I'll shoot!"

She looked deranged, said something in what sounded like Russian.

"Drop it!"

The young woman let go of the pitchfork. It clanged to the floor and she stood there trembling in shock and disbelief before she collapsed into a sobbing heap. That was when I saw her bare feet, all sliced up and draining blood.

It took a while for her to settle down and for paramedics to tend to her feet. In the ambulance on the way to Georgetown University Medical Center she gave me her initial statement in broken English.

Her name was Irina Popovitch. Twenty-four, she had been in the United States thirteen months on a work visa obtained through an agency in St. Petersburg, where she'd been assured she would find employment as a fashion model. They'd even paid her airfare.

Instead of glory on the fashion runways, she'd arrived to find that she had become the property of Russian organized crime figures who ran a string of high-class private brothels up and down the Eastern Seaboard: Boston, New York,

Philadelphia, Washington, Atlanta, Tampa, and Miami.

Popovitch had been to every one of them. The Russians evidently believed in moving the girls around in order to keep the clients, who paid upwards of two thousand dollars a visit, coming back for more. She'd been with this team of four women about a month. They stayed in a guarded apartment in Falls Church and commuted to work every day under the watchful eye of Dimitri, the well-dressed dead guy in the main room.

Around six forty-five that evening, twenty minutes after the arrival of the man we'd found dead in the first bedroom, Popovitch had welcomed Martin, her third client of the day, a man she'd seen once about a week before. She said Martin had asked Dimitri for her specifically.

Martin liked to take off his clothes first and have her tease him in her lingerie before they got down to business. That was what she was doing, teasing, when she heard the apartment buzzer. She was still teasing Martin when the music in the outer room was turned up very, very loud.

"That does not to make sense for me," Popovitch said, beginning to cry again. "Dimitri, he hate loud music and he hate hip-hop music. He say men with money enough for us are too old to like that shitty rap."

Streaks of mascara ran down her cheeks like spiderwebs. I got a wipe and cleaned her face, said, "So, you heard the music and you went to look?"

Popovitch nodded, sniffling. "After a minute, yes, because, well, my client he says he cannot do things he wants to with such music playing so loud. I go to bedroom door, and I don't know why, something says open just little bit."

Her face grew taut and her gaze fixed.

"You saw him?" I said. "The killer?"

She bobbed her head, crying again. "He wears business suit and hat like Indiana Jones. He carries two guns with these things to make no sound."

"Suppressors."

She took a deep, wavering breath. "He disappears into Marina's bedroom, and then I see down the hall my friend Lenka lying there in her blood."

Popovitch said she spun around and hissed to her naked client, "Run! He kills everyone!" She heard a scream from the other bedroom and ran for the window. She got her head and shoulders out the window, realized she was going to fall headfirst onto brick, and hesitated. Martin pushed her out from behind. She fell and hit her head.

Stunned, she nevertheless heard the music grow louder, understood that the door of her bedroom had opened. She heard her client say, "No, please!"

Then she got up, trying to find another place to hide. She said Dimitri kept a key to the basement door in a fake rock and she figured if she could get in there she was safe.

"I no know the glass is there," she said. "I run onto it, feel it cut, and want to yell, but I say nothing. I hear something back up at window, so I get down, cut myself more, but try to find key."

"Lucky you did," I said. "Why didn't you come upstairs once you heard the music stop?"

"I hear walking on floors, I hear voices," she said. "I no know who this is, where he is, so I stay put."

The ambulance stopped and then backed up to the emergency room entrance at Georgetown University Medical Center.

"How well did you see him?" I asked.

She thought about that. "He will know of me?"

"If you mean can we protect you, yes," I said firmly. "This is not Russia. Did you see him?"

Popovitch hesitated but then replied reluctantly, "Yes. Good in light from bathroom. But only from the side as he goes into Marina's bedroom."

The EMTs opened the rear doors to slide out her gurney. There was a female police officer waiting behind them.

"You come with me, Detective?" Irina asked in a pleading tone.

"The officer will stay with you," I assured her. "They'll fix your cuts, and I'm going to send an artist around to see you."

"I see this on television. They draw what I see, yes?"

"Exactly," I replied, and patted her on the shoulder. "You're a brave woman, Irina, and we're going to help you."

She started to cry again as the EMTs took her into the emergency room. "I just want to live in the United States, you know?"

I stood there a moment, feeling her pain. But by the time the doors had shut behind her, I was thinking that with any luck, by late that night we would have sketches of the killer from two different angles, and then the hunt for a mass murderer would really begin.

I was immediately overcome with doubt. Would

we have enough time? Who knew whether anyone would recognize the killer?

I sat on a bench outside the ER and phoned Bree. I just needed to hear her voice.

Chapter 63

FOR NEARLY TWO HOURS Bree had driven all over Southeast DC looking for Ava. She'd been everywhere she and Alex had gone in the past week, including the factory where the homeless guy said he'd seen Ava light Jane Doe on fire.

But there had been no sign of her.

Finally, around nine thirty, Bree pulled into a 7-Eleven parking lot on Eighth Street and rested her forehead on the steering wheel of her car. *Maybe Ava is gone,* she thought, feeling desperately sad at that idea.

She'd become very close to the girl during Ava's all-too-brief time in the Cross household, almost as if Ava were the younger sister she'd never had. To think that she might never see Ava again, never know what became of her, well, that was . . .

She flashed on the poor Bransons and the

Lancasters, grasping the depth and dimensions of their parental desperation and fear. Tears welled in Bree's eyes at the thought that those kids were going to be drowned tomorrow, and for several seconds she gave in to the misery.

But almost immediately she got angry. No, she was not giving up. Not yet. Not on those babies. And not on Ava.

Bree got out, went into the convenience store in search of comfort food. She bought a Coke and a bag of crunchy kettle-fried Zapp's Cajun-style potato chips, one of her few vices. Back in the car, she tore open the bag and snapped open the soda can. As she drank and crunched her way through the potato chips, she told herself she was going to have to think differently.

If Ava hadn't left Washington altogether, it made growing sense to Bree that the girl would at least have left Southeast, where drug dealers were hunting her. And Yolanda had said that Ava had been using painkillers like oxy and Percocet.

Once you latched on to those kind of drugs, it was hard to let go, Bree reasoned. Which meant that if Ava was still in the city, she'd be looking for a fix.

Bree had never worked narcotics and neither

had Alex, so she wasn't totally up to speed on where people scored these days. But she had a friend from the academy who'd worked drugs and gangs the past three years. She texted the detective, asking her where dealers worked in the city besides Southeast.

She was finishing the last crunchy Zapp's chip when her phone buzzed. She picked it up and read the reply. She drained her Coke can and started her car, hearing her phone ring. She clicked Answer and Speaker.

"Hey." It was Alex. "Where are you?"

"Out for a drive. You?"

"Georgetown Medical Center."

She felt her stomach knot. "You all right?"

"Just in need of a ride."

"I'll be there in fifteen minutes," Bree said. "I want to check one more place before I put Ava on the back burner."

"I'll be sitting outside the emergency room."

Chapter 64

FORTY MINUTES LATER WE were just north of Adams Morgan in a transitional neighborhood where enclaves of eight-hundred-thousand-dollar townhomes give way to a rougher side of the nation's capital. From Eighteenth Street we cruised east on Euclid, a narrow road with old redbrick row houses, oak trees, and older cars parked on both sides.

Ahead, near the intersection of Seventeenth, we could see the taillights of cars stopped in the road. This was where Bree's pal in narcotics had said there was a thriving open-air drug market catering to everyone from US Senate aides in search of a mild thrill to hard-core junkies on a jones for their next fix. And sure enough, as we got closer I could see figures darting up to the windows of the stopped cars.

"Should we stop?" Bree asked as we came within sight of the old Euclid Market, now boarded up and for lease. Five or six young men in hoodies were leaning against the wall, drinking Colt 45, smoking cigarettes, and watching us. Another band of guys stood on the opposite side of the intersection, dealing with the buyers coming in from the north.

"Go on through," I said, looking straight ahead. "We're better off talking to them on foot."

Bree nodded and we drove across Seventeenth, down the block past Mozart Place, and found a spot to park near the Children's Health Center. It was a quarter to twelve when we walked back toward the intersection, carrying that snapshot of Ava, months old now. Part of me wondered whether this was a wild-goose—

"There she is, Alex!" Bree cried, and pointed south on Seventeenth, to the west side of the street.

Ava was walking toward the dealers along the wall of the empty store. She must have heard Bree's voice, because she went on instant alert, scanned the area, and spotted me starting to trot in her direction.

She turned on a dime and exploded back the way she'd come.

"Ava!" I yelled, and took off after her.

"We just want to talk!" Bree shouted as she flanked Ava on the east sidewalk.

Ava sped up. She obviously knew this part of the city, because when she cleared the back of the Euclid Market, she darted west, jumping a low fence made of planks and dropping into an overgrown lot that had become a dump of sorts.

By the time I reached the lot, Ava had scrambled across two mattresses and was well up a mound of dirt and old construction debris. The abandoned lot sat at the corner of an alley that led back toward Eighteenth. That was where I thought she was heading. That was where Bree thought she was going, too, because I spotted my wife angling at the alleyway.

"Ava!" I shouted, trying to stop her.

But there was no stopping her, and she didn't go for the alley. Like a spooked squirrel, she sprang onto a chainlink fence at the rear of the lot, climbed it, then grabbed the top of a wooden fence beyond. She hauled herself over both fences into darkness.

I scrambled up to the first fence and looked over the second. Ava was across the backyard of one row house and climbing into the next.

"We want to help you!" I yelled.

But she never slowed. We had lost her all over again.

"At least she's here in DC," I said as we trudged back to the car. "As long as she stays, we'll find her again."

Bree, however, was quiet and somber the entire way home.

"She doesn't trust us anymore," she said as we climbed up onto the porch.

"I know," I said. "And I don't know why."

"Guilt?" Bree said, putting her key in the lock and opening the door into the front hallway.

It was past midnight and the house was dark. By my count we had about eighteen hours until Cam Nguyen and the babies would be killed.

I pulled out my phone to see if the police artists had e-mailed or texted me. They had not.

"Beer?" Bree asked.

"I don't think I could sleep without one," I said, turning on the light in the dining room.

She fished two beers out of the little fridge we were relying on during the remodel, opened one, and handed it to me.

The house phone rang. It surprised us not only because of the late hour but also because it seemed the only people who used the number anymore were telemarketers. I checked caller ID, didn't recognize the number, and answered harshly, "Kind of late to be selling something, isn't it?"

"It's me."

"Ava?" I said, punching on the speakerphone. "Where are you?"

"We'll come right away," Bree said anxiously.

"Please," Ava said, choking with tears. "Don't try to find me anymore. Please just forget me."

"Ava."

"It's the only thing you can do for me now," she said, and hung up.

Chapter 65

HAUNTED BY THOUGHTS OF Ava as a wanted felon, haunted by the looming execution of Cam Nguyen and the babies, we barely slept. Bree finally dozed off around dawn. But I was wide-awake when our bedroom door creaked slowly open around a quarter to seven.

"Dad . . ." Ali began in a soft voice.

There was no use arguing because I wasn't going to sleep as it was. I got up, holding my finger to my lips. Out in the hall I whispered, "Let me take a shower and I'll walk you to school."

He grinned at me and I saw that he'd lost another front tooth. I gestured at my own. "When did that happen?"

"Last night," he said. "Nana Mama said it happened too late for the tooth fairy to come."

"I heard she had strict rules," I replied. "The tooth fairy, I mean."

My youngest son nodded as if that were the most logical thing in the world and then went down the stairs toward the racket my grandmother was making as she whipped up breakfast.

Fifteen minutes later, after a quick shower, a shave, and a change of clothes, I turned the bathroom over to Bree and left our room. I stood on the landing at the top of the staircase, looking into Ali's room and watching him pull on a sweatshirt. All I could think about was Joss Branson and Evan Lancaster and whether some insane couple was going to drown them today and strangle a prostitute for no reason that I could figure.

"C'mon, little man, I've gotta move," I said.

"I'm moving!" Ali cried as he pushed his feet into his sneakers.

I shifted my attention to the staircase at the end of the hall that climbs to my attic office and frowned. Sawdust? I almost went over to see, but then Ali bounded out of his room, saying, "I'm ready!"

He threw his arms around my legs, smiled up at me, revealing his missing front teeth again, and said, "We gotta move!"

"That's right," I said, and hugged him to me.

We went out the front door with cries of "See you after school!" to Nana Mama. The builders were just arriving for the day, and I had a brief conversation with Billy DuPris, our contractor, who informed me that the plywood walls were going up around the addition today and the roof tomorrow.

"Dad, I'm going to be late," Ali said.

"Gotta move," I told DuPris, and we headed south toward Sojourner Truth, which is about seven blocks from my house.

As we walked, Ali held my hand, and my thoughts drifted to Ava and how she'd begged us to forget her. I noticed a panel van from a vacuum repair company parked on the opposite side of the street and thought someone in the neighborhood must have gotten into the business, because I'd seen it parked there before, sometime in the past—

"Dad?" Ali said.

"Huh?" I replied, looking down at him and realizing we'd gotten to the end of the block and had to cross the street. "Oh, sorry."

"Dad, you think a lot," he said as we walked on.

I smiled and said, "Sometimes too much."

We walked in silence for the next five blocks.

When we were almost to the school, Ali said, "I think a lot sometimes."

I looked down at him in wonder. You never knew what my son was going to say next. "Sometimes?"

"Yeah."

"You thinking now?"

"A lot."

"What are you thinking about?"

He fell silent.

"Zombies?" I guessed.

His head bobbed and he looked up at me, said, "And how they smell."

"Right. Not like something dead."

"Well, I don't know about all zombies. Just the one that was in the house."

"How could I forget?"

My son stopped outside the fence that surrounds the school playground and said, "You don't believe me, but I figured out what he smelled like, I mean *who* he smelled like."

"And who was that?"

"That guy who came to my school and talked to us about his company," Ali said, and curled up his nose. "He smelled weird, just like the zombie."

That stopped me. "What was this man's name?"

"I don't remember," Ali replied. "Just that he smelled weird. I could ask Mrs. Hutchins, though, and have her tell you."

"You do that," I said, and mussed up his hair. "Nana will be here when school gets out."

Chapter 66

I WATCHED MY LITTLE boy until he'd joined a group of his buddies gathered at the tetherball pole and then hurried home, trying to figure out what I was going to do first. The vacuum cleaner van was gone and a dark-blue Chevy Tahoe with tinted windows and District plates had taken the parking spot.

The sound of nail guns greeted me as I climbed the stairs up to the house, only to find Nana Mama coming out the front door in a tizzy.

"If they're going to do that all day, I'm leaving," she announced.

"Smart idea."

"Father Hannon asked for my help, anyway," she replied. "Getting ready for Good Friday and Easter services."

"Need a lift?"

317

"Absolutely not," she said, and went on down the stairs.

In the dining room, Bree was eating cereal and looking morose.

"Thinking about those babies?" I asked, pouring myself coffee.

"And Cam Nguyen," she replied, her face pinched. "I can't stand feeling helpless like this, knowing that—"

My cell phone rang.

"Got your fax on?" Sampson asked by way of greeting.

"Think so. I can check."

Sampson said we had artists' sketches on the way: the profile view from Irina Popovitch, who'd witnessed the brothel slayings, and the head-on perspective that Harry Barnes had gotten of the killer leaving the Superior Spa.

"Quintus's sending over the artists' sketches any minute."

"You seen them?"

"Not yet. When are you going in?"

"Straightaway," I said, and hung up.

Already heading for the stairs and the fax machine in my attic office, I called to Bree, telling her about the sketches about to come in.

"Be right up," she called after me.

I'd no sooner climbed to the attic and stepped into my office than I noticed something off. I couldn't place it at first but then saw that a penholder Damon had made for me when he was seven had been moved from beside the phone on my desk to the far end of the credenza. In the ten years I'd had it, I'd never moved it more than an inch.

I looked down, saw a few tiny specks of sawdust, and then startled when my cell phone buzzed, alerting me to a text. It was from Ali's teacher, Mrs. Hutchins. My head snapped back when I read it.

Our speaker last Thursday was Mr. Thierry Mulch.

Thierry Mulch? The same guy who'd sent me that letter with the—

The fax machine rang, connected, and started to print. I just stood there staring at the message and then stared at the penholder.

Over the sound of Bree coming up the stairs, I remembered Ali saying, "He smelled weird. Just like the zombie."

Had someone, Thierry Mulch, been in my house the night before last? Had Mulch moved my penholder?

Bree knocked, entered, said, "Sketches?"

Preoccupied, I gestured toward the fax, unable to shake the idea that the crazy man who'd pointed out the connection to the earlier massage parlor killings had been to my son's school, been close enough that Ali had smelled him, and then might have broken into my—

"This guy looks familiar," Bree said, excited.

"What?" I said, looking over to see her studying two drawings laid out on my desk. "Where?"

"I can't place him yet," she said, then tapped on the drawings. "But I know I've seen him somewhere in the last week or so."

"You're kidding."

"No, I swear."

I came around the desk beside her, wondering if I was going to be looking at the face of Thierry Mulch. I saw the two perspectives of the killer, one in a hoodie looking right at me, and the other wearing a suit and in profile.

Both drawings showed a baby-faced character in his late twenties.

Immediately I had the sense that I'd seen him before as well, but I couldn't place him at first. But then, in the blink of an eye, I saw him dressed differently and was assaulted by the images of several encounters I'd had with him recently, and felt no doubt.

"That creepy cold-blooded sonofabitch," I whispered. "He was right there in front of us the entire time."

Part Four

RECKLESS HEARTS

Chapter 67

IN UTTER DISBELIEF, MARCUS Sunday sat in the front seat of the blue Tahoe down the street from Cross's house, gaping at the live feed from the attic office streaming on Acadia's computer.

On-screen, Cross's wife said, "Who?"

"I'll explain on the way downtown," Cross said, grabbing up the drawings and exiting his office with Bree right behind.

"What's going on, Marcus?" Acadia said, confused. "Who was right there in front of them?"

"The massage parlor killer," Sunday said, feeling impressed and annoyed. Cross was indeed a worthy adversary, one to be respected, as all enemies must be if you intended to defeat them.

Cross had obviously taken the information from the Thierry Mulch letter and run with it a lot farther than he would have ever guessed. Dr. Alex had a suspect now. No doubt. For the first and only time since he'd decided to destroy Alex Cross, to make an example of the man, to demonstrate clearly the randomness and absurdity of life, the writer felt a pang of uncertainty.

If the detective could break open a case like this one—

"Here they come," Acadia said.

Cross and his wife ran off the porch, past the Dumpster, down the steps to the sidewalk, and away toward their car. Fighting off the urge to smash something, Sunday started the Tahoe, waited a second, and then threw his vehicle into gear.

It had all been going so well up until the past couple of minutes, he fumed. The audio bugs he'd put in the dining room and the front room two nights ago had been performing flawlessly, and they'd heard things since that with a little creativity would prove invaluable in the days to come.

Sunday had learned, for example, that Bree Stone was obsessed with and hunting for a teenage runaway named Ava, and that she and Cross had evidently talked to the girl the night before. Cross's son Ali, it turned out, was zombie mad, and the boy claimed to have smelled Sunday during his visit.

Was that possible? Did he have that distinctive an odor? Acadia said no, but he'd already changed deodorant and soap brands just in case.

They'd also learned that Cross's daughter had made the track team and had a chip on her shoulder concerning the amount of family time Dr. Alex regularly missed. And dear Nana Mama would be spending as much time at St. Anthony's as she was at home in the very near future, getting ready for the Easter celebration.

All this had been fantastic to learn. These facts had had his imagination running wild until Cross had gone up to his office and spotted the penholder out of place. That moment, caught on camera just before the fax machine rang, had been so perfect that Sunday had pumped his fist in victory and Acadia had clapped.

But then those police sketches had come in, and Cross had crowed about the killer being right in front of them the entire time, and had said nothing else!

"You probably should have put a bug in his car, sugar," Acadia offered.

"Gee, you think?" Sunday said.

"I do," Acadia said. "Where are we going?"

"Wherever they go, baby girl," Sunday said. "I want to see this killer now as much as they do."

"Kindred spirits?"

"Something like that."

Chapter 68

TWO HOURS LATER, FEELING handcuffed and shackled, Bree and I sat in an unmarked car down Tuckerman Street from an apartment building in the Brightwood neighborhood of Washington, not far from where Joss Branson had been taken from the day care center.

We had Captain Quintus on speakerphone and were engaged in a shouting match.

"What do you mean, you're getting blowback?" I demanded.

"There are lives at stake here!" Bree insisted. "Babies' lives!"

"You don't think I know that?" Quintus shot back. "But all you've really got at this point are those drawings and the fact that Carney seemed to show up around the crime scenes."

"Every crime scene! I saw him outside the spa,

and the Lancasters' house, and I swear I caught a glimpse of him in a Georgetown sweatshirt in the crowd outside the brothel. And Bree says she thinks Carney was the officer she ordered to help Mrs. Branson after she almost collapsed right after Joss was taken!"

"You're sure he wasn't dispatched to those scenes?" Quintus said.

"No, *he was not,* Captain," I retorted. "The first night he told me and Sampson that he'd heard about the Superior Spa on his scanner while driving home. At the Lancasters' he said he'd been dispatched for crowd control, but we just found out he was off-duty at the time."

"It's still not enough to perfect a search warrant. Find me more."

"Find us another judge!" I shouted, and hung up, wanting to punch something. We knew Carney was in his apartment. I'd used a burn phone to call his landline and he'd picked up about fifteen minutes ago. Were the babies in there? Was Cam Nguyen?

"How about we send someone up, listen for crying?" Bree suggested.

"Good idea, but we can't do it," I replied. "Carney knows us."

My wife threw up her hands in desperation. "So what do we do?"

"Unless Quintus finds a cooperative judge, we wait until Carney leaves for work, and then we break in."

"Times like these make me fall in love with you all over again, Dr. Cross."

I grinned and blew her a kiss. My phone rang. Sampson.

"John?"

"Okay, Alex," the big man said, breathing hard. "I've got a few things. Carney was a marine, did a tour in Afghanistan. Suffered a minor head injury due to an IED. Recovered enough to pass the physicals for Force Recon, Special Forces, but was turned down for unnamed reasons. He took an honorable discharge, became a security guard in Albuquerque around the time of the first shooting, kidnapping, and drowning. And he *was* on rookie probation with Tampa PD two years ago when the second round of killings and kidnappings went down. He took the job up here four months ago, better pay, same seniority."

"That's enough," I said. "Call Quintus, give him that."

Fifteen minutes later, the captain called. "You

got your warrant, Alex. Sampson's on his way to pick it up. He'll be there in twenty minutes, tops."

The minutes ticked by, and I had to force myself not to imagine what might be happening up in that apartment while we waited. The emotional part of me said, *Just go up there, knock down the door, and let the warrant come in behind you. Your word against Carney's on when it was served.* But a more rational voice in my head kept reminding me that we were so close to being legal that it wasn't worth risking the fruit of the poisonous—

"There he is!" Bree cried. "Carney's on the move!"

I looked up to see the young patrolman turn off the walkway to his apartment building and head away from us up the street dressed in civilian clothes: jeans, work boots, a plaid shirt, and a canvas jacket.

"He's carrying something under his arm," I said, grabbing a pair of binoculars and looking at him as he stopped beside a blue Chevy Impala and worked the key into the lock.

He opened the rear door, tossed in what he'd been carrying, then closed the door and circled the car.

"What was he carrying?" my wife asked.

"Empty, folded canvas duffel bags," I said, lowering my binoculars as Carney climbed into the driver's seat. "A bunch of them."

Bree understood and looked ill. "We can't wait for Sampson and the warrant, Alex. He's going somewhere to drown those babies and Cam Nguyen before he goes to work."

I agreed, started our car, and pulled out, saying, "Call John. Tell him to enter and search the apartment once he gets backup. And warn the captain."

Chapter 69

SUNDAY SAW CROSS PULL out of his parking space on Tuckerman Street and immediately followed half a block back.

"He's trailing that blue Impala," Acadia said.

"I've got them both," the writer replied.

"Go right," she said.

"I see it."

The writer took the right, kept well back in traffic, six or seven cars behind Cross, who was six or seven cars in back of the blue Impala. Was that the murderer driving? The thought gave Sunday chills.

Acadia evidently felt much the same way, because she asked, "Do you think he's like us?"

The writer glanced over, thinking once again how spooky it was that they thought so similarly, as if they were mirror images of the same person.

"He likes killing, certainly," Sunday replied.

"But I would imagine that it is compulsion and not enjoyment driving his darker activities."

Acadia nodded. "No choice in the matter. Not like us at all."

"A different subspecies," he offered.

"Fascinating," she replied.

They trailed the blue Impala and Cross's unmarked car north out of the District onto Maryland Route 97, which winds through the subdivisions of Wheaton, Glenmont, and Aspen Hill. It wasn't until Olney that farmland appeared.

There was less traffic on the road here and Sunday had to lag so far back that he lost sight of the blue Impala, and then of Cross's car after they'd both taken a left off the rural highway at Sunshine, heading west on Damascus Road.

He could see well down the road. They were gone. "Where'd they—"

"They must have gone to that reservoir back there," Acadia said. Sunday stomped on the parking brake and spun the wheel going forty. They went into a screeching U-turn that threw them into the opposite lane. He released the brake and hit the gas, looking for the road to—

"There it is!" Acadia cried. "Triadelphia Reservoir Road."

Sunday took the left without braking and shot up the dirt road, heading north once more. They passed one farm after another, separated by thick patches of timber. Where were they going? The reservoir?

He crested a rise in the road.

"Oops," Acadia said before Sunday said, "Fuck."

The unmarked car was parked off the shoulder not eighty yards ahead and twenty yards shy of where the woods gave way to hay fields. The detective and his wife were already out, doors shut. Bree Stone was holding a walkie-talkie and moving toward the front of the car, the edge of the woods, and the fields.

But Alex Cross? He was standing there looking right at them.

Chapter 70

I WATCHED THE DARK-BLUE Chevy Tahoe with the tinted windows and the DC plates pass by at a solid clip, giving me nothing more than a pair of silhouettes, a man and a woman. I started walking toward the fields, watching the SUV until it had passed the other end and a line of trees before disappearing around a bend in the road.

"What is it?" Bree asked.

"Probably nothing," I said, slowing as we reached the edge of the woods. "Lot of dark-blue Tahoes with tinted windows in DC. Whole fleet of them at the White House."

Beyond the field my eyes studied a long wall of pine trees, a windbreak of sorts that stretched from the road back toward an old farmhouse and an older barn surrounded by low brush. Through the binoculars, I could just make out the top of

Carney's Impala parked in the side yard by the house. From a long way off you could see that the white house paint was blistered or gone to bare clapboard. The roof of the barn looked like it had been hit by lightning at some point. There was a charred, gaping hole on one corner. The whole structure sagged left.

"They're in that house," Bree said.

"They have to be," I agreed, scanning the area with the glasses, understanding that we did not want to cross that open field to get to the farmhouse. We could be seen too easily.

My wife was thinking the same way and said, "We take the ditch on the left side of the road up to that tree line, then go across."

It made sense. We took off, running low at the left side of the road, and jumped down into the drainage ditch. Stooped over, even I couldn't be seen as we covered the hundred and fifty yards until the line of pine trees blocked any possible view of us from the farmhouse.

Moving along the road, hugging tight to the big conifers, we crept toward the farmyard and stopped behind the very last tree. Carney's Impala was parked next to the house and a door. The shades were drawn in every window. And what was that noise? Almost like chickens clucking?

"Cover me, then call for backup," I whispered, drawing my pistol and meaning to run around the pines, through the brush, and get to the side of the house as fast as possible.

But when I cut around the last tree, I ran directly into an explosion of cackling, squawking, and beating wings and flying feathers that became a flock of wild turkeys flushing all around me, ten or more.

I almost had a heart attack, so surprised and startled that it was at least ten seconds before Bree grabbed me by the elbow and together we sprinted around the back of the Impala and plastered ourselves against the side of the farmhouse.

"So much for being sneaky," I whispered, still shaking inside but aiming my pistol at the side door, expecting it to open at any moment. After that much racket, how couldn't Carney come to investigate?

But a minute passed, and then two. Was it possible he hadn't heard any of it? Where was—?

A man's voice, the words unclear but the tone threatening, echoed to us from inside the house. Then a woman's voice chimed in, equally abusive in tone.

Bree held up two fingers. Carney was in there with his accomplice. The woman who'd kidnapped the—

But then a second woman began making noises in a pleading tone.

A man yelled the first distinct words: "Shut up, you uncaring bitch!"

There was silence before babies began to bawl.

Chapter 71

"I'M GOING IN THERE right now," my wife whispered.

"I am, too," I murmured. "But let's do this by the book. Go around front, and through the door in thirty seconds. Remember, this guy is ex-marines. Very good with a gun."

Bree understood and in a crouch ran around the front of the house and up onto the dilapidated front porch. I sidled along beneath the windows, climbed the rickety back stoop, reached out with my left hand, and turned the knob until I heard it click. The door came loose.

Swinging it open, I did a quick head bob around the doorframe, and another, enough to tell me that the old kitchen was empty. The babies were still crying. My gun led as I stepped gingerly inside, seeing a cereal box and a used bowl with milk still in the bottom. The air smelled of food rotting.

The babies' crying grew louder, but the sound was weird, off, and coming from a room on the other side of the kitchen. Blood pounding in my temples, I heard the front door open and Bree take two creaking steps before a woman started yelling over the babies' cries.

"What did you expect?" she taunted. "After what you did to us? What did you expect?"

"Please!" the other woman cried. "I've done nothing to you. The babies have done nothing to you!"

"Liar!" a man roared, and I heard a loud slap.

Taking two quick steps to the doorway, I shouted, "Police!" and ducked into the room, expecting to see three adults and two babies.

Bree came in through another doorway. We stared at each other, and then at the ratty old couch, a coffee table, and a laptop computer, and no one else.

"Please, no more!" the woman sobbed, and I understood.

Going straight to the laptop, I spun it around. "Jesus."

Naked from the waist up, Cam Nguyen sat on a

chair at the center of the screen. She held the two crying children and was sobbing hysterically. Cribs flanked her. In the foreground, there was an old claw-foot bathtub. In the lower right-hand corner of the screen a red Record button glowed, and I understood. Carney wanted memories of his sick ceremony. Same reason he'd stolen the hard drive at the spa.

"Where is he?" Bree demanded, horrified. "Where's the woman? Where are they?"

"I don't know. The feed must be wireless, a—"

Suddenly we saw the back of Carney's head and his canvas jacket, and then the length of him. He was dragging a garden hose, which he dropped into the bathtub. He looked at Cam Nguyen and said, "You remember the tub, don't you, Mommy?"

Chapter 72

"HE'S GOING TO DROWN the babies in there," Bree said in a wavering whisper. "Where are they? Where's that room?"

I found the Mute button and hit it. "We have to move. We have to listen."

Given the way the babies and Cam Nguyen had been crying, we should have heard them if they had been anywhere in the main or upper floor of the farmhouse. But there was nothing but the gentle clacking of tree limbs outside.

I glanced back at the screen for some clue. But aside from the cribs, a table behind Cam, and the bathtub, the room was nondescript and small, with plain white walls. Carney came toward the camera and passed beneath it, disappearing from view.

I released the Mute button and heard that woman's voice coming from somewhere off-screen, saying, "That's it, Mommy. Be scared of the water, just like we were."

Then a man's voice followed, saying, "You didn't give us a chance, so we can't give you one, either."

"That wasn't Carney," I said.

Bree shook her head. "The other two must be in some kind of anteroom off that room. The barn?"

"Or the basement," I said.

"I'm going out . . . shit, I never called for backup," she said.

"Call on the way to the barn. I'm going downstairs. If you hear them, you call me, understand? Go through the kitchen and out that side door."

Bree nodded, turned, and left, while I went looking for a way downstairs, the ranting of various voices and the crying of Cam Nguyen and the babies on the computer making me more frantic than ever to find them before it was too late.

After two tries revealed only an empty pantry and a small closet, a door in the hallway off the kitchen opened onto a rickety wooden staircase. I listened. Nothing. I flipped on the electric switch. No lights, either.

Digging in my pocket, I came up with a Maglite and held it under the barrel of my pistol as I dropped down the staircase into a basement filled with moldering junk and rusting tools.

They have to be in the barn, I thought, and almost turned to climb out after Bree. Then my flashlight beam picked up footprints in the dust that quickly became a well-trodden path across the basement to an empty set of floor-to-ceiling wooden shelves. Why there? Had Carney emptied the shelves recently? What had been there?

For the second time, I almost turned around.

Then I felt the slight breeze hitting my cheeks. But it wasn't coming through the open door and down the stairs. It was blowing at me from the direction of the empty shelves. Moving fast now, I crossed to them, shining my light, seeing thick dust, and then fingerprints on the right side.

I reached out and tugged. The shelf barely moved. I set my pistol and flashlight down and grabbed it with both hands. The entire unit came free of the wall and swung toward me, moaning on rusting hinges.

"Alex?" Bree whispered over the radio. "I called Montgomery—"

I snatched up my radio, whispered, "Come back."

Nothing.

"Bree?"

Nothing.

I hesitated, ducked down into the narrow, low-ceilinged tunnel, and tried again. "Bree?"

But all I got in return that time was static.

Chapter 73

OUTSIDE IN THE MIST, Bree clicked on the Transmit button of her radio again but got zero. Her unit had died. She set it down on an old picnic table and hesitated, wondering whether to call Alex on his cell.

But then she heard something and all thoughts of calling her husband disappeared. It had been a brief noise that seemed to come from inside the old barn. Gun up, she angled fast through the high grass toward the near front corner of the sagging structure. Had that noise been the breeze whistling softly through the decrepit building? Or a muffled cry of desperation?

She stopped, listening, and then heard it again, short and almost squeaky, as if she was catching only the highest part of a longer cry. Up close, she could see how the barn had come off the sills and foundation in places. Was it safe?

The cry came a third time, louder, and Bree turned selfless. She was here to save those children from a madman. Nothing less would do.

She rounded the corner toward a set of big sliding doors and tried to push one open. It moved about eight inches before jamming in the mud. But it was enough for her to squeeze through into a dim space that smelled of old hay and spoiled leather.

Pigeons flushed from roosts on the beams above her and fled for that burned hole in the roof. Bree got out her Maglite and shined it around, seeing a loft, and a trail where lightning had spiraled from the roof down a massive wooden support post and scorched the floorboards.

The noise came louder now. Bree recognized words.

"Please!" Cam Nguyen was crying. "Please!"

It was coming from deep beneath the floorboards.

Bree shined her light, seeing gaps between the boards, and got on her knees, looking through the gaps to see a stone-walled basement cluttered with rusting old farm equipment.

There had to be a way down. She moved farther

into the barn, casting the light into every corner and stall, looking for a stairway or a trapdoor. But she found none. Maybe she had to go back outside, find an entrance to the lower level. She turned and headed toward the doors.

As she crossed the charred lighting scar on the barn floor, she heard cracking before planks broke away beneath her.

Chapter 74

I WOULD LATER LEARN that a man named Ezra Pike must have built the tunnel sometime in the late 1850s. Pike was a farmer on the land, a Quaker, an ardent abolitionist, and a vital cog in the Underground Railroad, which helped slaves reach Canada before and during the Civil War.

But that day, from my perspective, Pike's tunnel was being used as a pathway *to* enslavement, torture, and murder. I was having no part of it, and that steeled me, made me determined to rescue Cam Nguyen and those babies. I was fifty feet down the tunnel when I heard the babies squawking somewhere ahead of me. And then the muffled voices of Carney, Nguyen, and the other man and woman we hadn't seen yet.

Adjusting the beam, changing it to red, I cupped the bulb of the slender flashlight and stalked forward, then turned the light off altogether when the voices got loud enough to distinguish.

"Who's going to be first, Kenny-Two?" the woman asked.

"I hate to say it because it's so sad, sister, but it's the boy, of course," Carney replied. "Kevin was the first to go."

His sister? I thought. Kevin? I moved close enough to see light glowing through cracks in the plank wall that blocked the way.

"I went first?" the other man said in a wavering voice.

"I saw it with my own eyes," Carney replied in a grief-stricken voice. "She drowned you first, little brother. Mother of the year! Mother of us all!"

I pressed my eye to a slit in the wood and saw into a low-ceilinged space with a stone foundation, Ezra Pike's root cellar, a way station on the long road to freedom. Carney had recently built a crude room inside the root cellar that stuck out of the stonework to my left about fifteen feet. I could see exposed two-by-fours and thick foam insulation coating what would turn out to be plywood walls. Soundproofing, I guessed.

But for some reason Carney didn't care about

sound that day. He had left the steel door ajar. Light spilled out of the room into the main root cellar.

"So Kelli went into the water next?" Kevin asked.

"As soon as there were no more bubbles rising in the tub," Carney replied as if in awe. "She wanted us to go in reverse order of how we came into the world. Isn't that right, Mommy?"

My hands searched the corners of the door that blocked the tunnel, trying to find the mechanism that would open it. But I couldn't find it.

Carney said, "Mommy, give me Kevin to hold while you get down on your knees by the tub. You've got dirty work to do."

In desperation, I pushed against each edge of the wall. The left one budged just as Cam Nguyen screamed, "You're insane! I won't do it!"

The babies began to screech and cry. Over their wailing, from somewhere far above me, I thought I heard a crash.

Chapter 75

BREE FELT THE FLOOR giving way and instinctively threw her arms out wide. She fell through splintered wood that ripped at her legs, waist, and ribs before she slammed to a stop, trapped at her armpits. Her lower body and legs dangled in the basement below.

The impact had knocked the pistol from her hand. It lay a few inches away. But she still clutched the little Maglite.

She felt like she'd broken a rib, maybe two. And was that feeling blood?

Like ice fracturing, boards all around her started cracking and popping. For a terrifying moment she thought it would all collapse and she'd plunge through onto the rusting blade of some old piece of farm equipment in the darkness below her. But the boards held long enough for her to realize that she might escape if she acted quickly.

To get her elbows beneath her, she wiggled, strained, and struggled, trying to ignore the sharp pieces of wood biting at her from all sides like so many sharks' teeth. She made it to her elbows and stopped there, breathing hard and thinking for the first time that the floor busting must have made a terrible noise.

Had Carney heard it? Was he coming for her from wherever he was keeping Cam Nguyen and the babies? Would he spot her lower body, shoot first, and ask questions later?

Sweat poured off her brow and she began to breathe short and fast. She realized she was starting to panic and forced herself to take deep breaths, to calm down, to take things one step at a time.

She began to move her upper body back and forth, trying to get enough momentum to rock forward up onto her hands and then push herself up out of the hole. But she gasped in pain; one of the sharp pieces of wood had found her broken ribs. And she knew for certain now that she was bleeding. She could feel the blood soaking the side of her blouse.

Biting against the pain, ignoring the fact that she was wounded, Bree tried rocking to her left. It worked, giving her just enough room to sharply wrench her weight up onto her right elbow and then her right hand, which found one of the sharp pieces of wood sticking in her ribs. She pushed at it, trying to get it out of the way so she might rock to her right and get her left hand down.

But when she did, the piece of wood snapped away, taking another board with it.

Her right arm and shoulder scraped down through the hole. Her gun went through, too. She heard it clang below in the darkness.

Her left elbow and forearm slid toward gravity, and she began to thrash and grope wildly beneath her.

Chapter 76

FOR A SECOND OR two I thought Carney had heard the noise above me, Bree, no doubt, and I got up my gun, figuring he'd come out of the room to check. But the screaming of babies in that confined space must have masked the sound of the crash, because I heard the woman Kelli say, "Course you will do it, Mommy. You're a crack whore and we know what crack whores will do."

"When times get rough and the drugs get thin," Kevin added.

"I won't do it!" Cam Nguyen screeched, and I pushed at the passage door, getting it open enough for me to squeeze through into the root cellar.

"Then I'll make you, Mommy," Carney said, and I heard a sickening thud that set the babies off all over again.

"That'll fix her," Carney's sister said. "Fix her good, Kenny-Two."

Gun up, I took two steps toward the open door, sniffing the air, smelling body odor and diapers and fear.

"I'll get her on her knees," Carney's brother, Kevin, said.

I took three more soft steps and then a fourth sideways into the light that streamed from the door, looking straight into the chamber of horrors.

Cam Nguyen was slumped in a chair. Her head swung lazily the way a boxer's will when he's been dazed by a blow. Her nipples and lips had been smeared with lipstick, making them grotesquely large and gaudy. The babies squalled on the floor next to the tub, which was now close to full. But where were Carney and the others? They had to be either to the immediate left or right of the door.

I heard the rattle of metal to the left as I eased toward the doorway.

From what sounded like the same side, Carney said, "Is everybody in? The ceremony's about to begin."

The muzzle of my gun leading, I did a head bob left. My brain registered the fact that no one was there an instant before white fireworks went off in my head, blinding me as I stumbled forward and crumpled.

Chapter 77

GROPING CRAZILY BENEATH HER with her right hand, Bree felt the burned boards under her left elbow splinter and then collapse. As she fell, her right cheek struck the jagged edge of the hole, which stabbed and cut her. Her head twisted from the pain and her right arm snapped up to protect her face from further damage.

That reflex saved her life. She felt something hit her hard beneath her upper arm and elbow; and for an instant she was hung up on something metal, tubular and strong, like a pipe. The rest of her body swung forward beneath it, dislodging her, and she fell a third time.

She was only in the air a foot or two before her shoes smashed against the lip of something, which threw her forward, prone on a molded metal surface. The pain that shot up through her ribs was

z

360

electric, searing hot, and probing. Her face felt like she'd been clawed.

But Bree wasn't falling anymore and miraculously she'd managed to keep hold of the Maglite, which shone forward, revealing an old but gleaming Coca-Cola sign leaned up against the stone wall and boxes and piles of dusty junk. Shaking, wincing in pain, aware of the blood trickling down her cheeks, Bree shined the light around, and understood her location and just how close she'd come to dying.

She was up on the hood of a seatless and wheelless old tractor. Falling through the floor, she'd hung up on a roll bar meant to protect the driver. Immediately behind and below the tractor was a harrow with dozens of circular blades meant for breaking up sod. If she'd hit there instead of here, she would have been found impaled and dead.

"I won't do it!" Cam Nguyen screeched.

Bree heard her much more clearly that time, but again below her. Was there a subbasement? How in God's name would she get down there? Despite the blows she'd taken, gritting her teeth against the pain, she rolled over, sat up, and threw her legs over the tractor's dashboard.

Her feet found the base where the seat had once been attached. She stood there a moment, dripping blood but shining her light over the jumble of equipment, having no idea where to begin to look.

"No!" Cam Nguyen screamed, and now Bree could distinctly make out the sounds of the babies sobbing, as upset as if they were suffering colic.

I can't save them, she thought desperately, shining the light all around herself. *They're going to—*

Then she spotted something, that Coke sign, and took hope.

Chapter 78

I HIT THE FLOOR, not unconscious, but damn close from a blow to the back of my head. A boot connected with my lower back. Another hit higher and I convulsed. My vision returned, but it was off-kilter, wavering. I realized I still had my gun and tried to get turned to shoot, but the boot stomped down on my wrist, pinning it to the ground.

"Detective Cross?" Carney said. "What an unexpected surprise."

My vision cleared and I saw that the young officer was the *only* person in the room besides Cam Nguyen and the two crying babies. Carney's baby face was a mess of twitching muscles, thin lips, and wild eyes that aimed over the tritium sights of a 9mm pistol he had pointed directly at my head.

"It's over, Carney," I said. "Whatever this is, it is over!"

"It is never over!" he shouted. "It goes on and on and on!"

I saw his fingers flex toward the trigger.

"Other police are here," I said. "They're all around us."

"Bullshit," he said. "I would have heard the sirens."

"They came in silent," I insisted. "You'll never get out of here."

Carney seemed to find that funny. "Of course I'm getting out of here. There are tunnels all over the place. I'll simply do my business and slip away."

That thought seemed to distract him from killing me for the moment. He stomped on my fingers and I let go of the pistol. He kicked my weapon across the floor and followed it, splashing through the water that had begun to spill over the top of the tub. Carney picked my gun up, grinned, and kept it trained on me as he stalked toward Cam Nguyen, who wept and cowered away from him.

"Do it, Mommy!" he bellowed at her. "Do what you always do!"

The young officer's entire body seemed wracked with tremors then, and his posture shifted, turned feminine. So did his voice, which rose several octaves and became a woman's.

"Take the boy, Mother," Kelli said in a weird pleading tone. "Take Kevin before you take me."

With that Carney tossed my gun into the tub and with his free hand grabbed Cam Nguyen by the hair. Ramming his gun against her temple, he dragged her off the chair and threw her to her knees by the tub.

"Pick up my brother," Carney said in his sister's voice. "And put him in the water like the baby Moses or so help me God, Kenny-Two is going to turn your brain inside out."

"Please," Cam Nguyen began to sob. "I . . ."

Carney went through another of those minor seizures and I tried to get up and go for my gun. But I had to freeze when his eyes focused again and he raged at Nguyen, "Do it, Mommy. Or die!"

Shaking uncontrollably, sobbing from the depths of her soul, Cam Nguyen reached for one of the babies.

"That's Kelli," Carney growled. "Take Kevin first. Don't you remember?"

Her mouth chewed the air as she picked up poor little Evan Lancaster and held him out over the tub. Carney looked as if he were watching an old, familiar movie, his lips curled with pleasure, as if he were about to recite a favorite line.

"Put him to sleep, Mother," he said. "Put him to sleep. He'll stop crying."

The next ten seconds seemed like an hour.

Carney smashed the back of Cam Nguyen's left hand.

She howled in agony, dropped one hand that held the baby boy, but clutched him with the other by the side of his filthy little pajamas. Carney grabbed her right wrist to hammer her into dropping Evan Lancaster into the tub.

Chapter 79

THE EXPLOSION IN THAT confined space was deafening, disorienting.

Carney's right shoulder erupted in blood. He staggered against Cam Nguyen, who let go of Evan Lancaster. The baby fell into the tub.

Carney grabbed his gun with his left hand and tried to raise it.

The second shot shattered his left wrist before he could fire, and his gun fell into the bath after the baby. I shot up to my feet, going for Evan Lancaster, but Cam Nguyen was way ahead of me. She'd plunged headfirst into the tub and yanked up the sputtering boy before I got there.

Over the ringing in my ears I could hear Bree shouting, "On the ground, Officer Carney! Now! Any other move, I will kill you."

Carney looked at her like she was an apparition

in a nightmare. I saw why. My wife's face was completely swollen and lacerated. There were pieces of wood sticking out of her wounds, and blood ran like spiderwebs down over her face and shirt.

Despite my woozy head, I thrust my hand down into the tub, retrieved my service pistol, pointed it at Carney, and shouted, "You heard her. On the floor."

The tics and contortions of rage in the young officer's face began to disintegrate before he collapsed to his knees by the tub, looked up at the ceiling of the crude room, and moaned, "You said we weren't doing anything wrong, Mommy. You said they were just sleeping."

Chapter 80

MARCUS SUNDAY AND ACADIA Le Duc heard the sirens long before they saw the lights of the Montgomery County sheriff's cruisers and ambulances ripping up the slick dirt road toward the field and the farmhouse. The duo was up on a limestone outcropping across the road, back toward the reservoir. Sunday was using the binoculars to look down through the drizzle toward the old farm several hundred yards away.

"Shouldn't we get out of here, sugar?" Acadia asked.

"Why would we do that?" he replied calmly. "We're just hikers, or bird watchers, or both."

Sunday kept the binoculars trained on the cruisers as they turned onto the driveway.

"Those were shots down there a while back," Acadia complained. "I don't know how things went down at your house, but I was taught to stay away from police when there's been shooting going on."

"Your father the bootlegger taught you that?" he asked.

"And Mama," Acadia said. "She didn't trust any cop. I don't, either."

"My daddy took somewhat the opposite perspective," Sunday said, seeing the cruisers and ambulances stop in the overgrown farmyard. "He liked to study the people who might do him the most harm."

"He obviously never saw you coming," she replied.

"Oblivious," the writer agreed as Cross appeared from the house, followed by EMTs pushing a stretcher on which a sobbing young man lay. Bree Stone followed, carrying two babies in her arms. Behind her an EMT helped a young Asian woman wrapped in a blanket.

Sunday tilted his chin, said, "Bravo, Mr. and Mrs. Cross."

"What?" Acadia asked.

"It appears they've got the killer and rescued the babies and the missing prostitute."

Acadia gazed at him, said, "I must say, you surprise me, sugar."

"How's that?" Sunday replied, lowering the glasses and looking at her.

Acadia shrugged. "I figured you'd be upset because, I don't know, Dr. Cross just beat you there?"

"Did he?" the writer said. "I think not. Were it not for my letter, they would have been days behind the curve, and the Vietnamese girl and the babies would be dead."

"And how do you know that, sugar?" she asked skeptically.

"It has to do with certain timetables I noticed in the killer's pattern," he replied as if lecturing a student. "In brief, he killed them all about thirteen days and some-odd hours after the attack on the massage parlor. So clearly, I am responsible in no small way for their return to safety."

Acadia smiled slyly. "My hero again."

She slipped into his arms and pressed herself to him.

"And now?" she asked.

"And now we get down to it," Sunday replied. "We bring him to his knees."

Chapter 81

I STILL HAD A whopper of a headache two hours after Bree rescued me, and the hostages, and took a madman into custody. And my wife's face and ribs were killing her, even with the novocaine, the pain pills, the stitches, and the bandages.

But I don't think we'd ever been happier.

The truth is that many kidnapping victims don't make it home. At some point their captivity becomes their death, and there's nothing but heartache surrounding the discovery of a body. But at close to seven that Wednesday evening, we got to witness a miracle in the emergency room of Holy Cross Hospital, the same place the ambulance had taken Harold Barnes after his heart attack two days before.

Teddy and Crystal Branson burst in.

"Is it true?" Crystal said the second she saw

Bree. "Is Joss all right? Are you all right?"

"Broken ribs, a few stitches, but I'm fine. And Joss is a little hungry, a lot tired, and dealing with a mean diaper rash, but other than that, she's—"

Teddy Branson began to cry when his wife kissed Bree on her good cheek and sobbed, "Thank you, Detective. From the bottom of my heart, thank you. You've given me a reason to live again."

Twenty minutes later, we got to see the miracle repeated when the Lancasters came in to reunite with their son.

"I just want to hug you," Dr. Lancaster wept.

"Please don't," Bree said, laughing and wincing. "Go on, now, he's waiting for you."

"Detectives," her husband said. "We will never forget what you've done for us. We owe you everything."

Then he and his wife hurried toward the room where nurses were working on their baby boy.

"Pretty nice job, Alex," said Ned Mahoney, who'd driven the Lancasters over to the hospital.

"All thanks to my better half," I said, nodding to Bree, who walked over gingerly. "She really saved the day."

"Least I could do after what I went through to get to you," she said.

Bree had told me the entire story: how she'd fallen through the charred and rotting floor, lost her pistol and landed on the tractor; and how she'd almost given up hope of getting to the subbasement before she spotted her gun lying in the harrow discs; and then how she'd acted on a hunch, went to the old Coca-Cola sign—the only thing that seemed clean in the barn basement—and pushed it aside, finding a ring in the floor, a trapdoor that led to a ladder that dropped into an anteroom off the root cellar.

"Well, I wouldn't wish busted ribs on anyone," I said. "But I'm overjoyed you showed up when you did."

"Ahhh, that's so romantic," she said, laughed and winced again.

"I'll say it again, Alex Cross," Mahoney said. "You are a lucky guy."

"Don't I know it?" I said, and kissed my wife on the forehead.

"Carney?" Mahoney asked.

"They took him to the psych ward at St. Elizabeths," I replied.

"You going to do the evaluation?"

"I would think so."

"We need to go soon," Bree said. "I've got a

date with the couch and a big glass of wine. Maybe two."

"One minute," I said. "There's someone I want to talk to before we go."

Chapter 82

CAM NGUYEN DOZED, an IV in her arm, stitches in the back of her head, a cast around her broken hand.

Outside her room, I could hear the excited voices of the Bransons and the Lancasters celebrating their reunions with their babies. But here, around the college student turned prostitute, there was just the beeping of monitors and the dripping of whatever they'd put in her IV line.

I turned to leave, but she said behind me, "You're the one who saved us."

Going to stand by her, I said, "My wife did. We're both with Metro police."

"My head hurts."

"You suffered a moderate concussion," I said, and rubbed the back of my head where Carney had hit me. "Worse than mine."

Nodding slowly, Cam said, "He wanted me to drown those babies."

"I saw it, heard it. A horrible thing. But you're safe now, all three of you. And Carney's locked away in a padded room."

"That's his name, Carney?" she asked. "He talks like three or four different people."

"I'm beginning to understand that," I said, and noticed her eyes drooping. "I'll be back to talk to you tomorrow, okay?"

She nodded sleepily.

"Is there anyone I can call to say you're okay?"

"My par . . ." she managed before drifting away.

Outside, Bree was waiting. So was Mahoney, who said he'd drive us home. Given the way my head was feeling, I wasn't arguing. Neither was Bree.

Ten minutes later we were heading back into the city. I sat in the backseat. It was long past rush hour, but traffic was thick. Hundreds of cars went by us, each filled with their own drama, their own agenda, completely severed from the madness we'd been forced to confront and defeat that day.

It dawned on me then that the hardest part of my job was the separation from normal, the constant interaction with the bizarre and the troubling.

At some point that had to affect you, had to twist your mind, even if you were a highly trained and experienced psychologist. It had to turn you into someone else.

But not today, I told myself. *Not today.*

I remembered that I had the number of the restaurant Cam Nguyen's parents owned in California. I got out my cell, found the number in my recent contacts, and hit Call.

"Nguyen Pho Shop," a man said.

"Mr. Nguyen?"

"Yes, who this?"

"Detective Cross, sir. I called a couple of weeks ago about your daughter being missing?"

A pause. "She dead?"

"I'm very happy to say that we found her alive, Mr. Nguyen. She's been through hell and back, but she's very much alive."

The silence that followed surprised me. "Sir, do you understand what I—"

"She makes shame working as prostitute," he shot back. "Cam be better off dead."

He hung up on me.

Chapter 83

AT TWO P.M. HOLY Thursday, inside the psych ward at St. Elizabeths, Patrolman Kenneth Carney was strapped to a bed in a locked room having a murmured conversation with no one. The attending psychiatrist, Arthur Nelson, an old friend of mine, said that after surgeries on his hand and shoulder, Carney had been brought there for observation. Despite the drugs, he quickly went from disoriented to grief-stricken to violent. Nelson had ordered him into restraints.

"I'm recommending lithium once he's done with the opiates," Nelson said when I turned from the small bulletproof window set in the door.

"I'd like to talk to him now," I said.

Nelson raised an eyebrow but said, "Your call, Alex. You've dealt with more of the criminally insane than I have."

I looked over at Sampson, Bree, and Elaine Brown, an assistant district attorney who'd been assigned to the case. All three nodded.

"I'll have him brought to a treatment room," Nelson said.

We went out into a waiting area. Assistant DA Brown disappeared to make some phone calls. My head still ached. Of course it didn't help that Bree, Nana Mama, and I had polished off two bottles of Chianti the night before to dull the pain of our wounds and celebrate the fact that despite the way Cam Nguyen's father had reacted to his daughter's rescue, we'd solved an almost impossible case.

At least that was how Captain Quintus had described the investigation on the eleven o'clock news, adding that my wife would be receiving a special commendation for her heroic efforts. Both the Lancasters and the Bransons had appeared on camera as well, holding their babies and praising us and the department for making their families whole again.

As the news stories had noted, however, the exact motives behind Carney's actions remained murky. Which was why we were all at St. Elizabeths and not taking a hard-earned day off for a job well done.

Sampson's search of Carney's apartment had

turned up the 9mm pistol the officer had used to murder eight people in cold blood. He also found the ash-colored wig, the clothes, and even the makeup the hairless young man had applied to transform himself into Kelli Adams the kidnapper; as well as the hoodie, brown wig, and fake beard he'd used when roaming the streets as the mass murderer Kevin Olmstead.

But my partner discovered nothing concrete to explain Carney's insane behavior. Then again, that's why they're called crazy.

You have to think a little loony to talk with someone who is criminally insane, at least if you want to gain some real insight into his deep personality. Wishing to God I didn't have a headache, I tried to get myself to that crazy place, to remember everything I'd heard in the root cellar before he hit me, and then to imagine the subtext of that bizarre conversation.

I could see some of it, but there were big holes I couldn't explain.

"John," I said.

"Alex?" Sampson said.

"Call Mahoney and ask him to find out why Carney was turned down for marine recon after passing the physical requirements."

He nodded. "I have some marine friends at the Pentagon who might be able to help, too."

"Alex?" Dr. Nelson said, looking out at us from a doorway. "Patient is in room two on the right."

"You observing?" I asked, going by him.

"We all are. By video feed in my office."

"Good luck, baby," Bree said. Despite the wounds and the broken ribs, she'd refused anything more than Advil. It showed in the way she moved and spoke, stiff and slow.

I paused, took a deep breath, understood that this might be a bumpy ride, and went in to face Carney. He was restrained on the bed, looking off into space, when I took a seat opposite him. High behind me a camera rolled.

Studying the young officer a moment there in the bright light, hairless, baby-faced, I could see how with the right makeup and clothes he'd look feminine enough to fool another woman even at close quarters.

"Officer Carney," I began.

He looked over at me with disdain, said, "Wrong name."

"Okay," I replied. "Who am I talking to?"

Carney laughed, said, "Bang. Bang. As if you don't know."

Then I got it and said, "Oh, hello, Kevin."

Carney smiled, nodded, said, "See, I told 'em *you'd* know who *I* was."

Chapter 84

I CLEARED MY THROAT, said, "Told who? Kenny-Two? Kelli? Your brother and sister?"

"Who else? Officer Goody Two-Shoes?" Carney asked agreeably, then paused and gave me a suspicious look. "Why you asking about Kelli and Junior? Pay attention. You talking to me now, asshole!"

I held up my palms to him, said, "Just trying to understand the—"

Carney's agitated face became a sea of minor tics and palsies. His eyes quivered, got glassy, and then fluttered up toward their sockets, while his head arched and the muscles in his neck strained, making his veins bulge. For a second, fearing that he was going into an epileptic fit, I almost went to him.

But as suddenly as the attack had come on, in

less than five seconds, Carney's neck relaxed and his head lolled. He blinked lazily at me and then said in that raspy southern feminine voice I'd heard back inside the root cellar: "You'll have to excuse Kevin. My baby brother's faculties just aren't quite right."

I studied Carney, wondering whether this was an act or a genuine case of multiple personalities. If it was an act, it was a good one, because my experience and research have shown that people with real multiple personality disorder usually "switch" from one to another quite rapidly. The fluttering eyes and the facial tics fit as well. But the arching of his neck, I'd never seen before. In any case, I decided to indulge him.

"Well, Kelli," I said, "when you consider what Kevin did in the massage parlor and the brothel, I'd tend to agree with you."

Carney shook his head, added pity to Kelli's voice, and said, "Horrible thing what war can do to a young man, isn't it? The violence just twists them all up inside, spits them out. Makes you kind of understand when they come home and go off like that, you know, just killing everything that moves?"

The fit took him again, and when he rolled his

head forward the second time, he wore a tough, knowing expression.

"Don't listen to that psychobabble crap," he said in a voice much closer to his own. "Kevin likes to kill, pure and simple. Always has. Always will. And Kelli's a bit delusional, always out to save someone if I let her."

"Big brother Kenny-Two?" I asked.

"In the flesh," Carney replied, coughed, and then his left eye squinted as if it pained him.

"Your brother and sister look up to you," I said.

"They *better* look up to the first one out the chute," he said, chuckled, and then his left eye squinted in pain again.

"You hurting?"

"Lingering migraines," he said. "We all get 'em. Curse of the Carneys."

Thinking back to what I'd heard in the root cellar, and what Sampson had dug up, I hesitated fifteen, maybe twenty seconds before saying, "So tell me about the IED that got you in Afghanistan."

He squinted again, but this time as if he considered me a fool, and said, "How the Christ should I know? Ask the man in charge. He was there, not me."

Before I could reply to that, Carney's face

sagged, his eyes drifted and shut. His head rocked forward and then up like the head of a passenger drowsing on a plane.

Eyes open and incredulous, as if he'd been shaken from a deep sleep, he looked at me as if I were part of a lingering dream and then took in the bare room, the restraints, the hospital gown, and the bandages on his shoulder and wrist.

He seemed to startle fully awake then, acting bewildered and then agitated, struggling against the restraints for several seconds before succumbing to the pain of his wounds, turning very frightened and fixing his confused gaze on me.

"Detective Cross?" the young officer said. "Where am I, sir? What have I done to deserve this?"

Chapter 85

SEEING HOW UNHINGED OFFICER Carney was acting, the psychologist in me wanted to believe that he might have no idea of the things he had done. But the detective in me was much more skeptical.

"You saying you don't know why you're here, Officer?"

"Where am I, sir?" Carney asked again.

"Psych ward, St. Elizabeths Hospital."

"Psych?" he said, puzzled again. "No, that's not . . . No, I'm . . . I'm good. I, I checked out. I'm good. I'm good." He started to cry and then looked at me again. "They said I was good."

"Who said you were good?"

"Naval doctors. VA doctors. They cleared me years ago, said I was fine. No problems with the baseline. None."

"You mean a concussion baseline?" I asked.

He nodded.

"Tell me about the IED in Afghanistan."

"But what have I done, sir?"

"We'll get to that later, Officer. Where was that bomb?"

On a road southwest of Kandahar, deep in Helmand Province nine months into his tour of duty, Corporal Carney was riding as a top gunner in an armored car leading a line of trucks carrying supplies for several forward bases. The IED had been buried in the shoulder of the dirt road and detonated as he passed.

"Nothing hit me," Carney remembered. "No shrapnel or powder residue, just the explosive force, the waves of it going through my head. It was like I was there, alert, scoping for Taliban— hoorah—and then I wasn't. Woke up like thirty hours later on a medevac flight to Ramstein with a piece of my skull riding beside me."

Doctors told Carney he'd been bleeding from his nose and ears, and that he'd sustained a moderate closed-head brain injury. They'd removed the piece of skull to relieve pressure. After an initial recovery and second surgery to reattach the skull section in Germany, he was shipped on to the Balboa Naval Medical Center in San Diego, where he underwent extensive therapy.

"Five months and they said I was good to go," Carney said. "And I was. Went back to my unit, and was crushing PT in like a month."

"But you tried out for Force Recon and were denied?"

"Yes, sir."

"They give you a reason?"

"Given my medical history, Detective, they said they did not want to chance it."

"Make you angry? Sad?"

"Both," Carney admitted. "But I was only twenty-three. I could see an entire life out there before me. Still do. Please, Detective Cross, what did I do to get me put in here?"

It did me no good to hold back any longer, so I told him.

Carney became nauseated and vomited. "No," he moaned. "No, I couldn't. I would never do . . ." He looked up at me in abject despair. "Oh, my God, sir, what kind of monster have I become?"

Chapter 86

CARNEY WAS INCONSOLABLE AND began to struggle wildly. There was a knock on the door. Two nurses rushed in and started to work to calm him down before he could tear his wounds open or rip out his IV.

I went outside to find Dr. Nelson waiting with Bree and Assistant DA Brown. "I probably pushed him too hard," I said.

The psychiatrist nodded. "Especially given the surgeries last night."

"I'll come back in the morning?"

Nelson thought about that, said, "I'll let you know this evening."

"What am I supposed to tell my boss?" Brown asked, checking her watch.

"Tell him he's going to have to hold his horses a little while longer."

That did not sit well with the assistant DA, and she scowled.

"You believe him, Alex?" Bree asked.

"I don't know yet," I said.

"No doubt he's going for an insanity plea here," the prosecutor said.

"Maybe because he is insane, Counselor," my wife said, surprising me.

"You don't know that," Brown snapped.

"Neither do you," Bree said.

I said, "I'm not convinced this is entirely about a head injury."

"Why?" my wife and the prosecutor said at the same time.

"Because I can't see a link yet between the injury, the three other personalities, and the heinous things that have been done in this case."

Before anyone could reply, Sampson appeared, coming down the hallway in a hurry from the elevators. "You don't answer your phone?"

"Not when I'm interviewing a mass murderer and baby kidnapper."

"Yeah, well, I think I found some folks you're going to want to talk to before you go interviewing Officer Carney again."

He handed me two phone numbers, said, "My

contact says they're busy people. If you can't reach them at first, keep trying."

I did keep trying, all that afternoon and into the evening. But as of seven p.m., I had not yet heard back from Chief Petty Officer Sheldon Drury, stationed at Marine Corps Base Camp Pendleton, or Dr. Evelyn Owens of Balboa Hospital in San Diego.

"Dinner!" Nana Mama called.

The air smelled of meat frying and garlic, enough to tear me away from my phone. But Ali rolled over on his stomach on the couch and moaned, "Nana Mama, it's almost the end. Fifteen minutes? Please?"

"It's not fifteen minutes until the end of that episode and you know it, young man," my grand-mother shot back. "Now stop it and get to the dinner table. It's an important night."

I watched from the hallway as Ali groaned, shut off the television, and trudged to the table as if he carried the weight of the world. Jannie was already at the table, spooning out pork chops my grand-mother had pan-seared and then baked in a glass pan with sautéed sweet onions, olive oil, garlic, and a little Dijon mustard. With egg noodles, green beans, and fresh applesauce on the side, there are few dishes in the world that rival it. A cold Dr Pepper only adds to the experience. At least in my book.

In any case, my fifteen-year-old daughter was acting a hundred and eighty degrees different than she had a few nights before, now bubbly and open. Bree sported a new, smaller bandage on her face that showed just how swollen it had become. Her right eye was almost shut. She had to be in pain, but you never would have known it the way she engaged Jannie, getting her to talk about history and English—her favorite classes—and how the coach was expecting great things from her the following afternoon.

For once I just sat down and let them go on, listening to them babble while I dwelled on my sessions with Officer Kenneth Carney and his three alter egos. Was it real? Were there four people in his head? Or was this an elaborate—

"Alex?" Nana Mama said, breaking into my thoughts.

"Right here."

"The heck you are," she said, shaking a wooden spoon at me. "I asked you twice how many pork chops you wanted."

"I was giving it some thought. And I'll take two."

Bree, Jannie, and Ali were trying unsuccessfully to hide their smiles.

"Two it is," she said, and passed me my plate.

We said grace, thanked God for our many blessings, and prayed for Damon to have safe travels in the morning.

"What time's Damon get in?" Jannie asked, cutting her chop.

Bree replied before I could, saying, "He's getting the nine o'clock jitney to Albany. Train leaves at ten twenty. He changes in New York City and gets here around quarter to five. He'll be home in time for supper."

That thought made me very happy. I knew Damon loved being away at school, but I loved having my firstborn home under my roof.

"Speaking of suppers, Ali, do you know what tonight is?" Nana Mama asked.

"The night I have to wait until I finish *Walking Dead*?" he grumbled.

For a second there I thought my grandmother was going to lay into him as only a former high school vice principal can, but instead she said softly, "No."

In the silence that followed, I watched my son's head twist toward Nana Mama, who'd cradled her chin in her interlaced wrinkled fingers and watched him as if she were magically summoning his attention.

Then she smiled and said, "If you really think about it, the event we celebrate tonight was part of the very *first* zombie story, the best ever."

Chapter 87

OUTSIDE, DOWN THE STREET, in the back of the dark van that now sported a sign advertising a bogus paint company, Marcus Sunday was alone and listening in on the Cross family dinner conversation. Acadia Le Duc was long gone.

Sunday rolled his eyes as Nana enticed her grandson into the story of the Last Supper by selling it as a critical scene in a zombie tale, all the while feeling repulsed by the fact that Dr. Alex's entire clan was in there munching on fried pork chops.

Sunday hated pork. The whiff of a chop sizzling or a hock boiling set him on edge. So did the odor of bacon. Those thoughts took him back to the months after his father's death and the skeptical West Virginia state police detective who'd kept nosing around the Mulch farm, acting as if young Thierry Mulch was somehow responsible for his old man's having a heart attack and falling in among his pigs and having his remains gnawed to broken bones. It had taken DNA tests just to identify the old man.

The detective's name was Alan Jones, and Detective Jones had tried everything to get young Mulch to admit his involvement in his father's death, even bringing up the fact that his mother had abandoned the family and his father had recently shot down his idea of going to college to study, of all things, philosophy.

But eighteen-year-old Thierry had been too smart for Detective Jones, razor-focused on the long term. He had never once lost his cool, even when the detective had questioned his decision to sell his father's farm to a coal mining company that had been after the property for years, and to sell all the pigs.

"Why would you give all this up?" Detective Jones kept asking.

And every time, Mulch had told him the same thing: "Because I hate pigs and because I can."

Because I can. Wasn't that the reason you did anything in life? Sunday mused. For a moment he flashed on the industrial pig farm where he'd dumped Preston Elliot's body. Would there be anything left of him to find?

No, he thought. *Impossible.* His father had died in a sty holding twenty-four pigs and there had been little to analyze beyond shattered bones and teeth. There had to have been at least a thousand pigs in that barn where he'd dumped Preston Elliot. Maybe more. By now they'd long shit out the computer genius and rolled in it, the way pigs do.

Then Sunday startled from his thoughts and realized that Ali Cross was talking about him.

"Dad, if Jesus was a zombie," Ali was saying, "do you think he smelled like the one in here the other night, like that guy who came to my school?"

"You mean Thierry Mulch?" asked Cross.

"That *was* his name, Dad!" Ali cried. "Thierry Mulch. He really smelled bad, like Damon's basketball shoes. Must have been all that pig poop he grew up in."

Sunday flashed on a pretty redheaded girl who'd heaped scorn and laughter on him again and again during high school. He saw her again as an older woman pleading for the life of her husband and children.

Pleased by those memories, Sunday muttered, "Just wait, little Cross. You'll be getting a big whiff of me before you know it."

Chapter 88

SITTING AT THE DINING room table amid the laughter Ali's comment had triggered, I said, "He really told you he grew up on a pig farm?"

My younger son bobbed his head enthusiastically. "He said he hated it, but it was all good because he used the hate to get out of the pig poop."

Jannie grinned and punched Ali in the shoulder. "He did not."

"Did so!" Ali shouted at his sister before turning his protesting face in my direction. "Or something like that, Dad. Ask Mrs. Hutchins."

I gestured his way with my fork, said, "You know what? I just might do that."

Ali stuck his tongue out at Jannie, who groaned, "You are such a little brat sometimes."

"I am not, and you should go sit in pig poop somewhere," he shot back.

"That's enough!" Nana Mama cried, then stared at me. "The night that Jesus prayed in the garden and was betrayed and we're talking about pig poop?"

I stifled the urge to smile but threw a quick glare Ali's way and said, "Nana's right. That *is* enough. And if you want to finish your show before bedtime, you'd better get along with Jannie long enough to wash and dry the dishes."

"I hate washing dishes in the bathtub," Ali grumbled. "It's dumb."

"Think of washing dishes in the bathtub as pig you-know-what," Bree said. "Use it to be a better student."

"Wait, what?" Ali said, throwing up his hands. "How does that make any sense?"

I winked at my wife, said, "Nice try, but you should have quit while you were ahead."

Later, as the kids washed dishes in the bathtub, I couldn't help thinking again of the tub in the old root cellar and what might have happened if Bree hadn't discovered a trapdoor and a second way down from the barn.

I felt my wife's arm come around my waist. "Want to check the progress on the addition?"

Inspecting the new work was a welcome

change, something normal, not deviant, something understandable, not a mystery to solve. So I nodded and gave her a long, deep kiss.

"I didn't know you liked women who look like the Phantom of the Opera."

I looked at the bandage covering part of her face and laughed, said, "I think it's kind of sexy."

"Uh-huh," she said.

"Get a room, you two," Nana Mama said, chortling as she went by us toward the living room.

Ninety-something years old and she still had a wicked sense of humor. Another reason I loved my grandmother so much.

We went back into the dining room. While Bree separated the Velcro strips that held the big plastic sheets in place, I plugged in the extension cord and the work lights.

The builders had come a long way in the past two or three days. The windows were in and they'd begun to frame in the bases for the kitchen cabinetry. For the first time, I could see clearly what the added space was going to mean to our family.

"I'm beginning to like it," Bree said. "A lot."

"Me, too. A hassle with the cooking and the dishwashing, but I think we're going to be very happy when it's all said and done."

My wife nodded and looked around with a satisfied smile. "Nana said the electrician will be here on Monday and we need to mark where we want all the plugs and switches before then."

I'd never had anything built before, so this surprised me. "Contractor doesn't figure that out?"

"No," she replied. "He says it's on us."

"We could ask his advice, right?"

"Not until Monday," she said. "He told Nana he's taking his family to Delaware for the holiday because there's nothing more for his crew to do until the electrician's finished."

I took her in my arms, holding her gingerly because of the ribs, and said, "I love it when you talk construction."

Bree snickered, rolled her head around, and said, "Well, then, once Ali has finished his show and gone to bed, why don't we take Nana's advice?"

"Really? With your ribs like that?"

"We'll try, okay?"

"As long as you promise to use words like *hammer* and *nail* and *saw*."

"You have so little imagination, love of my life," my wife said, very amused. "I was thinking maybe a little plumbing and stud work?"

"Ooooh," I said before my cell phone rang.

"Don't," Bree said.

"Got to," I said, and answered. "Alex Cross."

"This is Evelyn Owens at Balboa Naval Medical Center. Am I calling at a good time?"

I looked mournfully at my wife, thought fleetingly of plumbing and stud work, but then said, "Yes, Dr. Owens. It's a very good time."

Chapter 89

I SHOWED UP AT St. Elizabeths around eight in the morning on Good Friday. Bree had decided to take the day off so she wouldn't miss Jannie's track meet. Sampson had a dentist appointment. And I hadn't bothered to contact DA Brown. I wanted Carney all to myself and to Dr. Nelson, who would tape and observe from his office.

When I entered the young patrolman's room, the head of his bed was raised. He wore hospital scrubs instead of a johnny, but his ankles were still lashed down. Even though Nelson said he had backed off on the painkillers, Carney looked like he'd just woken up after a night of very hard drinking, a night when he might have blacked out and gone on a rampage.

"Tell me about your mother," I said after I'd taken the chair opposite him.

Carney gazed over at me with zero affect for a beat before I caught the slightest ripple of hairless skin at his temples.

"She died when I was a baby," he said at last. "I never really knew her. Or my dad. He died in prison. I was an orphan. Ward of the State of Florida."

"Tough being cut off like that, no parents. Happened to me when I was ten. They put me in an orphanage until my grandmother came for me."

The young patrolman chewed on that, nodded. "I don't remember much of the orphanage. An older couple, the Carneys—Tim and Judy— adopted me when I was two. I grew up with them in Pensacola, joined the marines right out of high school. My adoptive parents died in a car crash around the same time I survived the bombing in Afghanistan. I didn't even find out they were gone until I got stateside."

"So you were orphaned twice?"

"Guess you could say that," Carney replied, and then pursed his lips. "Why are you asking me these things?"

Clearing my throat, I said, "I'm trying to see if what you believe is real jibes with what I know to be real."

Carney turned defensive. "What's that supposed to mean?"

"It means you're lying to me. Or at least that you've suppressed the facts so deep that your lies seem absolutely like the truth to you."

"No, I . . ." he said, shaking his head. "I don't know what you're talking about, Detective. What do you think I'm lying about?"

Diamond cutters will tell you that they'll study some raw gems for hours, even days, looking for the exact right place to break the stone open so all its brilliant facets are revealed. More often than not, I take the same approach: studying, probing, looking for that moment when I can challenge a subject on some point and use that sharp challenge to crack him and get him to confess. But my gut told me I did not have to wait, study, and draw Carney out—I already understood how to break him wide open.

"How'd your biological mother die?" I asked.

"Bicycle accident."

I shook my head. "Your mother was murdered, Officer Carney."

You'd have thought I'd slapped him. "What? No, that's not—"

"Your mother was murdered," I insisted. "And

your father killed her. That's why he went to the Polk Correctional Institution. That's why he died there."

Carney's head began to retreat. "No, that's not right."

"It *is* right," I replied calmly. "And the worst thing about it? You saw your father kill your mother. You saw him strangle her when you were three and a half, not a baby, Kenneth."

Carney stared at me as if I'd become some alien creature who'd come to haunt his nightmares. Seeing him right there on the verge of cracking, I hit him with the heaviest hammer and chisel I had in my bag.

"What else did you see that night?" I asked. "Why did your father kill your mother? Why did he strangle her like that?"

The tics came first this time, followed by beads of sweat that formed on Carney's naked head before his eyeballs rolled up ever so slightly and fluttered. His body arched as if he were right there on the verge of a convulsion, before it sagged and he slumped down and regarded me with a knowing smirk.

"Officer Goody Two-Shoes can't face the past," he said in a gruffer voice. "Never could. Never will, and that's a fact."

"But you can, right, Kenny-Two?"

"Course I can," he replied with that lazy smile I was learning to recognize. "I'm the lone survivor, Detective, the only one who really knows what happened."

"Kelli and Kevin don't know?"

"How could they? My baby sister and brother died that night, too."

Chapter 90

NEUROPSYCHOLOGIST EVELYN OWENS OF Balboa Naval Medical Center had told me much the same thing during our phone discussion. In the wake of the closed-head injury and after Carney had exhibited several short bouts of what appeared to be multiple personality disorder, Owens said she had dug deep into the wounded veteran's past. What she'd found was beyond disturbing.

According to Florida Child Welfare files, Carney's mother was named Kerry Ann Johns. On her sixteenth birthday, she had Kenneth. Two months shy of her twentieth birthday, she smoked crystal meth with Kenneth Peters Senior, her boyfriend and Kenneth Junior's father, walked into the emergency room at Tampa General Hospital, and soon after gave birth to twins: Kelli and Kevin.

They were nine weeks premature, habituated to meth, and quickly went into withdrawal. They spent nearly a month in the ICU before being placed in foster care.

After Johns and Peters were released from rehab, they petitioned for and got custody of Kenneth and the twins. Carney's biological parents managed to stay clean for a year. But caring for any child is difficult, much less three children, with two of them suffering from medical and developmental problems.

The stress became overwhelming, and Johns and Peters fell back into old habits. They began smoking meth again. To support their habits, Carney's father turned to burglary, and his mother to prostitution.

"She worked in a massage parlor?" I asked Kenny-Two.

"My father hated her for it," he replied bitterly.

"How about you?"

"Bitch was not exactly mother of the year, was she?"

"That why Kevin likes to shoot up places like the Superior Spa?"

Carney's eyes barely fluttered before his voice changed into the higher range of the Kevin personality. "Fucking A," he said. "Does a man good to see filthy whores and their customers begging and dying."

"So you see your mother in your victims?" I asked.

"Don't you?" he asked in a scoffing tone.

"Why did you take one of the hookers with you?"

He chuckled. "Kenny-Two says we got to get a mommy home with the kids before the ceremony can begin."

I thought about that and what I'd heard in the root cellar and said, "Tell me about that night, the first time the ceremony was performed."

Carney gazed without expression at me for several seconds before his eyes got lazy and his head bobbed. When he lifted his chin, his manner had turned feminine once more.

"Mama said she'd had enough of us," he said, sounding like Kelli again. "She gave us all cough medicine and told us we were going to take a bath. Kevin and I took the cough medicine like any good baby would. Kenny-Two spit it out."

"So *you* don't remember what happened?"

Carney's face looked haunted. "I remember seeing her smoking from a glass pipe and crying when she picked up Kevin and said she was going to give him a bath. When she came for me I remember looking for where my twin brother was and Mama said not to worry, that he'd had his diapers changed and gone to bed. Mama said it was time for my bath."

"And then what happened?"

No more than two beats passed with Carney's eyes shivering before he surfaced once more as Kenny-Two.

"She pushed Kelli under the water while I screamed at her, begging her not to do it," he said. "I'd seen her put Kevin back in his crib, all naked and wet and blue. I'd seen her pour the cleaning liquid on him. I knew what was happening."

"Because you didn't take the cough syrup?"

"Being contrary keeps you alive, ever notice that?"

"Or it kills you," I replied, and tapped my pen on my notepad. "Where was your father during all this?"

"Smoking glass somewhere on his way home," Kenny-Two replied in disgust. "He told the court he got to the apartment all wired, saw Kevin lying in his crib soaked in citrus cleaner my mom brought home from the massage parlor.

"Then my dad heard me screaming in the bathroom, pushed open the door, and seen what she'd done to Kelli, and what she was trying to do to me. My mom started crying, telling him everything was cleaner this way."

"Your dad snapped."

He nodded. "Choked my mom to death with the cord to her bathrobe while I watched."

I sat there a long while, trying to absorb it all, thinking about what drugs, a sordid night, and a traumatic brain injury had spawned. Sixteen dead men, women, and children in Albuquerque, Tampa, and DC. Every one of them had left behind lives torn apart as harshly as Carney's.

Aside from the senseless killings, the worst thing about it all was the fact that a few minutes later, Kenny-Two faded and the eager young man who'd fought for his country and dreamed of being a homicide detective resurfaced.

I gave him a summary of what his other personalities had told me and had to watch it torture him into wretchedness and despair. Carney hung his head and sobbed like an innocent man wrongly accused and doomed for it.

I stood, put my hand on his heaving good shoulder, and said, "I think it's time we took a break, Kenny. I'll be back to see you on Monday."

The young officer didn't acknowledge me, just continued to cry from deep, deep inside. I sighed and moved toward the door.

"Detective Cross?" he called after me in a trembling voice.

I paused at the door and looked back. "Yes?"

"Can they give the death penalty to someone like me?" he asked.

With more than two decades of police work behind me, I'd thought I'd grown calloused when it came to dealing with killers, insane and otherwise. But that moment devastated me because Carney's tone was desperate, wishful.

The poor bastard was asking me if there was any hope for a quick end to his suffering. And I had to shake my head and listen to his gut-shot moaning as I left.

Chapter 91

IT WAS FOGGY ON the campus of the Kraft School, which felt emptier than it had been during Acadia's prior visit. Many students had no doubt left already for the Easter holiday week. *So much the better,* she thought as she sipped from her third double espresso of the day and pretended to admire the architecture of the closest building. It would be easier to—

Damon Cross exited the far door of his dorm and set off on a paved path across the quad, carrying a Puma duffel bag and an orange backpack. Acadia moved diagonally toward the teenager, getting just ahead of him at an intersection of the paved paths. She never looked his way.

"Hi there, Ms. Mepps," Damon said behind her.

Acadia smiled to herself, then pivoted with a more quizzical expression, saw him, and acted surprised. "Now, look at this. I never expected to see you again, Mr. Damon Cross."

The teenage boy took that statement somewhat awkwardly.

"Well," Acadia said. "I just put down a deposit on my nephew's tuition."

"He got in that fast?"

"Smart boy, great grades, sugar," she replied. "How are you?"

"Good," he said with a hint of bashfulness. "I'm heading to catch the jitney to Albany and the train back home for nine days of sleep!"

Acadia smiled, said, "How much do the jitney and train cost?"

"You mean, like, together?" he asked, checking his watch.

"Yes."

"I dunno, sixty-eight for the train and like twenty for the jitney. Look, good seeing you, and glad your nephew was admitted, but I got to go."

"Maybe I can save you seventy dollars," Acadia said.

Damon had been turning. Now he halted, looked back. "Excuse me?"

"I am on my way to Virginia on business and have to go right through Washington," she said.

"You give me twenty dollars for gas and you pocket the difference."

Two other students, a boy and a girl, walked by, carrying their bags. The girl glanced at Acadia, said, "We've got to hurry, Damon."

"Okay, Silvia," he said, looking embarrassed. "I'll be right along." When they'd left, he looked at Acadia and said, "I dunno. I don't think so."

She shrugged. "Suit yourself. I could have used the company and some help driving. My left eye's been bothering me and it's a long way. Good-bye, Damon Cross. I wish my nephew was going to meet you."

Acadia started back in the direction of the admissions office, thinking that men are like boys in that they always want what they've been denied.

"Okay," Damon called before she'd gotten twenty yards on. "If I can help you with the driving because of your eye, and the gas, I guess it'll be fine."

She turned, grinning. "You don't know how much of a help this is."

"I should run up there and tell the jitney driver," he said.

"Do that, and I'll come around to pick you up," she said.

Ten minutes later, the jitney left. Acadia pulled up in front of Damon and said, "Get in."

"You want me to drive, Ms. Mepps?" he asked, putting his backpack and bag in the backseat.

"My eye's got at least an hour in it," she said as he got in and buckled his seat belt. "And call me Karla."

As she drove on, he said, "You know the way?"

"I got here, didn't I?"

"True," he said awkwardly.

"Latte?" she asked, gesturing to a center console and two to-go cups from the coffee shop across from the campus. "I figured to drink them both, but we can stop later."

"Oh," Damon said, and took the cup. "Thanks."

"Don't mention it," she said as he took a sip.

"If you don't mind me asking, what's wrong with your eye?"

"The doctor says it's strained," she replied. "But my family has a history of glaucoma, so I'm not sure."

"What's your job?" he asked, and took a longer draw on the coffee.

"I am a traveling saleswoman," Acadia replied, grateful that Sunday had convinced her to make her false identity deep. "I represent several fashion manufacturers up and down the East Coast."

"That's cool," Damon said.

"I like to think so," she said, and went on to move the focus off her and onto Damon, who warmed up and enthusiastically answered all her questions as they drove back roads west toward the New York State Thruway.

About thirty minutes into the drive, however, and soon after he'd finished his coffee, Damon's energy began to wane. He yawned. At a stop sign she caught him blinking several times as if he were confused about something.

Ten miles from Glenmont, she heard the first thickness in his tongue when he said, "I should probably call my dad, tell him I'll be home early."

"Cell service is horrible through here," she said. "I'd wait until we're on I-87. Good service there."

Damon's words were slurred when she took the exit ramp onto the thruway heading south. "You said, I drive . . . the interstate."

"Sorry, sugar," she said. "You've had much too much Rohypnol to be anywhere near the wheel of a car."

Acadia glanced over to find him staring with unfocused eyes.

"Roofie?" he said woozily. "That's . . . a date-rape drug."

"Yes, it is," Acadia said, patting his leg as he started to pass out. "But don't you worry your virgin little heart over it. You and I are going on a far stranger journey than sex."

Chapter 92

AROUND THE CORNER FROM the Cross residence, Sunday waited patiently in the van, which now sported a magnetic sign that read, SILVER SPRING ELECTRICAL CONTRACTORS AND REPAIR. It was a quarter to noon. The guys from Dear Old House were just leaving for the holiday weekend.

Things were falling neatly into place, he decided, putting the van in gear the second they left his view. Acadia had texted him that she'd picked up a friend and was on her way, already driving across the George Washington Bridge.

Now it was Sunday's turn to have a little fun.

The writer pulled into the parking spot the contractors had left and got out. He was wearing a set of green workman's clothes with a badge that identified him as Phil Nichols of Silver Spring Electrical and carrying a metal clipboard. Sunday bounded up the steps and gave a sharp rap on the door, then rang the bell. Moments later, Nana Mama came to the door in her church clothes, opened it on a safety chain, and said suspiciously, "May I help you?"

"Yes, ma'am," he said deferentially. "Sorry to disturb you, Mrs. Cross, but I'm the electrical sub on your addition. Did I miss the Dear Old House guys?"

"They just left," she said.

"Dang it," he said. "Well, I can probably look at it myself. Can I go around back? I won't be long. I'm just trying to get a general sense of where we are before heading down to St. Anthony's."

Cross's grandmother softened. "For the Stations of the Cross?" she asked.

"Yes, ma'am," he said. "I promise you I won't be long."

"You attend St. Anthony's?" she asked.

"Regularly? No," he said. "St. Tim's in Fairfax. But St. Anthony's is the only church doing the stations at a time I can go."

She nodded. "I'll see you there, then."

"That's nice," he said, smiled. "Am I good to make a quick check of the addition, then?"

She nodded. "Come around. I'll give you five

minutes. I have to be over at the church soon."

"No problem, ma'am," he said, turned, and walked off the porch and around the side of the house, remembering how he'd sprinted along this same route the night Ali Cross had spotted him. But when he got around the side, the plastic sheeting was gone. The addition walls were all up, the windows were in, and a steel door blocked access.

He heard the key in the dead bolt, put on his happy face. Nana Mama opened the door and waved him in, saying, "It's not too bad. They just swept it."

"This will take no time at all," he said, and went in.

Sunday spent about ten minutes looking around the addition, jotting notes as he exclaimed how nice the great room and the new kitchen were going to be. Rain had begun to patter on the roof when he beamed at Nana Mama and said, "That will do it until someone marks where you want the outlets, the switches, and whatnot."

"My grandson's planning to do all that tomorrow," the old woman said.

"Perfect," Sunday replied, made as if to leave, and then stopped. "Can I give you a ride, Mrs.

Cross? Do my good deed for the day in honor of the good Samaritan who helped our lord in his time of trouble?"

Nana Mama glanced at the roof, listened to the rain, and then nodded. "Very nice of you to offer. And I'm Regina Hope. Cross was my maiden name."

He stuck out his hand and shook hers, saying, "Wonderful to meet you, ma'am." He almost added, "I'm Thierry Mulch." But he caught himself, glanced at the badge, and said, "Phil Nichols."

"I'll get my umbrella, Mr. Nichols," she said.

"Do you want me to go around?" Sunday asked.

"No, no, walk through with me," she said. "You're parked right out front?"

"Yes, Mrs. Hope," he replied. "Thank you."

He continued on in this deferential way, holding the umbrella for Nana Mama and supporting her elbow as they made their way down the walkway and as she climbed into the van. Nana Mama looked around, saw that the van was neat as a pin, and nodded. "I do appreciate this, Mr. Nichols."

"Glad to do it, Mrs. Hope," he said, and shut the door.

Sunday walked around, got in. He fished in his

right-hand pants pocket, found the pen, and palmed it. Then he dug in his left pocket and came up with the keys. He started the van and pulled out of the spot.

"You'll have to go around the block," Cross's grandmother said. "St. Anthony's is back the other way."

"I thought so," he said, putting on the blinker and seeing her turn her head to look out the rain-streaked passenger-side window.

Sunday thumbed the pen's button, seeing the small hypodermic needle drip for an instant before he stabbed it into her thigh and drove a small dose of Rohypnol into her. Nana Mama screamed and tried to reach for the syringe.

But Sunday let go of it and used his forearm to pin the old woman against the seat until she lost consciousness.

Chapter 93

THREE HOURS LATER, ALI Cross skipped across the playground at Sojourner Truth School. Nine whole days of vacation! They weren't going to Florida or anything like that. But Damon was coming home, and he'd have his big brother to hang out and play basketball with—

The little cell his father had given him rang. He stopped and answered.

"Dad?"

"How'd you guess?"

"You're the only one who ever calls this phone," Ali said.

"Oh, right," his dad replied. "You on your way to St. Anthony's?"

"Yes," Ali said impatiently. "Where are you?"

"Heading to Jannie's track meet."

"I'd rather do that than go to church," Ali said.

"You weren't listening this morning. Stations of the Cross are over by now. You're coming to the track meet *with* Nana Mama."

"Oh," Ali said, sort of remembering that his father had said something about that at breakfast. "Okay. Nana will be there?"

"Probably inside."

"When's Damon getting home?"

"In time for dinner. Got to go."

"Gotta move!"

He and his dad were laughing as they hung up.

Most of the kids had already cleared the playground. Heading out through the gate in the fence onto Franklin Street, Ali turned away from home and had soon crossed the intersection and headed north on the east side of Twelfth Street toward St. Anthony's, some eight blocks away.

He'd crossed Hamlin Street and was walking by a funeral home when a panel van came roaring up alongside him. "Hey, kid! You Ali Cross?"

Ali stopped, looked over, saw through the open window of the van that his great-grandmother was slumped in the front seat, out cold. The guy in the sunglasses driving looked worried.

"I was bringing her from church to find you and she passed out," he yelled. "Get in, we got to get her to the hospital!"

Ali didn't think. He bolted for the van, opened the side door, and jumped in, seeing computers and electrical gear bolted onto shelves. The van was moving the second he closed it.

"What happened to her?" Ali said fearfully. He was crouched on his knees now between and behind the front seats.

"Heart," the driver said. "I don't know."

"Nana!" Ali said, shaking his great-grand-mother's shoulder. "Nana, wake up."

But she didn't move. "Oh, no," he moaned. "Is she dead?"

"No," the driver said. "She's breathing. I think. Check."

Ali struggled to stand, to lean over the seat to see if that was true. That was when the boy smelled the zombie at the wheel. The look of shock on Ali's face was so deep that Sunday caught it. Cross's younger son tried to push himself backward and opened his mouth to scream. Sunday was ready.

Quick as a whip, he raised an aerosol can and sprayed the boy in the face with vaporized chloroform. The boy staggered backward, smashed off one of the shelves, and collapsed on the floor of the van.

Sunday opened a window and kept an eye on Ali in the rearview mirror as he drove toward St. Anthony's Church. The chloroform would not last long.

He pulled in and parked in the small lot behind the church. Within three minutes he'd injected Ali with about the same amount of Rohypnol as he'd given his great-grandmother, enough to keep them both out a good twelve hours.

Before he drove on, he texted Acadia: Got two. Your play.

Chapter 94

JANNIE WAS ALL WARMED up, stripped down out of her sweats, and making little sprints to get her muscles firing. My daughter was as tall as or taller than the other girls warming up for the quarter-mile. But she was easily the thinnest girl out there, as well as the youngest athlete in the entire event, the first meet of the year, a prestige invitational on Benjamin Banneker High's home track.

Sitting in the stands, I checked my watch, said, "Ali and Nana are going to miss this if they don't get here soon."

"They're probably caught in traffic," Bree said, shading her eyes from the afternoon sun. "Call them."

Reaching for my phone, I heard the starter call out: "Take your mark."

"Too late, here we go," Bree said as the seven girls in the race moved toward the starting line. Jannie was in lane two, well back in the stagger.

"She told me at breakfast that she's got no expectations," I said, despite the fact that my stomach was doing flip-flops, the way it always does when I see one of my kids about to compete. "Her coach said this is just for the experience."

"That why you're practicing your ballet pose?" my wife asked.

"Just trying to see a little better," I replied.

"Alex, you're six three, you can *always* see a little better."

"Set," the starter said, raising the gun.

The gun went off and they sprang off the line, driving their arms and legs down the straightaway toward the first curve. Once around the track as fast as you can go, the quarter-mile takes speed, strength, and guts.

My daughter had gone to the starting line remarkably relaxed, but the second the pistol fired, the intensity exploded out of her with such force that it caught me completely off-guard.

So did her speed, which was evident almost immediately as she began to make up the stagger and run the curve. When they entered the backstretch, Jannie was barely third and boxed in by the second- and fourth-place runners. I wasn't thinking strategy, just praying that she hadn't blown her wind in that first hundred and ten yards.

But again to my surprise, Jannie ran with the older girls stride for stride down the backstretch, and she didn't look like she was straining at all. Then they entered the far turn, still in that tight bunch with Jannie boxed in third, jostling with the elbows of the second- and fourth-place runners. I felt certain she'd stay boxed as they exited the curve and headed toward home.

Then the girl in second place, a senior from College Park, made her move, trying to get ahead of the leader, a senior from Eastern High. The girl in front sped up and gave no ground, but the give-and-take opened up a gap between the second- and fourth-place girls.

Jannie seized on the opportunity like a cagy veteran. She leaped diagonally through the opening. Showing strength and guts I'd never known she had, my daughter gritted her teeth, dug deep, and ran like there was a lunatic with a blowtorch chasing her.

She caught and passed the girl from College Park with sixty yards to go and ran neck and neck with the senior from Eastern, who was a fighter, too. She held Jannie off until the thirty-yard line, where my baby girl hit the afterburners and broke the tape two full body lengths ahead.

Chapter 95

BREE AND I WENT wild, or at least as wild as two bruised and injured people can, cheering and whooping it up along with hundreds of Jannie's schoolmates who were stomping their approval on the metal grandstands and clapping wildly.

Down on the track, the coach was hugging Jannie. The other competitors in the race were eyeing her in shock and awe. My daughter was at least three years younger than them, a girl against women, and she'd blown their doors in. I still couldn't believe it as Bree and I made our way down to the track.

Jannie came toward me with the coach in tow. She had tears in her eyes.

"Did you see it?" she asked.

"Every incredible second of it."

"Fifty-four nine," said the coach, an earnest guy in his late thirties who looked shocked. "Paul Anderson. Honor to meet you, sir, ma'am. Saw you both on the news the other night."

Bree touched her facial bandages and smiled. "What's fifty-four nine?"

"Why, her time," Anderson said, beaming.

"That's good?" I asked.

"Mr. Cross, that's one-point-twenty-five seconds off the national high school record of fifty-three sixty-five, set back in 1979!" Anderson said. "It's also now the school record!"

"That *is* good," Bree said.

"At fifteen? In her first race?" Coach Anderson cried. "It's ridiculous! And I'm telling you, that wasn't the strongest I've seen Jannie run. Not by a long shot."

This was all staggering news, hard to wrap my head around. I knew it was a big deal that she'd made the Banneker track team, but this?

"So what exactly are you saying?"

He leaned over the fence and replied, "Get ready for every NCAA Division One track coach to come to watch her run and knock at your door with scholarship money. Get ready to watch her smash records in the coming years. Your daughter, Detective, is a running marvel."

Glancing at Jannie, who was grinning, her eyes shiny, I said, "Don't let it go to your head."

"I promise," she said, and laughed.

"We'll all talk later," Coach Anderson said. "I've still got athletes in the last few events."

"Absolutely," I said, then looked at my daughter in wonder. "Where did that come from?"

She shrugged. "I have absolutely no idea. I've always been fast, but I dunno, something clicked last year, and running just felt different."

"God's given you a remarkable gift," Bree said. "You're obligated to work hard to make that gift as big as it can be. You know that, right?"

Jannie nodded and glanced at me.

"She's right," I said, and tried to lean over and kiss Jannie.

But she pulled back, acting embarrassed, and whispered, "Dad. C'mon."

"Sorry," I said. "I was overwhelmed by the moment."

"Need a ride home?" Bree asked, trying to defuse the awkwardness.

Looking uncomfortable, Jannie said, "I should finish watching the meet. Be part of the team."

"You should," I said, checked my watch. It was

ten past four. "I'm going to Union Station to get Damon."

"I'm going to get dinner," my wife said. "See you in an hour?"

"Hour, hour and a half," I said.

We headed toward the exit. We were almost out when I said, "Wait, I should tell Jannie that if Nana Mama and Ali show up they should all take a taxi home."

But when I turned, I saw something I wasn't expecting at all. My baby girl, my track prodigy, was talking to a very tall, very muscular, very handsome boy, and she was smiling wider than she had been winning the race.

"I thought there might be something going on there," Bree said. "His name's Will Crawford. He's the captain of the team."

This whole teenage daughter thing was new to me. So was the idea of boys in her life. Honestly, I felt like I was constantly in unexplored terrain with Jannie. "So what should I do?"

"My advice?" Bree said. "Give her some space. Send her a text and walk away."

Chapter 96

DAMON WAS SUPPOSED TO arrive at Union Station at four forty-five.

I got to the station with four minutes to spare and jogged through the grand main hall, remembering the last time I was in the rail depot, back on Christmas Day, when a terrorist named Hala al-Dossari tried to bomb the place.

Al-Dossari was currently behind bars in a federal supermax facility in Kansas, but she would always haunt Union Station, at least in my mind.

Approaching the Amtrak ticket counter, I glanced up at the arrivals and departure board and saw that Damon's train was right on time and passengers would arrive through gate G.

Hey bud, I texted him. I'll be right at the top of the stairs.

I expected some kind of rapid response. After

all, that was what Jannie had given me, answering my text about Ali and Nana Mama within thirty seconds. But I got nothing back from Damon. Then again, he rarely answered his phone. Why was I paying fifty bucks a month so he could have the damn thing if he—

The train's arrival was announced, and quickly passengers began to pour up the stairs through gate G. But they were all gone within ten minutes. I walked down the stairs and found the porter, who said he'd just walked the length of the train and it was empty except for Amtrak personnel.

Had Damon missed it? Wouldn't he have called? Or texted?

I tried his cell and was immediately switched to voice mail, which meant either the phone was off or the battery was dead. But couldn't he have borrowed someone else's phone? He knew I'd be waiting. I'd told him so the other night.

Maybe he had missed it and was taking the next express train, or a local. I went back up into the main hall to the ticket counter and asked the teller if he could check to see if Damon had gotten on the train at Albany.

"Can't do that," the teller said snippily. "Right-to-privacy laws."

I showed him my badge, and he sniffed. "It's a federal law, Detective."

"Do me a favor?" I asked.

"If I can," he said, in a way that said he wouldn't.

"Call Amtrak Police Captain Seymour Johnson for me?"

The teller stiffened. "I know who he is."

"I bet you do."

Captain Johnson owed me big-time for my role in helping to unravel and thwart the al-Dossari bomb plot, and ten minutes later he looked up from his computer and shook his head. "He's not in the system, Alex."

Okay, I thought, trying to remain calm. *Where is he? Where could he be?*

I thought of calling Bree and Jannie to see if they'd heard from him, but it seemed unlikely. If anyone, he would have tried to contact me. I scrolled through my contacts list and found the number of the Kraft School. I got a recording that said the school was in recess for the Easter holiday and told me to push zero in an emergency.

A security guard named Whitfield answered in a bored tone. I identified myself as Damon Cross's father and explained the situation.

"Oh, you know kids," Whitfield replied. "He probably—"

"Could you check his room, please?"

The guard hesitated. "I don't know if I can—"

"Mr. Whitfield," I said, hugely irritated. "Is it not true that one of your fellow guards was killed in the past week?"

That got to him. "Yes. But that has nothing—"

"Mr. Whitfield, I am a homicide detective, so we're going to go with my instincts here. I want you to go and check my son's room and then get back to me. And I want the name of the jitney service he was supposed to have used to get to Albany. Or I'll track down the headmaster and see what he can do."

"I'll call you back in ten minutes," Whitfield said, and hung up.

I called Bree and was relieved when she picked up. "Where are you?"

"Almost home from Maine Avenue Fish Market with crabs and a jar of Blue Crab Bay boil seasonings. Damon's favorite."

I told her about Damon not making any train from Albany that morning.

"But where would he go?"

"I'm trying to figure that out," I said.

"Keep me posted," she said. "But Alex, Damon is a big boy who can take care of himself. Let's not panic yet. He probably got a ride and forgot to tell you."

But as I hung up, I had the growing, oppressive sense that something could be going very wrong in my son's life. I flashed on his late mother, saw her holding him as a baby. That only fueled my fears.

Where are you Damon? Where are you, son?

Please, God, make my boy okay.

Chapter 97

JANNIE CROSS HAD NEVER felt like this before. It was as if in one day, one afternoon really, she'd become a different kind of creature, like a caterpillar becoming a butterfly in 54.9 seconds. This morning she'd come to school as Jannie Cross, the only freshman varsity runner, and she'd just left, heading toward the Howard University Metro station with people calling her a phenom and Will Crawford asking if she was interested in going to the senior prom.

The senior prom! With Will Crawford!

It was easily the greatest day of her life, exhilarating and scary and fun and too many other emotions to count. *Could it get any better than this? Was what Coach Anderson said true? Could I break more records? Run in college? Or even go to the Olympics?*

That last question sent shivers down her spine.

Could I do that? Run at that level? Faster than anyone in the world?

Jannie felt indescribably warm and complete at that idea. It was as if she'd found her purpose and identity in life, doing something that she loved, something that made her very, very happy. The fact that her dad had been there to see it was so good. And Bree, too. It was all good, all—

"Jannie Cross?" a woman asked in a soft southern drawl.

Jannie startled and looked up. She was still two blocks from the Metro station. There was a very pretty woman with curly blond hair, in jeans and a leather jacket, in front of her at the curb, holding a car door open.

"Yes?" Jannie said, feeling uncertain about the situation.

"My name's Dee-Dee," she said. "I'm a friend of your brother Damon. And, well, you were the first person he wanted to see when he got home."

Jannie cocked her head, confused. "He's in there? Damon?"

"Still asleep after helping me on the long drive from school," the woman said so softly that Jannie was forced to come closer to hear. "I think he had a long night with his friends."

445

"I thought my dad was picking him up at the train station," Jannie said, taking several steps toward the car. She looked into the backseat and saw Damon sleeping on a pillow leaned up against the rear right window.

"I was coming right through DC," Dee-Dee said. "And he helped with gas and driving, but before he went to sleep, he forgot to give me your address."

"That's easy," Jannie said. "I'll show you."

Pleased, the woman closed the rear door and opened the front passenger door. "Thank you so much. He was actually very excited to be coming home, before he hit the snooze button."

Jannie's head was so full of thoughts and dreams that she barely heard the woman. It was enough that her big brother was in the car and she could wake him and tell him all that had happened that day.

She climbed into the front seat and was putting on her safety belt when she finally realized that something was off about the situation. "How did you know where I—?"

When the needle jabbed into the side of her neck, Jannie made a yipping noise, like a puppy that's had its paw stepped on, and almost immediately saw dots and then blackness.

Chapter 98

AT THAT SAME MOMENT, Marcus Sunday waited in the shadows where the new addition met the old house. Thanks to Nana Mama's key, he'd been able to sneak in the back a solid half hour before Bree Stone returned home. He'd gone upstairs and printed a few items, and then had returned here to wait.

Through the plastic sheeting that sealed off the construction site, he watched Cross's wife enter the dining area, moving stiffly, her face bandaged. She'd been hurt somewhere in her core, he thought. That was good. A trained cop is a difficult person to manage. An injured cop not so much.

Bree put two sacks of blue crabs on the dining room table and then set about filling a big pot with water to put on the little two-burner they'd been using. Gingerly she removed her jacket. She was wearing her shoulder holster, left side, the injured side, so she'd have to reach across her body to draw.

Sunday was so close to the second-biggest prize of the day that he had to fight not to hyperventilate. The writer lived for these kinds of moments, when he was free, unencumbered by any convention whatsoever, a stranger in many ways even to himself.

Boundaries? Limits? There were none now, as far as he was concerned. *No reason to be subtle here,* he thought. *When you get the chance, you take her.*

But Sunday was cunning enough to understand that he couldn't act like a bull in a china shop. He had to do this cleanly, with no noise that might alert Bree before it was too late.

She turned on the burners, put a lid on the pot, and went upstairs to change. She was deeply favoring her left side. Good. All good.

Sunday knew from experience that the long Velcro strips that sealed off the Visqueen sheets might be loud enough to be heard upstairs.

Instead of chancing that, he got out a utility knife with a fresh blade, and a 9mm Beretta, and waited. The hypodermic needle with the Rohypnol was in his shirt pocket, ready to go.

Now all he needed was for Bree to return to see

if the pot was boiling. Five minutes later, he heard the staircase creak and the padding of feet. Cross's wife walked right into the dining room, right to the pot. She had her back to him, wore sandals, yoga pants, and a loose blouse. No holster. No gun.

In two silent diagonal downward slashes, Sunday opened a large triangle of the sheeting. It flapped forward, leaving the writer a gaping hole through which to aim. "You watch pots, they never boil," he growled at her.

Bree jumped and knocked into the pot. It fell. The heated water poured all around the bags of crabs. She tried to turn around, but Sunday was already through the sheeting and right behind her, the muzzle of the Beretta pressed to the nape of her neck. "Don't do it," he said. "Or I'll be forced to kill you."

"Who are you?" she demanded.

"You'll find out soon enough," he replied, kicking her feet apart and feeling for a second weapon at her ankle. But she'd taken both holsters off upstairs.

"What do you want?" she said. "Do you know who I am? Who lives here?"

"I know exactly who lives here," Sunday replied. "So listen. We're going out through the addition and the gate into the alley. If you value your family, you'll do exactly as I say. Now, back through that hole in the plastic."

Bree hesitated and he pushed her roughly in the ribs, showing her that he understood where her balance points were, that he understood where her injuries lay. From that point on, Cross's wife did as he instructed, leading the way through the addition to the steel door and out into the backyard.

It was just before dark and the neighborhood was alive with dogs barking, moms calling their children to dinner, baseballs striking leather mitts. But the only thing Sunday was focused on as they made their way to the rear gate was the smell of Bree Stone. That, as much as the threat of violence, aroused him. When he and Acadia were finally alone, they'd tear each other apart.

When they got to the gate, he said, "Open it."

Bree hesitated, said, "I'm a cop. You know what they do to people who mess with cops?"

"I know what I'm going to do if you mess with me," Sunday said.

Cross's wife threw the latch and pulled open the gate.

"Slow left," he said. "Go to the back of the van and open the door."

The alley was quiet, dark, and empty. His vehicle was ten yards away. Sunday knew that if Bree were to try a countermeasure, she would do so climbing into the van, as much out of panic as opportunity.

For a moment as she climbs in she'll be higher than me, he thought. *She'll also be seeing her stepson and Cross's grandmother.*

Sure enough, when Bree opened the door and started to get in, she spotted Ali and Nana Mama, passed out, duct tape across their mouths and around their wrists and ankles. She tried to mule-kick Sunday, but he'd already anticipated that move and eased off to the side. With her leg fully extended, he stuck the hypodermic needle through the stretchy fabric of her yoga pants and buried it and the drug in her right haunch. Bree gave a kind of half scream and fell forward on her broken ribs, out cold.

Sunday pushed her legs in, calmly shut the rear door, got into the driver's seat, and left. When he was well away from the Cross household, he checked his phone and saw that he had a new text from Acadia: **Done. Moving.**

Right behind you, he replied.

Tucking his phone back in his breast pocket

and putting the van in drive, he thought: *Let the enormity of his plight take hold in Cross's vivid imagination, let him wallow in it a good while before Thierry Mulch flips the switch and shows Dr. Alex his new and stark reality.*

Part Five

THE ZOMBIE WALKS

Chapter 99

AROUND SEVEN THAT EVENING, I came home to find the door unlocked and the front rooms of the house dark and silent. I stepped into the front hall and called out, "Anybody home?"

I heard them then, making noises like the clicking of many dead phone lines, or cigarette lighters being struck one after the other. When I flipped on the hall light, six or seven blue crabs scuttled away along the floorboards, claws raised, snapping as they went. There were more loose crabs in the television room and more still in the dining room, some on their backs on the rug, having fallen from the table where the two-burner stove still burned. Our crab pot lay on the floor, water spilled all around it.

My mind seemed to go into slow motion then, seeing the sliced plastic sheeting that separated the new addition from the old house, noticing the sawdust in the water, putting together the puzzle pieces until I grasped the scene the way one might watching a movie. But it was not real. Not real at all.

My voice, sounding far away, echoed in my head as I read the scene: Bree had set the crabs on the table and was heating the water, expecting us all soon for dinner. But someone had come from behind my wife, from back in the addition, and there'd been a struggle. The pot had been upset, hot water spilled, and the crabs somehow freed.

Frightened of what other secrets my house might now be holding, I turned and ran through the crabs and up the stairs. My wife's service weapon and backup pistol were sitting on the shelf where she kept them, along with her badge.

Whoever grabbed Bree knew her routine, I thought. Waited for her to stow her guns before making his move. Was Bree alone? Or was everyone here when it happened?

She'd been alone, I decided. If Ali had been here, the television would have been on. If Jannie had been here, I'd have seen her laptop somewhere close. If my grandmother had been here, I'd have seen some evidence of her, the knitting bag, something.

I tried to stay calm, but there was a sudden terrible weight in the house where I'd spent so many happy years. The air in my bedroom felt pressurized, as if it were seawater and I was a hundred feet down, fighting for every breath.

What the hell was going on? Where was Damon? Where was my wife? Jannie? Ali? Nana?

I had the overwhelming sense that I was in danger of drowning as my mind tried to answer the single question that came to dominate my thinking: *What has happened to my family and why?*

Sampson, I thought. *Someone clearheaded. He can help me figure out—*

My cell phone buzzed, alerting me to a text message. Grabbing it from my pocket, I looked at the sender and felt a rush of joy. Jannie had sent me a—

Two photographs came in. I opened them, seeing Bree, Ali, and Nana Mama in the first, and Damon and Jannie in the second. They all appeared unconscious, with duct tape wrapped about their wrists and ankles and strips of it stretched across their mouths.

A message accompanied the second picture, the one of Damon and Jannie: Don't even think about calling Sampson, or your other friends with Metro and the FBI. Look around. You are alone now, Cross. And I am watching you. If you try to bring in reinforcements to your cause, your family dies, simple as that. Do not leave your home. Await further instructions to follow—T.M.

"T.M.," I said, feeling scalded inside. "Thierry Mulch."

Chapter 100

MULCH, THE FACELESS PHANTOM who'd been lurking at the periphery of my life the last two weeks—sending crude letters, speaking at my son's school, for God's sake—now had my children, my wife, and my grandmother. That reality pounded through my head like so many wild horses. I got woozy and nauseated. I sat on the edge of my bed and massaged my temples with the heels of my palms, thinking: *Who is he, Mulch?* That Internet entrepreneur from Southern California who'd gone to Ali's school? Or one of the other Thierry Mulches I'd found on the Web?

And what was his motive? Why was he doing this to me? What sort of leverage was he looking for? Was this for himself, or on behalf of a third party?

But it was the peril that my family faced that

finally hit me like a shock wave off a roadside bomb. My imagination conjured up ten or more terrible endings for my wife, my children, my grandmother. Each of them felt like a concussion, one after another, so bad I feared I might crack like Carney had, splinter into several people, strangers every one.

Then my rational side stepped up, demanding that I detach from what might be happening to them, that I address the evidence and the facts. They were the only paths that might lead me to Mulch and my family.

Call Sampson. Call Quintus. Call Mahoney. Get them involved. You need manpower, and you need it now.

But Mulch had said he'd kill my family if I made that move. And he'd said he'd be watching, that he would know. Was he boasting? Bluffing?

No, I decided, he was clever enough to kidnap my entire family in an afternoon. It suggested planning. A lot of planning. So if he said he'd be watching, he'd be watching.

But how would he know if I contacted outside help?

I got to my feet then, turned off the light in the bedroom, crossed to the window, eased back the drapes, and looked down on Fifth Street. It was nearly nine by then and the sidewalks were quiet. Cars choked both sides of the street. Though the oak leaves were out, I could still see a long way east and west.

Retrieving a pair of binoculars from the closet where Bree and I kept our weapons, I began studying each vehicle in turn, looking for someone inside, or anything out of the ordinary. But I spotted no one near or in their cars on the half-block to either side of our place.

Had Mulch rented a house or apartment that had views of mine? I peered out at each house, using the binoculars to look for someone looking back at me. I did the same from Jannie's room, above the side yard, and from Nana Mama's room, which faces the back and the alley. I looked out every window and had suspicions about neighbors I'd known for years.

Nothing. No one.

Had I seen anything strange in the neighborhood recently? I supposed our construction project was the biggest change. But then I thought of that vacuum repair van I'd been seeing around. And that blue Tahoe with the tinted windows. Who owned them?

I went downstairs, spooking more of the crabs, went to the television room, and looked out the front windows, which offered a low-angle view of the street. Neither the Tahoe nor the van was there, as far as I could see.

Okay, then how else could Mulch know if I've contacted Metro or the FBI? Then it hit me. Ali had said he'd smelled Mulch in here. Why would Mulch have taken a chance like that, broken into my house with two armed police officers inside?

To bug the place, I thought. So he could watch me right now, after he'd taken my family, after he'd told me he had them.

I began to look about slowly, as if the walls had eyes and ears.

Chapter 101

I SUDDENLY WANTED TO tear my house apart, find the bugs and—

Stop!

Stop looking around! I yelled at myself silently. *If Mulch has bugs in here, he's watching you or hearing you. If you start an obvious search, who knows what he might do?*

Your family dies, simple as that.

For many moments I just stood there in the television room, staring dully at one of the blue crabs as it crept into the darkness behind our couch. The whole situation suddenly seemed to have been designed with diabolical forethought.

Mulch shows himself to me through a letter, taunts me, and depicts me in a cartoon with a huge penis perched on by birds. Then he goes to give a motivational speech at my son's school. How did that happen? Who arranged it? Then he kidnaps my entire family and threatens to kill them if I act to save them or bring in help. Crueler still, Mulch watches, or listens to me, as I wrestle with my demons. It smacked of sadism at some level. Mental torture, certainly.

My house became overwhelmingly claustrophobic at that point, and I craved fresh air the way a desert nomad seeks water. But I refused to grab a jacket and go out into the night. For reasons I couldn't explain, fleeing the house felt like surrender, and I was not surrendering to this man, whoever he was, whatever his ultimate motives were.

I was going to fight for my family, but I was going to have to do it in a way that didn't seem like fighting. So I did what any normal person would do: I went hunting for the crabs that had taken over the lower floor of the house, grabbing up the ones in the hallway and dropping them into a brown paper bag and then moving the furniture to track down the rest of the escapees.

All the while I looked for signs of electronic transmitters, but frustratingly found none. It occurred to me that Mulch might have put them high up where they couldn't be easily seen, but where they might provide a wide-angle view of the room. But sure as I was that they were there, I couldn't spot them.

I didn't feel like eating anything, so I stuck the crabs in the refrigerator and sat at the dining room table, looking at the pictures Mulch had sent me using Jannie's phone. At first I just looked at each of them, wondering bitterly if this would be the last image I'd have of my wife, my kids, the grandmother who'd raised me.

Then I thought: *Jannie's phone.*

Trying not to act purposeful, I got up from the table and turned off the light. I turned off every light in my house and then eased off my shoes. In the pitch black I padded like a cat up the stairs to my office.

But hadn't Mulch been in here? I stood in the doorway, thinking of how Damon's Christmas penholder had been moved, feeling certain that Mulch had moved it, which meant he'd been behind my desk, possibly even monkeyed with the computer. Should I take the chance?

I wanted to log on to a website called PhoneSniffer.com. Two years ago, I'd installed an app from the company on Jannie's and Ali's cell phones. Both phones came with GPS chips in them that communicated through the app to the

PhoneSniffer site. The last twenty-four hours of activity were visible at any given moment, and archival history was available on request.

But did I dare call up the website here?

No, I decided at last. I needed to be sure. I needed to get out of my house and to a computer I knew was clean without being spotted by Mulch.

Reluctantly, I turned and left my office. I changed into dark clothes and forced myself to lie down on my bed, to avoid thoughts of my hostage family, and to doze until the blackest hours before dawn.

At three a.m. I made my move, exiting the house through Ali's window on a bar-and-chain fire escape ladder we kept rolled up in his closet. I got off in the walkway between our house and the Hendersons' place next door. Instead of heading for the street or the gate to the alley, I struggled over the fence into the Hendersons' yard, grateful that their oldest son, Pete, had taken his Rottweiler, Knot Head, away with him to college.

I climbed the fence into the Olsons' yard and another into the Lakes', using my peripheral vision to navigate, not daring to flick on my Maglite. A lock hung in the gate mechanism, but the hasp wasn't shut. I lifted it out and stepped into the alleyway, looking everywhere for a long moment before heading quickly north, keeping to the shadows. I walked ten blocks before I dared to hail a cab.

Terry Simmons, the cop on duty at the rear entrance to Metro headquarters, was surprised when I walked up at three forty and presented my badge.

"Kind of early, Detective," he said, pressing a button to let me through.

"Couldn't sleep," I said. "How long's your duty?"

"Seven a.m.," Simmons said. "Week's over for me."

"And it feels like mine's just beginning," I said, heading toward the elevators.

Ten minutes later, I was drinking coffee from a vending machine, wondering if I dared call John Sampson while waiting for the record of my children's activities to load. Was it possible that Mulch had bugged Sampson's place, too? Mulch had mentioned specifically that I was not to contact my partner. Was that a bluff? Or something he could know?

Confused on that issue, I focused on the PhoneSniffer site, which now showed Jannie's position every fifteen minutes since four a.m. on

Good Friday. Ali's doings were there as well.

My daughter's movements had been entirely predictable, based on what I already knew. She'd left the house at seven forty, gone to school, and moved to the track in the early afternoon. It wasn't until late in the afternoon that things got disturbing.

PhoneSniffer had Jannie leaving Banneker High, heading toward the Howard University Metro station, about forty minutes after I'd left her to pick up Damon at Union Station. Two blocks shy of the Metro stop, my daughter got into a vehicle. By the time her phone had transmitted her position again, she was crossing the Fourteenth Street Bridge, heading into Virginia.

That was the last signal for almost two hours until Mulch sent the photographs of my family. PhoneSniffer pegged the phone's position on Baron Cameron Avenue, heading into Reston, Virginia. There had been no more transmissions since then.

Ali's last known location was two blocks from school, heading in the direction of the church shortly after school let out. Then he simply vanished from the tracking system. Mulch had to have taken their phones and disabled them. This was a dead end.

I was about to call a number at Verizon that would put me in touch with a police liaison so I could get a last fix on Bree, Damon, and Nana Mama, when I suddenly remembered my wife saying something about downloading the PhoneSniffer app onto my grandmother's phone soon after she'd had heart problems the year before.

I went to the account page, and sure enough, there was a tracker app on Nana Mama's phone. Calling up the page, I was surprised and happy to see that it was still on and had been sending out her position all day and night. The last transmission had been sent only three minutes before.

I clicked on the location, saw it magnified on the screen against Google Maps, and felt terrified for her.

Chapter 102

IN THE GROUND FOG and the first dawn light, the tens of thousands of simple white gravestones looked like row after row of broken teeth, stretching in every direction as I ran along a path through Arlington National Cemetery.

When I'd pulled up at the gate at 5:30 a.m., an armed member of the US Army's Old Guard had come out of a booth shaking his head, said, "We don't open until eight, sir."

I'd showed him my badge and identification and told him I was searching for my grandmother. But he'd refused me entry until I explained that she was ninety-some years old and suffered from dementia.

A little stretching of the truth often works wonders.

"My granddad's got the same sorry thing,

Detective, and he's only seventy-eight," the sentry said. "Can't let you drive in, but you can go search on foot."

I showed the soldier Nana Mama's position on my cell phone screen. According to PhoneSniffer, she'd been there since six thirty the evening before. The guard studied the location and told me that she was in section 60, an unfortunately popular place in Arlington these days. Section 60 was where they buried soldiers, airmen, sailors, and marines who had died in the global war on terror. The day before, the sentry said, ten men had been laid to rest there.

That thought only added to my worry as I began to weave my way through the gravestones of section 60, using the map to guide me. When I got to the location of all the transmissions from Nana Mama's phone in the prior eleven hours, I found three fresh graves.

For a sickening few moments, my mind reeled with the idea that my grandmother might be dead and buried there. But then I remembered that funerals at Arlington are highly orchestrated affairs attended by members of the Old Guard, who often give the dead a twenty-one-gun salute. There was no way Nana Mama was here.

Her cell phone, however, had to be. Gravestones had not been erected, but all three burial sites were covered with fake grass, flower memorials, and small American flags stuck upright in loose soil at the heads of the graves.

Feeling like a ghoul, and asking forgiveness from the spirits of the fallen soldiers, I put on latex gloves and began to carefully search among the flowers. I found the phone twenty minutes later, but not in any of the bouquets or vases.

When I lifted the fake grass at the foot of the middle grave, the phone was just lying there inside a sandwich-size Ziploc bag. I crouched, took a picture with my camera phone, and then picked the bag up, studying the phone, which was dark. I turned the bag over. There was a small envelope in there, too. It was addressed to "Dr. Alex."

I felt angry. Some sick freak was playing me, and I hated it.

But I set those feelings aside and fished out the envelope. It had not been sealed and contained a child's birthday-party invitation with little bunches of balloons in the corners. There was no date, time, or place entered on the dotted lines, just these words scrawled in an odd script: "You disappoint me, Cross. I told you to stay at home and await further instructions, and here I find you out looking for your family. Go home, or suffer the consequences. Look at the picture on the phone and go home."

Grinding my teeth, not wanting to look at the photograph, I nevertheless thumbed the button that activated the screen.

Nana Mama was lashed to a chair. Her head was slumped forward on her chest. A person— head and body outside the photograph—stood next to her, holding a bolt-action hunting rifle, pressing the muzzle to the side of her neck.

Chapter 103

I DID AS THE man said. I went home and spent most of the day there, but not before taking a chance and making a short stop at DC's new state-of-the-art crime lab on E Street in Southwest.

The MPD was in the process of moving from having sworn officers running the lab to employing skilled and degreed civilians who were increasingly taking over the forensics end of investigation in the nation's capital. But I still knew people in the lab, and when I asked after the manager on duty I got lucky.

Five minutes later I was behind closed doors in the spanking-new office of Lieutenant Commander Alison Whitehead, an old friend and colleague who owed me a favor or three. Without revealing exactly what was happening, I got Whitehead to sign a requisition slip giving me access to several pieces of equipment that I believed might help my situation. The entire visit took less than fifteen minutes.

So I was well within the time parameters of a trip between Arlington National Cemetery and home. Twice during the drive, John Sampson called, and twice I ignored him. I parked the unmarked car in front of the house and went past the construction Dumpster and inside, hearing the phone ringing from the porch.

When I got inside, my partner and best friend was leaving a message about Easter dinner tomorrow. I'd forgotten that Bree and Nana Mama had invited them. Billie wanted to know what to bring.

"Call me so I can get her off my back," Sampson said, and hung up.

I smelled something faintly putrid in the air then. At first, I flashed on my son, Ali, and thought Mulch might be in the house, but then I realized that one of the crabs must have gotten behind something and died.

It worked in my favor. Grumbling about the dead crab gave me cover to move furniture and clamber around the house, carrying a small handheld device that measured radio waves and electrical activity.

I found the first bug around 10 a.m. It was a tiny audio unit pinned to the upholstery on the back of one of the couch cushions. Barely giving it a glance, I set the cushion back in place as if I'd seen nothing.

That was a good thing, because I realized soon after that there was a camera of some kind in the bristles of the small broom we use once in a blue moon when we have a fire in the fireplace.

The optical bug in one of Nana Mama's spider plants was located thirty minutes later, soon after I began picking up activity from the ceiling light over the dining room table. Luckily, the dead crab wasn't a foot away from the camera, under a stand my grandmother uses for her houseplants.

Making a show of it, I picked the crab up by its claw and held it away from me as if it were a skunk. After putting it in a plastic bag and going out back to dump it in the trash can, I went upstairs and through my bedroom, grateful to find no bugs there.

My attic office was a different story. Pacing back and forth as if in a total fret, I was able to locate a listening bug attached to my wedding picture and a fiber-optic camera between two old homicide textbooks on the highest shelf of my choked bookcases.

By then it was noon, I'd been up for thirty hours, and I was completely exhausted. But I felt as if I was making up some ground. I knew where Mulch could see or hear me. I also knew exactly where he couldn't.

From now on, I decided, I was going to become a creature of the dead zones in my house, making only sporadic trips to the dining room, the television room, and my office.

I yawned in the general direction of the camera in my office and then went downstairs to my bedroom. The pillows still smelled of Bree when I lay down and looked at my cell phone and the Ziploc bag that held my grandmother's.

Theoretically, my phone was clean. As far as I knew, unless Mulch was some kind of Houdini, it had not been tampered with, which meant I was probably free to send text messages, or even to call from my bathroom with the shower on full blast. But what if Mulch was sophisticated, using intercept technology to monitor any transmissions from inside my house?

There had to be a way for me to communicate

with John Sampson and Ned Mahoney without triggering a reprisal from Mulch. If a man says he's going to kill your family, the last thing you want to do is risk a false move.

My indecision turned to drowsiness and I fell into a troubled sleep in which a faceless man with flaming-red hair taunted me as I tried to run after my family, who were sprinting around Banneker High's track. But try as I might, I gained no ground, not even on my grandmother.

That was when I realized that Mulch had attached strings to my arms, legs, and head. Still running, I looked over my shoulder and up to see the strings stretching high into the sky, where they met a crossbar held by white-gloved hands.

Aside from the red hair and a polka-dot bow tie, all I could see of the puppeteer was a mouth populated by the gravestones of Arlington National Cemetery.

Church bells tolled in the distance.

The bells became my doorbell ringing downstairs and I roused groggily, realizing I'd been asleep for hours. It was nearly seven in the evening.

Somebody started knocking, and then I heard John Sampson's voice calling up through the open bedroom window, "Alex? Bree? Anybody home?"

I snapped wide-awake, thinking, *What if Mulch could hear that? What if he thinks I called my partner?*

Chapter 104

FOR A SECOND I was frozen, staring at my phone and at Nana Mama's inside the Ziploc bag. The plan came to me in an instant, and rather than questioning it, evaluating it, I ran with it.

"Be right down," I yelled toward the window.

I picked up the Ziploc bag and palmed it. Then I took a big breath and went downstairs, remembering the placement of the optical bugs. If I was right, Mulch had no view of the front hallway, though he could probably hear any conversation at the front door.

Time for a little disinformation, I thought, turned the handle, and swung the door open so I was looking through the screen.

"Hi, John," I said in a purposefully weak voice.

"You haven't been answering your phone, and my wife's in a tizzy about what we're supposed to be bringing for Easter dinner," Sampson said, studying me through the screen. "Don't you listen to your messages?"

"Not when I've got four people puking their insides out," I said. "Damon brought some nasty stomach bug home from school. Norovirus or something. It's killing Bree with the cracked ribs and all."

Sampson took a step back with a foul look on his face. "You got it?"

"Not yet," I replied. "But I've been up all night with everyone else."

Sampson took another step back, and I took that as a cue to open the screen door and step out onto the porch, saying, "Easter dinner's touch and go for the time being, John. Could be one of those eighteen-hour viruses, though."

"Hate those things," my partner said. "Had one in Cancún last year that laid me flat, and I'm not up to repeating that scene anytime soon."

"Don't blame you," I said loudly, and took several steps toward him, offering my hand so he could see the Ziploc bag and the phone inside. He glanced at it, showed no reaction, just reached for my hand.

Stepping in to throw my arm around him in a

guy's hug, I whispered, "Thierry Mulch, the guy who sent me the bizarre letter about the massage parlor killings, has taken my family hostage. Look at the picture on the phone. They're all like that. My house is bugged. Not certain about my cell. Mulch says he'll kill them if I contact police or the FBI. Hang back for now. And pray."

"For sure, Alex," Sampson said in a normal voice, stepping back nice and relaxed, as if he heard that sort of dire message every day. "I know Billie still wants to make the green beans and bacon dish you all like."

"Bacon might be tough on their stomachs," I said, turning to go back inside. "I'll let you know."

"All right," Sampson said. "Have a good evening."

"Long as I'm not moving buckets around I'll be fine," I said, and shut the door. Pausing there, I listened to Sampson's footsteps fade away and started toward the stairs and the bedroom.

But then my phone vibrated. A text from Bree: You were told not to contact police. You were told the penalty.

I immediately texted back, He's my partner, Mulch. He came asking about Easter dinner. I did not call him. Repeat: I did not call him.

For several agonizing minutes I got no reply, then my phone buzzed with a second text from Bree: **Suffer the consequences, Cross.**

Before I could do a thing, my phone buzzed again—a picture with a time stamp, taken just moments before.

Nana Mama lay sprawled on her side on a cement floor. There was a pool of blood beneath her slack, spattered face, and a gaping wound on the left side of her head, just above the ear.

Chapter 105

IT WAS LIKE SOMEONE had struck me in the stomach with an axe blade.

Doubled over, I whimpered in a child's voice, "No. Please, dear God, no."

I staggered forward, trying to sit on the stairs, but the disbelief and grief were overwhelming, and I lurched into the banister. Falling to the hallway floor, feeling gutted, I sobbed my heart out.

For more than three decades, Nana Mama had been my rock, my anchor, more so than any of my wives or significant others. She'd rescued me from the orphanage. She'd pushed and cajoled me through school, and had seen me receive my PhD in psychology.

My grandmother was right there when I wed my first wife, Maria, and rocked Damon and Jannie for hours when they were babies. She held my hand at Maria's funeral, and helped me through the tough times after Ali's mother left me. She had been overjoyed the day I married Bree. Throughout Nana Mama's entire life, she'd been open and kind and tough to everyone, family and friends, and especially to me.

I'd always thought of her as immortal somehow.

And now, Regina Cross Hope was gone in a pool of blood, lying on some cold cement floor in God only knew what basement or empty building, a bullet through her head courtesy of a psychopath named Mulch whom I knew next to nothing about.

But I instantly hated Mulch. I had never really hated any of the bloodthirsty lunatics I'd faced in the past, preferring to look at them as disturbed creatures I was charged with capturing. But Mulch felt beyond Gary Soneji. He felt beyond Michael "The Butcher" Sullivan, too.

Killing my grandmother, Mulch had gone for the jugular, and I wanted to fight back, throttle him with my bare hands. Knowing he was listening, I almost screamed out how much I loathed him, how much I wanted to kill him, but something deep inside me had me biting my tongue, still hoping that somehow I'd be able to turn the electronic bugs against him.

Nausea welled inside me. Crawling to the downstairs bathroom, I threw up again and again, trying to get rid of something worse than any stomach bug. Gasping, covered in sweat, I sat with my back to the wall by the toilet, wondering if I should just call Sampson where Mulch could hear me and openly declare war on the coward who'd just executed a ninety-one-year-old woman in cold blood.

But for almost an hour, my thoughts and actions would not track. Every time I tried to formulate a plan, my brain peeled off and found that image of Nana Mama dead of a gunshot wound in a garish light. It paralyzed me.

The second photograph came an hour later. This time Bree had taken the bullet, lying on her side like Nana Mama in a pool of her own blood, the gunshot wound visible behind her left ear.

I could not control my agony in any way, shape, or form. It simply devoured me and I began screaming for my dead wife from the depths of my soul.

"Stop it!" I shouted when the initial shock had passed. "Don't do this, Mulch! No more!"

Trembling from head to toe, fighting off the urge to vomit again, I wiped aside my tears with my sleeve and texted him back on Bree's phone. **Please, Mulch. I'll do anything you say. Just stop killing them.**

Feeling scorched inside, I stared at my phone and then went into the dining room where Mulch could see me. I crossed to the spider plant and looked directly into the camera lens. I cried out to Mulch to spare my children from my grandmother's fate and my wife's. I begged him until I was hoarse, and I texted him over and over again: **Have mercy on them. Have mercy on my children.**

At nine o'clock I got a picture sent from Jannie's phone. It was my son Damon, executed in the same manner, sprawled on his side in his own blood. My disbelief became a raw, tearing sensation, as if someone were literally skinning me alive and disemboweling me at the same time.

Damon. My firstborn. My son. My—

My mind collapsed inward, forgot time, and I saw Damon as an infant, sleeping in the swing Maria had found in a secondhand store, and me sitting by his side, thinking that I had never seen anything so beautiful. Then there he was as a Little Leaguer, unsure up there on the mound, looking to me in the stands for support. And Damon as I'd last seen him up on the Kraft School campus after winning a basketball game in the final seconds with a perfect three-point jumper.

GONE.

GONE.

The word began ringing in my head, like a huge bell tolling, and with each peal—GONE—I got weaker, and weaker, dissolving, turning primitive, unable and unwilling to move a muscle, knowing that no matter what I did, no matter what I said, Thierry Mulch was bent on killing them all.

I left the dining room and went upstairs. I lay on my bed, looking up at the ceiling, feeling as if someone had been harvesting chunks of my brain, seeing everything in my room as if down a long, dark tunnel that was closing with every minute that passed.

At ten o'clock that Saturday night, the photograph of Jannie came. Same position. Same shot to the head. A girl who hours earlier had been told that her life could be extraordinary, that her talent was almost unlimited, was gone.

GONE.

GONE.

It was my only thought.

GONE.

GONE.

Ali died at one minute before eleven, according to the time stamp. My little boy's eyes were open and vacant, an expression I'd seen on scores of corpses over the years.

GONE.

My entire family was GONE. For a long time I lay curled up in a fetal position on the bed. Then, around midnight, though I was still unable to think at all, my legs swung off the bed as if of their own accord. I stood up, seeing everything around me as if through a scratched and blurry lens.

There was no conscious thought at that point, but my brain was not dead. Fully infected by the overwhelming virus of loss, my mind turned reptilian, and the reptile commanded me to walk.

Chapter 106

DROPPING THE PHONE, I trudged out the front door of my house, left it open to the wind of a coming storm. I walked in a state of total shock through the streets of Washington, alternately catatonic and then overwhelmed by grief, sobbing my heart out. People who passed me on the sidewalks seemed creatures from another lifetime. Their laughter was like some foreign language I'd never understand again.

By two Easter morning the streets were deserted. By three, they were empty and dark, and thunderstorms lashed the city.

I'd been walking like that for hours by then but didn't feel hungry, or thirsty, or tired in any way. When lightning bolts ripped the sky and thunder clapped right over my head, I barely flinched. Not even the pouring rain could slow me or soothe the agony burning through every inch of my body.

I heard my little boy's voice telling me that the only way to kill a zombie was to destroy its brain.

Is this what Thierry Mulch wanted?

Mulch had destroyed everything I loved, everything I believed in. He'd left me a dead, soulless man doomed to endless, meaningless movement. I started hoping that he or some anonymous street predator would appear in my path at last and blow my head off with a shotgun, or crush it with an axe.

In search of that kind of predator, I walked into the worst neighborhoods in DC, desperate for an end to my suffering. But street after street was empty. Everyone had gone inside.

Some internal guidance system brought me later to a known crack and meth house about twenty blocks from my home. I walked through the living dead in that place, seeing the open sores on their skin, the sunken eye sockets, and their rotten teeth, envying the way some of them were drifting on their drugs and others were so far gone that reality didn't register at all.

One filthy woman who looked older than my grandmother but was probably a few years younger than Bree glanced up from her glass pipe when I stopped in front of her. Her nose was gushing. Her lips were split and bleeding.

"Whaddya want?" she demanded.

"I want to die," I told her.

"Join the club, honey," she replied, cackled, and went back to smoking her glass pipe.

"I have money," I said to her and four or five other people who were lying around in their various stupors. "I want to die."

Pulling a roll of bills out of my pocket, I held it up and asked, "Who's brave enough to kill the zombie?"

Several people lying on a mattress stirred and came alert. One guy in a ratty T-shirt and grimy hair looked at the money hungrily. "How much?"

"All of it," I said dully.

I heard a gravelly voice behind me say, "I'll take that deal."

Then I heard a faint whistle as something swung violently through the air before cracking against the back of my skull not far from where Carney had hit me. Everything exploded and I fell into the deepest darkness I've ever known.

Chapter 107

I WANTED TO STAY there in that darkness, surrender to nothingness.

So there was no joy when I came to with a searing pain in my head and realized to my dismay that I was still alive. Lying in the filth in the crack house, suffering the second blow to my head in several days, I felt the room swirl like a ship in a whirlpool as I begged God to end the pain, to take me back down into that blackness that had been such a relief.

Opening my eyes, I had trouble focusing for several long minutes. Everything just kept blipping and slipping by me like one of those filmstrips we used to watch in elementary school. When I finally was able to stop the room from spinning, I thought it was empty except for that woman, who looked a hundred years old. She was passed out a few feet from me, twitching, drooling, but still clutching her pipe and butane lighter.

Reaching around the back of my head, I felt coagulating blood and a nasty knot where I'd been hit. The money was gone. So were my shoes. But my wallet and badge had been placed neatly beside me.

Getting to my hands and knees, I felt woozy, sick, and the room reeled like a kite in a gale. I fell back on my side, fighting off the urge to puke.

"Why do you want to die, Alex?" a voice asked.

I knew that voice, though I couldn't place it. My head felt ten times its size and pounded when I turned it toward a dark corner of the room, where a gaunt young woman with close-cropped bleached-blond hair, dark makeup, and several nose piercings was looking at me, a lit cigarette dangling from her lips.

For several confused seconds I had no idea who she was. Then she rolled her head at me as she exhaled her drag of smoke, and I knew her.

"Ava?" I grunted.

"Don't call me that," she snapped. "I'm Bee now, like the bug."

"Bee," I said, hanging my head and closing my eyes.

"You shouldn't be in a place like this," Ava said.

I opened my eyes, seeing two of her. "And you should?"

"Got nothing better because I deserve nothing better," Ava said, spitting out the words. "But you, you got everything, Alex, so pick up your badge and wallet and get out of here before something really bad happens to you."

When I shook my head it felt like paint cans were swinging from side to side inside my skull. "I've got nothing anymore."

"C'mon," she said, taking a drag. "You have Bree, Nana Mama, and—"

A rage built in me. "No," I said. "They're all dead, Ava."

She could tell by my tone that it was true. The color drained from her face and she stared at me dully for a long while through the smoke curling in her eyes. Tears began to well and drip down her cheeks. Then she stabbed the butt out angrily and got to her feet as if to go.

"Help me home," I said.

"I can't do that. It will be day soon and I have to get safe."

I blinked, said, "Get me safe first. Please? I think . . . I know I have a concussion. And I'm bleeding."

You could tell she was struggling, wanting to leave, wanting—

"Just get me home," I said. "And I'll tell you what happened to Bree."

And then we were two survivors trudging through the predawn streets of Washington. As small as she was, Ava managed to keep me upright as we walked toward my home. The sidewalk seemed like the rolling deck of a ship in hard seas.

But I told Ava everything: how this insane man Mulch had bugged my home, kidnapped every member of my family, and then executed them because John Sampson had come to my door. He'd even sent me pictures on my cell phone. Twice during the telling I broke down so badly I had to hold on to a street sign to keep from collapsing.

The whole time, Ava said nothing, as if this kind of tragedy was to be borne in silence and then never spoken of again. I don't know how she did it, but she got me to the house. The storms had passed and the first light of dawn was showing in the night sky. The front door was still open. Spring-green oak leaves floated in a puddle in the hallway.

I stood there, gazing stupidly at the leaves floating, until Ava said, "Where do you want me to take you, Alex?"

"Upstairs," I said.

"You sure you don't want a doctor?"

"No," I said as my house began to move. "I just need to lie down."

And then, somehow, she'd shut the front door behind us and had gotten me up the staircase and into my bed on my back. The room spun slowly like a carousel.

"Ava?" I asked, trying to focus on her to make the whirling stop for good.

I could see she was annoyed at me.

"Bee?" I said.

"Yeah?"

"Did you kill that girl and burn her body in the factory?"

"What?" she said angrily. "No! Elise, she was my friend."

"We have evidence at the scene, your ID and that sweater Nana Mama gave you."

"Someone must have planted it there."

"We have an eyewitness," I said. "A homeless man named Everett Prough."

Ava looked disgusted and furious now. "Of course Everett said I did it. Of course he put my things there and told you that."

"What? Why?" I asked, confused again.

"That homeless getup is Prough's disguise, Alex," she said. "He's a pimp and an ice dealer, but no one looks at him twice when he's dressed like a bum. Elise owed him money, but only half as much as I owed him. Prough killed Elise and set her body on fire as a warning to me."

She began to sob. "I caused it."

Even with my blurry vision and my bruised brain, I could see that she was telling the truth. I wanted to tell her she hadn't caused Elise's death, and to come forward and testify against Prough to avenge her friend. I wanted to tell her that she would be protected and that she wouldn't have to run anymore.

But was that true? My own family . . .

I swooned, remembered something about concussions. I wanted to say, "Don't let me sleep, Bee." But all I got out was "Don't let me go . . ."

The last thing I remember was Ava standing in the doorway staring back at me, hoodie up, chewing her thumbnail and looking like she was getting ready to run.

Chapter 108

IN THE NIGHTMARE THAT followed many hours later, a blurry figure I knew as Mulch raced through the crack house after smashing my head and stealing my money. Like some cartoon character, I took the hit and still was able to get to my feet and chase him outside, except we were no longer in DC but up on that abandoned farm where Carney had taken Cam Nguyen and the babies.

Mulch went into the farmhouse, giving me just a glimpse of that shock of red hair, and I pursued him down into the basement and through the secret passage. When I left the tunnel and entered the root cellar, Mulch was gone.

But the room Carney had built inside the root cellar was still there in my dream, and light shone inside. I stepped into the light, peered into the room, and saw my family laid out side by side on the floor by the bathtub, all of them in the same position I'd seen in the pictures, lying on their sides, faces turned left, dead, bloody, and head-shot.

Their milky eyes were all open, and their blank stares a universal accusation: I had failed to protect them. I had allowed this to happen. The harshest expression was Nana Mama's, as if she'd become ashamed of me, as if her life raising me, and protecting me, had mattered not at all when she was in dire need.

That crushed me. I fell to my knees, arms wide, weeping and begging for her forgiveness, and for Bree's forgiveness, and Damon's, Jannie's, and Ali's. But they just stared at me with their milky eyes, their expressions never changing, and I began to convulse with pain and loss, heaving and sobbing and thinking that this brutal feeling would never, ever end.

Then I heard splashing and looked through my tears at the bathtub, where Mulch had risen up out of the water carrying a hunting rifle. His face was a brilliant aluminum light above that polka-dot bow tie and that shock of red hair, and his voice came to me like a shortwave radio transmission.

"I had to shoot them like that, you know,"

Mulch said. "If you head-shoot them, they can never become zombies."

I said nothing, just stared into the blinding light of his face.

After several seconds, Mulch said, "I figured you'd thank me, Cross."

"Why?" I whispered.

"For saving them from the doom of the walking dead."

"No, why are you doing this *to me*?"

Mulch laughed with irony in his voice, said, "I'm doing it for the only reason anyone does anything. Because I can." He started to laugh again, caustically.

"Who are you?" I demanded.

Mulch seemed to think about that. "I'm whoever you believe me to be."

"Why don't you kill me?"

"Why does a cat play with a mouse?" Mulch replied.

"So you *will* kill me?"

"Of course."

"When?" I said.

"I think it's time right now," Mulch said matter-of-factly. "Lie down there beside your wife and your grandmother, on your side, right cheek in that perfect puddle of blood, staring left into oblivion."

I got down without hesitation, gazing one last heartbreaking time at my family, each one of them in turn, before twisting my head from them, eyes wide open and aware of the muzzle of the rifle swinging past my face.

"Shoot straight," I choked.

"I always do," Mulch said, and pulled the trigger.

Chapter 109

THERE WAS A SOUND like an artillery shell going off in my head, and a wicked electrical pain that fragmented into different arms of excruciating energy that spiked out with fingers in all directions, as if Mulch had shot me with a lightning bolt and not a .30-06.

The lightning came not through that gaping bullet hole I expected on the left side of my head, but from low and at the back of my head, right where someone had hit me in the crack house.

Then I smelled ammonia and jerked toward confused consciousness.

"Alex?"

Wincing at the pulsing pain at the back of my head, I felt my eyes come open blurrily, seeing three figures that soon became Ava, John Sampson,

503

and Ned Mahoney. We were all in my bedroom. The door was shut.

"What . . . ?" I started to say. "How . . . ?"

Sampson tossed a smelling salt capsule away and threw a thumb at Ava, saying in a low voice, "Real smart girl here, Alex. You don't know the half of it, but eventually she came and got us."

I blinked, felt fire in my eyes. "Eventually? What time is it? What day?"

"Easter Sunday," Mahoney said. "Six in the evening. You've been out about thirteen hours."

Almost a day had passed since Nana Mama died, I thought, wanting to cry again, realizing that each coming hour would bring one tragic reminder after another.

"Mulch killed them all," I said to Sampson and Mahoney. "Executed them with a hunting rifle in cold blood."

"Maybe," Ava said. "Maybe not."

Suddenly and irrationally angry, I twisted my pounding head at the teenager and snapped, "What's that supposed to mean?"

Ava shrank, started to move toward the door.

"Hear her out, Alex," Mahoney said. "She's got us convinced."

"Convinced of what?" I demanded. "That

Mulch had a partner who performed the executions?"

"No, Alex," Sampson said. "Ava's convinced us that your family's still alive."

Chapter 110

I REFUSED TO BELIEVE it. The idea that they had somehow all survived gunshots to the head required more hope than I had left in my heart, maybe more hope than was left in the universe.

But then Ava explained that she'd left me passed out on the bed, intending to take off and then call 911 down the road. As she passed the doorway into the television room, however, she saw my phone lying on the carpet.

As dark as it sounds, Ava wanted to see the pictures I'd described, and she picked up the phone. Mindful of Mulch's camera trained on her from the bristles of the fireplace broom, she'd gone halfway up the stairs and started to look at them.

"Why did you do that?" I asked, irritated again.

"I dunno," Ava said, shrugging. "Interested?"

"Whatever, it's a damn good thing she did, Alex," Mahoney said.

Sampson nodded. "Though we would have figured it out eventually."

"Figured out what?" I demanded.

The FBI agent pulled out an iPad and called up every picture Mulch had sent me so that they were all visible, side by side. He held the screen out to me. I couldn't bear to look at them until he said, "Notice anything odd when you look at them all at once?"

Steeling myself, ignoring the pain in my skull, I forced my gaze onto Nana Mama's corpse, and then Bree's, Damon's, Jannie's, and Ali's. They were all in virtually the same position.

"Mulch killed them in a ritualistic manner," I said. "Fetishizing their death."

"I thought about that," Ava said.

I looked at her again, this time in surprise. "*You* did?"

"I used to listen to you talk to Bree about your jobs," she said defensively. "And, I dunno, the pictures seemed *too* ritualistic."

Before I could reply, Sampson twirled his finger, said, "Get to it, Ava."

Ava nodded, stepped up beside the bed. She

took the iPad from Mahoney, tapped at the screen, and then turned the device so I saw it horizontally. The pictures of Bree and Jannie showed in split screen one atop the other. Ava gestured to the gunshot wounds, said, "They're the same."

"Of course they look alike," I said. "He shot them in the same place."

"They're the same," she insisted, and then pointed to the blood pooled around their faces. "It's pretty much the same here, too, like the same amount of blood, and the shape of it. And notice these spatters?"

I didn't see it at first, but then I flashed on my nightmare, and how Mulch had told me to assume the same position in *that perfect puddle of blood.* My subconscious had seen what Ava had seen. It had been trying to tell me the same thing.

I nodded in shock. "They're nearly identical."

Sampson said, "Ava spotted it, snuck out, and brought your phone to my house. I'd been at work with Ned since you gave me Nana Mama's phone yesterday evening. Billie brought Ava to us downtown, and she quickly convinced us after we blew the pictures up on a computer screen."

Mahoney nodded. "I had the skeleton crew on duty at Quantico do a quick analysis to confirm our take. There's no doubt that every one of those pictures was Photoshopped. A very good job, but Photoshopped."

A glimmer of optimism began to glow in my chest. Was it possible? Were they alive? Could they be?

Chapter 111

THEN THE SKEPTIC IN me took hold, said, "Why would Mulch do this?"

"Trying to break you, I suspect," Mahoney said.

"But why?" I insisted.

"You'll be able to ask him when we find him," Sampson said. "And by the way, we believe his name is not Thierry Mulch. It's Preston Elliot; he's a graduate student in computer science at Georgetown."

My head hurt again. "Wait, what?"

Mahoney said, "John called me right after you gave him Nana Mama's phone. We've been on Mulch ever since, and on you, by the way."

I squinted at him. "How's that?"

"Well, what did you think, that we weren't going to get your house under surveillance?" the FBI agent replied. "We had two teams trailing you on your long walk last night. We honestly had no idea what you were up to, and you weren't answering your phone, so we figured Mulch had contacted you and you were going to meet him."

It took a few moments for that to sink in, but then I said, "But how do you know Mulch's real name is Preston Elliot?"

"DNA, luck, a sex crimes report out of Alexandria, and complaints in Georgetown and Bethesda," Sampson replied, frowning. "But not in that order."

He explained that one of the first things he and Mahoney had done was to run criminal database searches on Thierry Mulch.

Sampson added, "We got our first break through a rape case in Alexandria last week. A woman named Claudia Dickerson, twenty-eight, a CPA, reported that a man who kept referring to himself as Mr. Mulch had attacked her and her boyfriend, Richard Nelson, at her front door. Mulch forced them inside her apartment, knocked Nelson cold, and then raped Ms. Dickerson from behind. She never saw his face, but he left DNA."

"Has it been analyzed yet?" I asked.

"Not completely," Mahoney said, holding up one hand. "But give us a minute or so here to finish telling you what we do know."

Sampson said, "We came across Mulch's name two other times in the databases. He caused a stink at the Four Seasons in Georgetown about two weeks ago. Same guy Ali described: tall, red hair, bow tie. He also took a Bentley out for a test drive from Euro-Motorcars in Bethesda, an eight-hour test drive. And we contacted the principal at Ali's school. She said he'd approached her by e-mail and directed her to a website about his social media company and its new app for kids. He said he wanted to inspire kids and pick their brains, so she agreed to let him come speak. She also sent us a copy of Mulch's California driver's license. Fake, by the way. There's no such Mulch on record out there."

Mahoney turned the iPad again and I came face to face with Thierry Mulch for the first time. Rooster-red hair. Bushy red eyebrows. Abe Lincoln beard. A lazy expression.

"You have a picture of Preston Elliot?"

The FBI agent nodded, typed on the iPad again, came up with the computer scientist's Georgetown ID, said, "We think he's wearing a disguise in the driver's license photo, but they're roughly the same height and weight, and look at the other facial features."

I did, and saw striking similarities in the cheekbones and along the jawline. I looked at the eyes and knew they were the same person. "And you have DNA evidence that directly links the rape to Preston Elliot?"

Sampson said, "We do, and you're not going to believe how."

He explained that he'd found a report from the lab on my desk, an analysis of the semen and vaginal traces found at the scene of Mandy Bell Lee's attorney's death.

"Are you saying Mulch killed Tim Jackson?"

"We're saying that Preston Elliot killed Tim Jackson," Mahoney replied. "We got a dead-on match between the semen taken from the attorney's hotel room and the DNA samples FBI agents took from Elliot's hairbrush after he was reported missing last week. And the vaginal secretions on Jackson's pants match DNA samples taken from Claudia Dickerson, the rape victim. By the way, the rape and Jackson's murder took place within hours of each other."

For several moments, I didn't reply, and then I

said, "Why would Elliot smear Jackson with the evidence of a rape?"

"Could have just been on Elliot's pants and he rubbed up against Jackson while he was poisoning him," Sampson said.

My head hurt too much to think critically about that possibility. I said, "My family *is* alive."

They all nodded. "As far as we know," Mahoney said.

"So what are we going to do?"

The FBI agent said, "Launch an investigation as if they'd been murdered. Don't let on that we know they're alive, leaving you to act the mourner out of his mind here in the house where Elliot/Mulch can watch you."

Sampson said, "We think he wants to watch you suffer, Alex."

"But why?" I asked again. "I don't know this guy Elliot."

"Like John said, you'll get to ask him about his motives when we catch him," Mahoney replied.

"And I just go on about my life in the meantime?"

Ava said, "No, you go on with the life of a man who's just lost everything. You go on as a victim, Alex."

"Couldn't have said it better myself," Sampson remarked with a soft smile at Ava.

Mahoney added, "In the meantime, we work the murder and Mulch angle and wait for Elliot to make a move, surface, maybe even contact you under a different name."

I flashed on Nana Mama, Bree, Damon, Jannie, and Ali, said, "And my family?"

"We do everything in our power to find them and bring them home safe," Sampson said. "And we pray."

Chapter 112

THAT MISSION GAVE ME renewed strength, and an easing of the pain in my head. I said, "Okay, we'll do it your way for the time being. Wait, how did you both get in here? Wouldn't Mulch or Elliot have seen you on camera?"

"No, I thought of that," Ava said. "They came in the way I went out: across the roof of your addition."

"Like I said, smart girl," Sampson added.

"Plan on leaving the same way?"

"As a matter of fact," Mahoney said, and tossed me a disposable cell phone. "Use that when you need to talk, and for God's sake, keep it on you."

I caught the phone and swung my legs off the bed, feeling a rush of agony at the back of my head. "I'm probably going to need stitches."

"Ava will take you to the ER once we're gone," Sampson said.

I looked at her. "You're staying?"

"Can't leave you alone with a nasty concussion, can I?" Ava said.

I smiled, said, "I suppose not." Then I looked at my best friend, said, "When you get the chance, tell Captain Quintus to have an arrest warrant drawn up for Everett Prough, a homeless guy cum pimp and ice dealer who hangs around that abandoned factory where we found the burned Jane Doe, who now has a name: Elise . . ."

I glanced at Ava, who said, "Littlefield."

"Elise Littlefield," Sampson said, and wrote it down. "Okay."

We shook hands, and then Ava and I waited several minutes for Mahoney and Sampson to get down off the roof of the addition and leave by the back gate.

I hugged Ava, said, "Thank you."

Ava was stiff at first but then softened, said, "No, thank *you*, Alex. I should have come to you and Bree sooner. But I was ashamed of what I'd become after everything you'd done for me."

"Water under the bridge," I said, and let her go. "Right now, we've got other things to think about."

Ava made a show of helping me down the stairs, and I acted the shattered, injured, and demoralized victim while we intentionally made a tour of the dining and television room, looking for my jacket.

A good part of me wanted to grab up one of the cameras, look into the lens, and tell Preston Elliot I was coming for him. But I kept my cool and went with Ava out onto the front porch.

The air was clean after the previous night's thunderstorms, and you could still smell the scent of Easter hams cooking somewhere on the block. I thought of how this holiday should have been celebrated with the ones I love all around me. It filled me with rage.

Looking at the night sky and the glittering stars, I vowed to Nana Mama, Bree, Damon, Jannie, and Ali that I would not rest until I'd found them all and brought them home.

Then I crossed my heart and followed Ava down onto the sidewalk.

THE STORY CONTINUES IN

HOPE TO DIE

COMING NOVEMBER 2014

STAND-ALONE THRILLERS

Sail (*with Howard Roughan*) • Swimsuit (*with Maxine Paetro*) •
Don't Blink (*with Howard Roughan*) • Postcard Killers (*with Liza Marklund*) • Toys (*with Neil McMahon*) • Now You See Her (*with Michael Ledwidge*) • Kill Me If You Can (*with Marshall Karp*) •
Guilty Wives (*with David Ellis*) • Zoo (*with Michael Ledwidge*) •
Second Honeymoon (*with Howard Roughan*) • Mistress (*with David Ellis*) • Invisible (*with David Ellis*)

NON-FICTION

Torn Apart (*with Hal and Cory Friedman*) •
The Murder of King Tut (*with Martin Dugard*)

ROMANCE

Sundays at Tiffany's (*with Gabrielle Charbonnet*) •
The Christmas Wedding (*with Richard DiLallo*) •
First Love (*with Emily Raymond*)

FAMILY OF PAGE-TURNERS

MAXIMUM RIDE SERIES

The Angel Experiment • School's Out Forever •
Saving the World and Other Extreme Sports •
The Final Warning • Max • Fang • Angel •
Nevermore

DANIEL X SERIES

The Dangerous Days of Daniel X (*with Michael Ledwidge*) •
Watch the Skies (*with Ned Rust*) • Demons and Druids
(*with Adam Sadler*) • Game Over (*with Ned Rust*) •
Armageddon (*with Chris Grabenstein*)

WITCH & WIZARD SERIES

Witch & Wizard (*with Gabrielle Charbonnet*) •
The Gift (*with Ned Rust*) •
The Fire (*with Jill Dembowski*) •
The Kiss (*with Jill Dembowski*)

MIDDLE SCHOOL NOVELS

Middle School: The Worst Years of My Life (*with Chris Tebbetts*) • Middle School: Get Me Out of Here! (*with Chris Tebbetts*) • Middle School: My Brother Is a Big, Fat Liar (*with Lisa Papademetriou*) • Middle School: How I Survived Bullies, Broccoli, and Snake Hill (*with Chris Tebbetts*) • Middle School: Ultimate Showdown (*with Julia Bergen*) • Middle School: Save Rafe! (*with Chris Tebbetts*)

I FUNNY SERIES

I Funny (*with Chris Grabenstein*) •
I Even Funnier (*with Chris Grabenstein*)

TREASURE HUNTERS

Treasure Hunters (*with Chris Grabenstein*)

CONFESSIONS SERIES

Confessions of a Murder Suspect (*with Maxine Paetro*) •
Confessions: The Private School Murders (*with Maxine Paetro*)

GRAPHIC NOVELS

Daniel X: Alien Hunter (*with Leopoldo Gout*) •
Maximum Ride: Manga Vol. 1–7 (*with NaRae Lee*)

For more information about James Patterson's novels, visit www.jamespatterson.co.uk

Or become a fan on Facebook